LOVE
EVERLASTING

Books by Tracie Peterson

www.traciepeterson.com

BRIDES OF SEATTLE

Steadfast Heart
Refining Fire
Love Everlasting

LONE STAR BRIDES

A Sensible Arrangement
A Moment in Time
A Matter of Heart

LAND OF SHINING WATER

The Icecutter's Daughter • The Quarry-man's Bride • The Miner's Lady

LAND OF THE LONE STAR

Chasing the Sun • Touching the Sky • Taming the Wind

BRIDAL VEIL ISLAND*

To Have and To Hold • To Love and Cherish • To Honor and Trust

STRIKING A MATCH

Embers of Love • Hearts Aglow • Hope Rekindled

SONG OF ALASKA

Dawn's Prelude • Morning's Refrain • Twilight's Serenade

ALASKAN QUEST

Summer of the Midnight Sun
Under the Northern Lights
Whispers of Winter
Alaskan Quest (3 in 1)

BRIDES OF GALLATIN COUNTY

A Promise to Believe In
A Love to Last Forever
A Dream to Call My Own

THE BROADMOOR LEGACY*

A Daughter's Inheritance
An Unexpected Love
A Surrendered Heart

BELLS OF LOWELL*

Daughter of the Loom • A Fragile Design • These Tangled Threads

LIGHTS OF LOWELL*

A Tapestry of Hope • A Love Woven True • The Pattern of Her Heart

DESERT ROSES

Shadows of the Canyon • Across the Years • Beneath a Harvest Sky

HEIRS OF MONTANA

Land of My Heart • The Coming Storm
To Dream Anew • The Hope Within

LADIES OF LIBERTY

A Lady of High Regard • A Lady of Hidden Intent
A Lady of Secret Devotion

RIBBONS OF STEEL**

Distant Dreams • A Hope Beyond • A Promise for Tomorrow

RIBBONS WEST**

Westward the Dream • Separate Roads • Ties That Bind

WESTWARD CHRONICLES

A Shelter of Hope • Hidden in a Whisper • A Veiled Reflection

YUKON QUEST

Treasures of the North • Ashes and Ice • Rivers of Gold

*A Slender Thread • All Things Hidden**** • House of Secrets*
What She Left for Me • Where My Heart Belongs

*with Judith Miller **with Judith Pella ***with Kimberley Woodhouse

BRIDES *of* SEATTLE,
BOOK THREE

LOVE
EVERLASTING

TRACIE
PETERSON

BETHANYHOUSE

a division of Baker Publishing Group
Minneapolis, Minnesota

© 2015 by Peterson Ink, Inc.

Published by Bethany House Publishers
11400 Hampshire Avenue South
Bloomington, Minnesota 55438
www.bethanyhouse.com

Bethany House Publishers is a division of
Baker Publishing Group, Grand Rapids, Michigan

Printed in the United States of America

Library of Congress Cataloging-in-Publication Data
Peterson, Tracie.
    Love everlasting / Tracie Peterson.
        pages ; cm. — (Brides of Seattle ; book three)
    Summary: "After the great fire that destroyed much of Seattle in 1889, Abri-anna Cunningham recognizes that her longtime friendship with Wade Acker-man is changing, but she finds herself overwhelmed by her conflicting feelings and the pursuit of another relentless suitor"— Provided by publisher.
        ISBN 978-0-7642-1305-2 (cloth : alk. paper)
        ISBN 978-0-7642-1063-1 (pbk.)
        ISBN 978-0-7642-1306-9 (large-print pbk.)
        I. Title.
PS3566.E7717L68 2015
813'.54—dc23   2015009358

Scripture quotations are from the King James Version of the Bible.

This is a work of historical reconstruction; the appearances of certain historical figures are therefore inevitable. All other characters, however, are products of the author's imagination, and any resemblance to actual persons, living or dead, is coincidental.

Cover design by LOOK Design Studio
Cover photography by Aimee Christensen

15 16 17 18 19 20 21   7 6 5 4 3 2 1

In memory of Sharon Asmus,
a phenomenal editor and friend.
You will be missed.

1

Surprise!"

Abrianna Cunningham's heart leapt to her throat as she jumped back against the wall. Her hand flew to her breast. Goodness. Why did people think it amusing or even desirable to frighten a person half to death on such occasions?

"Happy Birthday!" the crowd called in unison.

She willed her heart to slow. "I am deeply touched." And she was. "But honestly, I think such surprises are quite a shock to one's system. I once read that a man died from just such a shock, though I think that was a bit dire. As I recall, he was startled by a burglar demanding he hand over his money. Nevertheless, it was a similar stupefaction, and he wasn't much older than me. Although perhaps he had a weaker heart." Abrianna looked at the others. There were looks of joy mingled with confusion. It would seem that the entire Madison Bridal School had turned out to honor her.

"Nevermind." Abrianna smiled at the two dozen people gathered for the celebration. "I fear I am given to digress, but I am honored that you would plan such a wonderful surprise." Several of the bridal school students clapped in joy and ushered her toward the table where a large cake awaited.

"We helped with the baking," one of the girls announced, "but Mrs. Madison did all the decorating."

Abrianna's three aunts stood behind the adorned table, each smiling in her own way. Miriam Madison, owner of the Madison Bridal School, looked rather severe, but she always did. With her gray hair secured in a tight bun and her mouth almost always in a straight line, even when smiling, Aunt Miriam's appearance suggested she was never quite happy. However, Abrianna knew better. Aunt Selma, Aunt Miriam's dear friend, stood to one side, her closed mouth bent upward as a horseshoe might. There was a definite gleam in her eyes. Aunt Poisie stood on the opposite side. As the younger sister of Miriam Madison, she had the job of sharing all the emotions her sister held back. Her smile was given with great abandon and looked as though she had just heard a very humorous joke. All so different, yet so dear.

"Don't you love how beautiful it all is?" Clara asked. As one of the more outspoken and flirtatious of the bridal students, she was generally first to make her presence known. "Miss Poisie and I gathered the flowers."

"Well, we all helped with the decorating, and Mrs. Gibson made the linens," Elizabeth, another student offered.

Abrianna nodded. "I can see Aunt Miriam's beloved Minton china has been chosen for this affair." She put her hand again to her heart. "I know just how special those dishes are to you, Aunt Miriam. I am honored that you would use them for my birthday. But I would be completely devastated should they be so much as chipped."

"I believe everyone will be careful, Abrianna," her father said, coming forward. "Happy Birthday." He put his arm around her and gave a squeeze. "You look a lot like your ma." He winked. "Minus the red hair, of course. That is now and ever will be your mark of honor." After being absent most of her life, Jay Cunningham seemed quite caught up in the moment.

"Thank you, Father. Although I hardly see my hair as something to bring me honor." She touched her hand to the hastily coiffed gathering of curls. "Mostly, it has seemed a curse."

"Nonsense. You are beautiful."

"I keep trying to tell her that." Wade Ackerman stepped up to join them while the bridal school students buzzed around them like bees in a hive, helping get the cake served and punch poured.

Abrianna felt her heart skip a beat at Wade's closeness. She had come to realize, just a little more than a month ago, that she was very much in love with her lifelong friend. To her surprise, he leaned over and boldly kissed her cheek.

"You are the prettiest girl here," he whispered.

"Indeed," her father said with a quick glance around the room. "But I'm prejudiced."

"Mr. Cunningham," Aunt Poisie said, coming to them looking worried, "I wonder if I could impose on you to help me bring in ice for the punch?"

"Of course." He too kissed Abrianna's cheek. "Duty calls." He then extended his arm for Aunt Poisie to take. "Lead the way, dear lady."

James Bowes Cunningham was—in spite of his difficult life— a rather handsome man who had returned to Abrianna after a lifetime absence. She and her aunts had long thought him dead. Having been falsely accused of murder and imprisoned for almost twenty years, Jay, as he preferred to be called, had allowed his family to think him deceased to spare them shame.

Abrianna found his reappearance in her life to only add to the confusion of her age.

And that confusion, this mastery of intricate exhaustion, culminated with Wade Ackerman. She braved a sidelong glance at the young man she'd known all of her life. He had been a brother and dear friend to her in his association with her aunts, but now . . . oh, now things were ever so different.

She felt her cheeks grow hot when Wade caught her glance and winked. Ducking her head, Abrianna fought her emotions. Now she was in love with Wade. What in the world was she to do about that?

"I'm so happy for you," Elizabeth declared. "Everything will change for you now that you are of age and in love." She giggled and added in a whisper. "Love changes everything."

Abrianna frowned. Just what she was afraid of. Her friendship with Wade was a foundation that she understood and counted on. Her aunts were most precious, but they were old, and their ideals and concerns harkened back to another age. Wade, on the other hand, had been privy to her innermost secrets and ambitions. Their friendship was the one thing she didn't wish to see change.

"Mr. Ackerman, I am so pleased to find you here tonight," Clara said, sidling up to him opposite Abrianna. She batted her eyes and fanned herself. "My, it is warm tonight. Maybe a little stroll in the garden would be nice." Her expression betrayed her desire that Wade offer to accompany her.

"As low cut as that bodice is, I'm surprised you haven't taken a chill." Abrianna shook her head in disapproval.

Clara giggled. "Oh, Abrianna, you do go on. The bodice isn't at all scandalous. It's quite fashionable."

"Not by Aunt Miriam's standards. I'm surprised you were allowed downstairs."

Clara gave a coy smile. "Well, she didn't realize I planned to wear this particular gown. I only purchased it yesterday. What say you, Mr. Ackerman? Don't you think it quite lovely?"

Wade looked to the ceiling. "I know little about fashion, but I do know Mrs. Madison's rules about modesty."

"Oh, that's just because she's old." Clara gave a twirl. "I'm young, and I want to attire myself in the latest fashion to enhance my beauty."

Abrianna noticed the way the bodice strained against Clara's well-endowed bosom. "I'd be careful about moving too much or too quick. Maybe you should retrieve a shawl."

"No. Clara needs to go change her gown altogether." They all turned to find Aunt Miriam looking on in disapproval. "We shall discuss this further tomorrow, but for now you will go upstairs and make a better choice."

Clara pouted, pursing her lips. "But I shall miss the party."

"You should have thought of that before making such a display." Aunt Miriam fixed the girl with one of her looks that Abrianna knew only too well. With her arched brow and narrowed eyes, Aunt Miriam could look quite imposing. She would not be moved by Clara's childish moping.

"Well, fine!" Clara's tone of exasperation and crestfallen expression put closure on the matter as she turned and stomped out of the room.

"You two need to get a piece of cake and some punch," Aunt Miriam said in a more pleasant tone. "After all, it's not every day that one celebrates her twenty-first birthday."

"It certainly isn't," Kolbein Booth declared. He and his wife, Lenore, joined the trio. "Happy birthday, Abrianna." He lifted her hand and kissed it.

Lenore, her longtime friend, waited her turn and then

embraced Abrianna. "Happy birthday. This is such a grand occasion, and you certainly deserve it." She leaned closer and whispered, "I was glad to see you get rid of Clara. That dress was positively scandalous."

"Indeed. But it is just one of many shocks I've had tonight."

"I'll get us some cake," Wade said. "How about it, Kolbein? Join me?"

"I will. That cake looks much too good to pass up. I heard someone say it has strawberry preserves in between the layers." He patted his stomach. "If I keep eating like this I'll be a fat old man in no time."

Abrianna stepped back as the men made their way to the table.

Lenore took hold of her arm. "You mentioned shock. I do hope nothing's wrong. Your aunts were quite excited to plan this celebration for you."

Another friend, Militine Patton, joined them. "I didn't mean to eavesdrop, but you have to know this party has completely occupied your aunts since the Fourth of July party was completed."

Abrianna smiled. "They are dears. I suppose it isn't every day that your ward turns twenty-one. It was very kind of all of you to join in the festivities. I feel quite beloved. I have never had so much attention put upon me—well, at least not this pleasant type of attention. Goodness, I've had more than my share of unpleasant attention, as you both know, and often by no fault of my own."

"Well that's of little concern now." Lenore patted her arm. "It's a wonderful party, and of course . . . there's Wade. Has he proposed yet?"

Abrianna bit her lower lip. Word had gotten around rather

fast that Wade and Abrianna had indeed admitted feelings for each other that went far beyond the friendship they'd known. Lenore and Militine had been her immediate confidantes. To them she shared her confused emotions where Wade was concerned. Both assured her that this kind of change was no cause for alarm. They further suggested she enjoy rather than dread the change. Lenore put it in most eloquent words: "Love is always a mixed bowl of fruit. Some pieces are tart and others sweet." Abrianna didn't bother to add that some also could be full of worms.

The men returned with the cake. She sampled a forkful and found it a wonderful concoction of strawberries and whipped butter frosting layered between moist white cake. Across the room the bridal students got up a game of charades, and the party atmosphere was soon alive with whimsical laughter as each lady vied to act out her secret. From time to time someone came up to congratulate Abrianna and wish her well. It was a lovely party, but Abrianna found it hard to concentrate. Everything was happening much too quickly. Her father's return. Her change of heart toward Wade, and now coming of age. Could life become any more complicated?

"I would like to speak to you in the parlor," Aunt Miriam declared in her authoritative manner. "You may join us as well, Militine and Lenore." She looked to Wade and Kolbein who were now discussing something with Militine's husband, Thane. "You three, as well."

She led the way to the parlor while Abrianna began to fret. What was this all about? Why was Aunt Miriam sequestering them away from the others? Abrianna bit her lip and made her way into the parlor to find Aunt Selma and Aunt Poisie, as well as her father, already waiting. She scanned her memory for something she might have done to cause reprimand, but it seemed unlikely that Aunt Miriam would confront her on her birthday.

"Please come stand here, Abrianna," instructed Aunt Miriam.

Every gaze was now upon her, and Abrianna felt her face flush. Goodness, but this was enough to put a person into a state of apoplexy, although she'd never been in one before and really wasn't at all certain what the symptoms would feel like.

Life could be full of extremely vexing and embarrassing moments, and this definitely appeared to rate right at the top of her list. Of course, that time earlier in the summer when she'd had to discard her skirt and swim to safety when the great Seattle fire threatened to consume both her and Wade was probably her most recent humiliation. Thankfully, her aunts had been understanding.

"As you know, Abrianna became our responsibility upon the death of her mother," Aunt Miriam began.

"God rest her soul," Aunt Poisie declared.

"Amen," Aunt Miriam and Aunt Selma offered their customary reply.

"We had thought her father to have perished, as well," Aunt Miriam continued, "but are happy to realize that he had not." The aunts looked to Abrianna's father and gave a brief nod.

"In taking charge of Abrianna, we devoted ourselves to benefitting her throughout her life," Aunt Miriam added. "We worked to give her a solid education, teaching her ourselves rather than allowing her to be misled by public schools."

Aunt Poisie bobbed her head in her usual manner and gave a toothy smile. Aunt Selma looked quite satisfied, no doubt congratulating herself on the fact that she had spared Abrianna a lifetime of unlearning what she considered to be outrageous, ungodly claims by leading educators and scientists of the day.

". . . and because of this, we now have a gift for Abrianna. One that we have prepared for throughout the years."

Abrianna hadn't heard the entirety of Aunt Miriam's comment, but smiled nevertheless as the women beckoned her forward. Aunt Miriam handed her an envelope.

"You will find all of the details inside, but Mr. Booth can better explain, should you have questions."

"Questions?" Abrianna asked. She looked around her as if for explanation. Lenore's husband came forward with a grin.

"It means that you are now self-sufficient—a woman of means."

Abrianna shook her head. "I don't understand."

"Were you not listening?" Aunt Miriam asked, raising a brow. "No, I suppose your mind was filled with thoughts of fancy." She sounded harsh, but Abrianna saw the amusement in her eyes. "I said that we have put aside an inheritance for you." She looked to Kolbein. "Mr. Booth helped us to manage and invest the money we faithfully put aside. He has agreed to continue assisting you."

"I don't know what to say." She looked from her aunts to Kolbein. "What must I do?"

"Not a thing," Kolbein said, laughing. "You simply allow me to go on making wise choices for you, or I could probably help Wade to better understand the workings of the investments."

"No thank you," Wade said. "I think the paper work is best left to those with that kind of education. I know my limitations. Besides, this is Abrianna's money, and I won't have anyone accusing me of trying to take it out of her hands."

"No one who knows you would ever think that," Lenore replied. "You are a man above reproach, Wade. We have long appreciated that about you."

To Abrianna, it seemed the world had once again turned upside down. "Thank you, Aunts," she finally managed to murmur. "I am in such a state of shock that I have no other words."

"Now there's a first," Wade teased. The others laughed.

They soon rejoined the bridal students, who now entertained with songs and piano pieces. What might have otherwise been a simple celebration in another year turned into an afternoon of revelry. Abrianna couldn't help find herself caught up in the merriment. After all, fussing and worrying over the future wouldn't resolve the matter in a single day. It would no doubt take weeks if not months of pondering. Of course, she would do what she could to lessen that time.

She was glad when she spied Kolbein standing alone. She needed to discuss a great many matters with him and the most pressing couldn't wait. She had received yet another invitation for an outing with Priam Welby. Some months earlier, Welby had convinced her that she should court him in return for his help in furnishing a facility for the homeless and friendless. He had known her passion for ministering to those poor souls, and prior to the great fire that had destroyed downtown Seattle, Abrianna had even known him to donate money to the cause from time to time.

When he had proposed a contract between them, a contract that would allow Abrianna the means by which to help her old sailors and indigent citizens while giving Welby the right to court her, she had thought it utter foolishness. But she had been so long praying for an answer as to how she could better help those poor people that Welby's proposition seemed like answered prayer. Aunt Miriam had long taught her that answers to prayer didn't always come in an expected form. Because of that, Abrianna had to allow that God might very well have sent Priam Welby as His answer.

"Kolbein, do you have a moment?"

He nodded and led her to the far side of the room. "I'm sure you have a lot of questions."

"I suppose I should. To be honest, I'm in such a fitful state of confusion, I don't know if anything I say will make sense. You know, I once heard tell of a man who, upon receiving a great shock, was forever unable to even remember his address without prompts. Do you suppose I shall succumb to such madness?"

He laughed. "Abrianna, you will never succumb to madness of any kind. To do that would require you yielding control, and I've yet to see you do that in any area of your life, save perhaps your encounters with the Almighty, and even then I'm somewhat certain you barter with Him."

"Oh, you do have a poor opinion of me." Abrianna shook her head. "Perhaps I shouldn't even ask for your help."

"I have only the best opinion of you, Abrianna. I have always admired your strength. Now what can I do for you? Did you want to discuss your inheritance?"

"No." She shook her head again. "I want to dissolve the contract with Mr. Welby."

"Ah yes. I presumed that would be forthcoming and have already arranged the papers for you to sign dissolving the agreement. He won't be happy about it, you know."

"His happiness is not my responsibility. Besides, he knows full well I only agreed to court him because he offered help for the poor. I made it quite clear that I would never love him nor would I pretend to court him with any thought of marriage. He was the one who was deluded in thinking that he could somehow win me over. And now, given my recent . . . discovery of feelings for Wade, I cannot court Mr. Welby."

Kolbein chuckled. "Not unless Wade were to come along, and I doubt Welby would be tolerant of that."

"No, I'm certain he wouldn't. Mr. Welby doesn't seem to be tolerant of much."

Her words appeared to sober Kolbein. "He is known for being vindictive, Abrianna. I can't say what he might do to attempt punishment for your change of heart."

"I do not think he will attempt anything. I was never meant for Mr. Welby, and I told him so. Why he thought he could win me over is quite beyond me. He did not appeal to me in the least, especially given his big ears, although I truly would never let that be a reason for rejecting someone's love, if I loved him in return. Which, of course, I don't." She gave a heavy sigh. "I will rely upon you to finalize the matter."

"I am your humble servant," Kolbein declared with an exaggerated bow.

"I haven't had you to myself all day." Wade led Abrianna out onto the wraparound porch. The sun hung low in the sky and painted the horizon in hues of orange and red. "I can't remember us having a moment alone since the Fourth of July." He grinned. "A day I still reflect on with great pleasure."

"It was quite the affair. My birthday party, that is. Well, the Fourth of July was quite a wondrous event, as well." She fell silent.

Abrianna looked tired, and Wade felt selfish for demanding her time. But she was all he could think of these days. The only soul in the world he wanted to be with. With great care Wade tucked her arm in his and walked to the farthest point away from the front of the house. The porch offered them a private yet respectable place to share a moment alone, and Wade intended to take full advantage of it.

"We need to talk."

She looked up and nodded. "I suppose we do."

"With the long hours I've been putting in helping with the rebuilding of the city, we've hardly been alone. And when I am here, you seem busy or have already gone to your room for the night." He reached out and lifted her chin with his finger. "You aren't avoiding me, are you?"

"Maybe."

He hadn't expected her answer. "Why?"

"I don't know." She pulled away and walked to the porch rail. "I suppose I'm very confused. This is all so new to me. One minute we're good friends, and the next you kiss me and everything changes. Stuff and nonsense. I can't even look at you without all sorts of thoughts rushing through my head."

He chuckled. "We're still good friends, Abrianna." He moved toward her. "Nothing will ever change that."

She turned and held out her hands as if to ward him off. "How can you be certain of that? After . . . well, after we . . . well, I think of you quite differently now."

He grinned. "I'm thinking of you pretty differently, too. But they're all very good thoughts. I love you."

She nodded. "I know you do, and I love you, Wade." Her expression puzzled him.

"You look like you're about to face a battle rather than a wedding."

"Wedding? We haven't talked about a wedding." She shook her head. "I vacillate between having a stomachache and then a headache. One minute I feel exhausted and the next I could climb a mountain. If this is love, then I'm not at all sure I am going to enjoy it."

He suppressed a grin. She would never understand his amusement with her. "Oh, Abrianna, you're making this much more complicated than it needs to be."

"Well, it's just that everything I knew to be stable in my life has turned upside down. I feel so . . . so . . . misplaced." She shook her head again. "I don't expect you to understand. I don't understand it myself. Goodness knows, I've tried. I've even written out lists. I could show them to you to prove myself."

This time he couldn't suppress his amusement and laughed. "Abrianna, I believe you. I can see that you're confused. What I want you to know, however, is that despite all these changes, you are still the same. I'm still the same. That's not going to change."

"Of course it will." She gave him an indignant glare. "Only dead things don't change. I'm not the same person I was five years ago. You are completely different than you were back then. I would never have dreamed of kissing you. I recall your being a pest to me, always ruining my plans."

"For your own good." He took a step back. "Honestly, Abrianna, you make it sound like falling in love is the end of something rather than the beginning."

She turned away from him, and all those cinnamon-colored curls rippled down her back, begging his touch. Wade held himself in check. If he touched her now, she might go back to avoiding him, and he didn't want to risk that.

"I'm afraid of that very thing. I like what we have, Wade. You are the only person in the world I feel I can be completely honest with. You can be very harsh with me, but I always know it's done out of concern for my well-being and not because you are striving to make me into someone else, as my aunts do."

"No one wants you to be someone else, Abrianna. Your aunts have only tried to make you the best person you can be."

She continued staring out toward the bay and the setting sun. Wade wanted to offer her something that would put her mind at ease, but he was rather baffled. He had fought for some time against the feelings he had for Abrianna, and now that he knew she felt the same way, he didn't want to lose a moment in planning for their future. Abrianna, on the other hand, was fixed on the past.

Without warning, she turned to face him. "What if we're wrong? What if that kiss was just a coincidence? What if because we were in a celebratory mood and everyone was having a good time, the kiss only seemed right? Goodness, it could have just been the night air. Aunt Poisie always said the sea breezes could stir up one's blood."

Wade closed the short distance between them and pulled Abrianna into his arms. His hand cradled her head as he lowered his mouth to hers, determined to prove their love had nothing to do with night air. He felt her melt against him, her hands going up to the back of his neck. His pulse quickened.

Sea breezes indeed. "Does that help answer your thoughts of coincidence?" he asked after making certain she was thoroughly kissed.

She didn't try to get away from him or break his hold. She just laid her head upon his shoulder and gave the tiniest of nods. "It does. It's just as I feared."

"Just as you feared?" He lifted her face to meet his gaze. "And what is that?"

She blushed and looked away. "I like very much when you do that."

He laughed and touched her lips with his finger. "I like it very much, as well. And once we are married, I plan to do it often, so you might as well get used to the idea."

2

B ut I have no desire to end our arrangement." Priam Welby fixed Kolbein Booth with a hard stare. "She agreed to give me a chance."

"The contract clearly states that either party may dissolve it at any time. Miss Cunningham is otherwise engaged and can no longer allow for your courtship."

"Otherwise engaged?"

Booth nodded. "I believe, although it hasn't been formally announced, that she and Wade Ackerman will marry."

Welby brought his fist down on the desk. "I won't stand for this. I'll go and speak to her myself."

"As her counsel, Miss Cunningham asked me to handle this matter. I don't believe she wants to see you."

"I don't care. I think those old ladies have clouded her mind so much she doesn't know what she wants." He rose from his desk. "I won't sit idly by and lose her."

"You can't lose what you never had, Welby." Booth remained sitting, as if he were somehow Welby's superior. It irritated Priam to no end that where legal responsibility was concerned,

Abrianna was free and clear to walk away from all that he had planned. Especially now.

"I don't expect you to understand." Welby decided to take another line. "I have feelings . . . very deep feelings for her."

"She's a wonderful young woman, to be sure. My wife and I are very fond of her. But her heart belongs to another. That's hardly something you can change."

Priam smiled. "I've seen it happen before. I'm certain I can figure out a way to persuade Abrianna to give me another chance."

Booth got to his feet. "I wouldn't count on that. You don't know Abrianna very well at all if you think she'll just put aside her feelings for Wade. They've a long history together. She trusts him, something I doubt she'll ever do with you."

Welby narrowed his eyes. Booth appeared smug, in fact, delighted at the turn of events. "You and that pack of prudish nannies might well think you can control everything around Abrianna, but you can't. I will do whatever it takes to win her heart."

To Welby's utter frustration, Booth shrugged. "Waste your time and efforts if that's your desire, but it isn't going to happen. For a long while now I've seen the love those two have for each other. It's based on things you will never understand. Time. Trust. Spiritual ideals." He started for the office door but stopped short and turned to face Welby again. His eyes narrowed.

"You might have fooled the women of the Madison Bridal School with your façade of disgust at the girls found in your basement last June, but you and I both know it was you who put them there."

Welby considered the Chinese girls he'd imported to be sold to the highest bidder for their virginal purity. They would have brought him a pretty penny, but Abrianna had found them and set them free, even as the fire ensued and destroyed his building. To convince her of his innocence in the matter, he had played indignant and shocked, then hired a missionary woman to escort them back to China. All in order to impress Abrianna and her meddling aunts.

"You have no proof of that, Mr. Booth. I would suggest that rather than malign my good name, you would do better to keep such thoughts to yourself. I would hate to have to file a lawsuit against you."

To his surprise, Booth only smiled. "You do what you think you have to where I'm concerned. But I would advise you to leave Miss Cunningham alone. I don't think you want to have to tangle with not only Wade but also Abrianna's father. They are both rather protective and will not stand for your interference. Good day to you, sir."

Welby watched the man leave without awaiting his dismissal. He wasn't used to such blatant disregard. Booth would pay for his attitude and words. Welby would see to it if it was the last thing he did. But for now, he needed to figure out a plan for taking Abrianna away from Mr. Ackerman.

Only a week earlier Priam had forced information from a man very much indebted to him. A banker who knew many details of the Madison Bridal School finances relayed the details of an inheritance—a tidy sum—to go to Abrianna upon her twenty-first birthday. That sum would have allowed Priam to finalize plans for crushing his father.

Priam walked to the window of his office and gazed out. His house, located away from the bay area on Denny Hill, had suffered no fire damage. Even the smoke seemed minimal, and his servants had worked wonders to negate the stench.

All of Seattle lay below in various stages of destruction and repair. There was still a great deal of the burned city to be cleared, but already thousands of bricks were being laid out for new businesses. For the time, most businessmen set up shop in large serviceable tents, but Welby knew that given the things he'd heard, Seattle would be remade in as little time as humanly possible.

He'd toyed with the idea of leaving the area. Taking his insurance money and heading back east with the rest of his fortune to see the look on his father's face when he came to realize that the industry and properties he'd spent a lifetime building up were now in the hands of the son he'd disowned. But Priam was never one to run from a challenge once he set his mind to it, and he had set his mind on Abrianna Cunningham.

It wasn't for love. That ridiculous emotion got way too much attention. No, his interest in her first arose in order to get her aunts to sell him their downtown building. Once they agreed to do that, without Abrianna having to compromise her wishes and court him, Welby realized he was rather obsessed with the redheaded hoyden, as he'd come to call her. He'd never met anyone quite like her. She spoke her mind and was able to stand up to most anyone, including him. Not only that, but Priam found her to be a challenge, one he intended to meet and conquer.

Tea could be such a droll affair, even if it did involve her dearest friend. Abrianna sighed and picked a piece of lint off her gown as Lenore chatted with Aunt Miriam. The lightweight creation of white dotted Swiss trimmed in bold swaths of yellow and green was one of her favorites. And not just because it didn't need a bustle. But that did make it praiseworthy, indeed.

Oh, the atrocities women went through to look fashionable. Not that Abrianna didn't appreciate her extensive wardrobe, thanks to Lenore's generosity with hand-me-downs. Lenore's mother abhorred any woman who would wear the same gown over and over like a fisherman's wife. She raised her daughter to dress in the most fashionable attire available, and that influence hadn't ended with Lenore's marriage. Yes, Abrianna had much to be thankful for. Especially gowns without bustles.

Aunt Poisie pushed in the tea cart, reminding Abrianna of the onion man who used to go from door to door with his wheelbarrow full of product. The thought almost caused her to giggle out loud, and she barely controlled herself as Aunt Miriam began to pour.

"I do hope your husband's law firm has plans to rebuild." Aunt Miriam handed Lenore a cup and saucer.

"Oh, they are already well into it," she assured. "The plans were approved by the city, and building will commence right away."

"Goodness, it's only been two months." Aunt Poisie's face expressed her wonder. "You would think such matters would take a great deal more time, but I suppose the modern way of doing things causes people to always be in a rush. I do hope they take time to consider using quality materials. We wouldn't want the buildings to fall down around us because they're in too big of a hurry. Do you think there are requirements for such things?" Aunt Poisie paused for but a moment. No doubt she expected her sister to berate her for such a lengthy comment. However, when Aunt Miriam said nothing, she continued. "I suppose there must be a great many rules. Seattle is all about change these days. The newspaper said the city plans to connect Front Street to Commercial Street." She shook her head in what appeared to be exasperation. "I fear I will never get used to that."

Abrianna grinned and met Lenore's gaze. There was a twinkle in those brown eyes that let Abrianna know she wasn't alone in her amused assessment of Aunt Poisie's worries.

"I suppose it will take time," Lenore admitted, after sampling the tea. "I'm certain there will be a great many changes. However, Kolbein tells me that the entire city is determined to rebuild better and bigger. And they plan it to be done within the year."

"The year!" Aunt Selma declared. "Why, that doesn't even seem reasonable. How will they ever ensure safety? I cannot think such rebuilding could be done that quickly. The very laws of nature would suggest otherwise. It sounds to me to be the work of Darwinists." She nodded so fast her neat little bun bobbed and looked ready to come undone. "They believe"—her voice grew hushed—"that everything evolves in order to survive. At least that was what Mr. Gibson used to say."

"God rest his soul." Aunt Poisie took her cup of tea.

"Amen." Aunt Miriam and Aunt Selma nodded most solemnly.

Abrianna accepted a cup of tea from her aunt and slumped back in the chair in a most unladylike manner. From childhood, she'd been taught that ladies did not sit in a chair—they perched lightly, as if ready to spring up at any moment. Such perching did not lend itself to comfort and relaxation.

"Sit up straight, Abrianna. You'll ruin your posture," Aunt Miriam admonished.

Abrianna sighed and straightened but didn't perch. A girl could only do so much. "Wade says that everyone is anxious to see things back to normal. There are workers coming all the way from California to lend a hand. He says that anyone who wants a job can have one, and I know that many of those who visited the food house before it burned are now employed, despite their age and condition."

"It is good for a man to have work." Aunt Selma's brow furrowed as if in deep thought. "I often thought if Mr. Gibson . . ." She paused, raised an eyebrow, and looked to Aunt Poisie, who seemed to have been daydreaming.

"Oh dear. God rest his soul," she sputtered.

"Amen," Aunt Selma declared. "If he had kept busier with physical labor rather than all that reading, his soul's destination might not be in question. As it is, I find it necessary to plead with God on his behalf every night during my prayers."

Abrianna and Lenore exchanged a smile. The eccentricity of the old ladies never ceased to amuse them. Their oddities were endearing but could also be attached to lengthy lessons of lost souls and opportunities unwisely ignored.

The ladies sipped their tea and shared around a plate of cookies. Abrianna glanced at the mantel clock. How long before she could dismiss herself from the gathering and get on to more important things? She had promised bread to three of her old sailors who had been turned away from the food kitchens downtown for rowdy behavior.

Without warning, Lenore put her cup aside and looked to Abrianna. "I have an announcement to make." She glanced back to the older women. "And I wanted you all to be among the first to know."

"Do tell." Aunt Miriam seemed most interested.

Abrianna looked to Lenore in surprise. "Go on. You have us quite captive."

Lenore smiled and put her hand to her waist. "I am with child."

The cup clattered against the saucer, and Abrianna very nearly dumped the contents on her gown. "A baby?" She lowered her cup to the table.

Lenore nodded, unable to hide her pleasure. "The doctor believes I will be delivered in December."

"Oh, goodness. What glorious news. A baby." Aunt Poisie set her cup aside. She clapped her hands in excitement. "It's been ever so long since we've had a baby about."

"It has indeed," Aunt Miriam replied. "This is a wonderful blessing from the Lord."

"To be sure." Aunt Selma nodded in agreement. "For truly only God can create life, unlike what Mr. Darwin and his cronies believe."

"Do they truly believe they can create life?" Aunt Poisie looked quite grave.

Aunt Selma shrugged and gave a wave of her hand. "Who knows what deceptions they believe? I can only imagine that they are steeped in their experiments for just such purposes. Mark my words, one day they will attempt to create life without the benefit of a mother or father."

For several moments no one said anything. Abrianna found herself quite mixed in her thoughts. Lenore had always been such a dear friend, and while marriage kept her rather busy in the running of her household, she always made time to visit with Abrianna. A baby would no doubt change things once again.

"Kolbein and I are so very happy," Lenore continued. "We plan to tell my parents over dinner this evening."

"No doubt they will rejoice with you," Aunt Miriam said. She looked to the other women. "We shall have to put forth efforts to help Lenore make a complete wardrobe for the little one."

"One can never have too many diapers," Aunt Selma threw in.

"At one time, I thought two dozen to be more than sufficient." She shook her head in a most serious manner. "But I was sadly mistaken, and I would not want you to be likewise."

Lenore nodded. "Thank you for telling me. I will make certain to have more than two dozen."

"And blankets," Aunt Miriam added. "In this damp climate it's important to have plenty of blankets."

"Oh, and I will crochet the most delightful booties." Aunt Poisie all but danced out of her chair, nearly stepping on one of the cats. She bustled about the room in animated delight. "This is like having Christmas in August. I will make you a dozen pair in all colors. That way no matter whether it's a boy or girl, you will have an adequate number."

Abrianna listened in fascinated silence. She looked at her friend with new eyes, wondering how it could be that Lenore could be so changed and yet the same. She was radiant. That much was certain. Abrianna had credited it to nothing more than the afternoon warmth, but now it was quite clear that the babe she carried was the reason.

Then a thought came to mind. Would she and Wade have children right away? Lenore and Kolbein had not been married a year, and already they were expecting their first child. The thought seemed quite daunting to Abrianna. Marriage would surely be change enough, and while Wade hadn't formally asked for her hand, she knew it was assumed they would wed. Would he want children right away? Oh, but there were so many unanswered questions. When the excitement finally died down and her aunts removed themselves to give the younger women time to visit alone, Abrianna couldn't help but ask a question.

"Are you . . . and Kolbein . . . well, are you surprised that this has happened so soon after marrying?"

Lenore laughed and shook her head. "We've wanted it since our wedding night." She put her hand momentarily to her mouth and lowered her voice. "I suppose that sounds rather scandalous."

"Are you at all afraid?"

"Afraid? Of what?" Lenore seemed genuine in her confusion.

"Of the change. Of everything that will be different with a baby to care for. It will no longer be just you and Kolbein. Now there will be a baby to take up your time."

"I see that as a most wonderful blessing." She gazed toward the ceiling, and Abrianna did likewise, wondering if there was a spider. But Lenore just sighed and closed her eyes. "I hope it's a boy. I hope he looks just like Kolbein."

"Mustache and all?" Abrianna teased. She still couldn't quite grasp the excitement of her friend and chewed her lip to refrain from further comment.

Lenore lowered her head and opened her eyes. "Honestly, Abrianna, you do say the silliest things sometimes. But enough about my news. Let us talk about you and Wade. Have you set a date for your wedding? You know I shall be deeply wounded if I am not chosen to stand up with you."

Abrianna slouched back in the chair, thankful that Aunt Miriam was gone. "I don't know what to tell you. We haven't really talked about it. Wade's been so busy, and I . . . well . . . I still don't know what to make of this all."

"What do you mean?"

A sigh escaped Abrianna's lips. "My situation is not like yours. You and Kolbein fell in love at first glance. I always thought that rather romantic and quite special. But Wade and I have been lifelong friends."

"And that is remarkable," Lenore replied. "How wonderful to have that foundation for a marriage."

"Is it?" Abrianna twisted handfuls of her skirt. "I'm not so sure. I mean . . . well. . . ." She didn't know how to put it into words without sounding fretfully ignorant.

"What is it, Abrianna? You do love him, don't you?"

Lenore looked at her oddly, and Abrianna felt she must do what she could to ease her friend's concerns. "Of course I love him. But I've loved him as a brother and a friend for as long as I remember. To love him otherwise . . ." Her cheeks flushed, and she could feel the heat of her embarrassment.

"Are you worried about . . . being . . . physical?" Lenore asked in a hushed tone.

Abrianna shrugged. "I don't think that's what this is about, although I can say that is a mystery to me that I prefer not to contemplate at the moment. I suppose my worry is about what will happen to our friendship."

"Why, it will grow stronger and deeper," Lenore replied. "You are such a silly goose. You are worried over nothing at all. Your love will only make your friendship better. We have long seen that Wade was over the moon about you, and now that you realize he holds your heart, nothing could ever be better."

It seemed that Abrianna could not find words to express the depths of her concern. "But marriage . . . loving someone in such a different and intimate way . . . it can't help but minimalize the feelings that were there before."

"Why? Why should there be any minimalizing of the heart? Your love has grown from a blossom of friendship. You have nurtured it with trust and healthy watering of honesty and compassion. Now it has bloomed in full to become the sweetest and most beautiful of flowers."

"But flowers don't remain long after full bloom," Abrianna said. "Don't you ever worry about . . . well . . . becoming like other married people? I mean, look at your parents as an example. You've often said yourself that they sometimes go days without really sharing time together. I would never want that to happen. I love spending time with Wade. I find him fascinating to talk to. He treats me like an equal—well, most of the time. He tells me things that are happening in the world without concern that he will shock or disturb my delicate sensibilities."

Lenore gave an unladylike snort. "That's because you have no delicate sensibilities, Abrianna. You were born with an eagerness to meet the world head on, and God help the man or woman who tries to force you into a mold that society could approve."

"Am I truly that bad?" Her friend's comment caused Abrianna to wonder if she was the misbehaving rebel she'd often been accused of being.

"It's not at all bad." Lenore shook her head. "You misunderstand my words. I mean them as a compliment. I've always admired your boldness. I have even envied your ability to deal with people, and your compassion for the needy humbles me. I do not believe you to be bad in any way, Abrianna. I simply want to encourage you to look forward to this next step in life. To become a wife is most fulfilling."

Abrianna decided to say nothing more on the matter, although she was most tempted to ask Lenore to give greater detail about her comment on wifely fulfillment.

"Let us put aside such worries and speak about the joys," Lenore suggested. "Have you thought of what kind of wedding gown you would like? Every girl dreams of such a gown, and you surely must have thoughts for your own."

Not wanting Lenore to think less of her, Abrianna nodded. "The gown would be a very special thing to plan. I know my aunts will want to have a hand in its creation."

"I think we should get started right away on preparation. You will no doubt want to marry before the year's out. Oh, do wait until after the baby is born so I might be allowed to stand up with you. You do want me to be your matron of honor, don't you?"

"Of course." Abrianna's stomach flipped at the very thought of arranging a wedding. Goodness, but why did these things have to be so complicated? A gown to plan and a date to set. No doubt there would be parties and appointments to figure out. Where were they to live after they were married? What would her role be in helping the needy?

"I think you should have a gown of satin. It will probably be chilly when you marry, so you'll want to have a long sleeve. It should be very flat but ornate in the front, with a bustled back and long sweeping train."

Lenore continued to share her thoughts, but at the mention of the word *bustle* Abrianna couldn't help but wonder if she was too old to run away from home.

3

Jay Cunningham climbed the porch steps at the back of the house and admitted himself into the kitchen. The wafting aroma of fresh baked bread and brewed coffee reminded him that he'd not eaten since supper the night before. It wasn't at all hard to put aside thoughts of Seattle's restoration or of winter rains when a hearty meal awaited him.

"Mr. Jay, you come eat. I make you plenty good breakfast," Liang, the Chinese house girl announced.

"I'm pert near starved to death," Jay said with a smile for the dark-eyed girl. She was just a youngster, no more than fifteen or sixteen, he guessed, but he'd never known anyone to work harder.

He took a seat at the kitchen table where he usually took his morning meal and waited while Liang went to retrieve a plate that was warming on the stove.

"I make you crispy bacon and egg toast." She put the plate in front of him. "I bring you coffee, too."

Jay had once marveled at Liang's attempt at eggs in a basket, and since that time the girl often repeated the treat. He picked up a fork and broke the yolk of the egg nestled in the center of a large piece of toasted bread.

"It plenty hot." Liang put a mug in front of Jay. "You be careful."

He laughed. "I will. This looks mighty fine, Liang. Thank you."

"Missy Abrianna say you also like donuts."

He took a bite of the eggs and toast, then nodded. He washed down the bite with the steaming coffee. "I do. My mama used to make them when I was a boy."

"We gonna show the girls how to make them today. I save you some."

"I would like that, Liang. You're mighty good to me."

The girl beamed. "I mighty good to everyone."

Chuckling, Jay turned his attention back to the food. He was to drive Miss Poisie to town and wasn't at all sure when she expected to leave. He was on his second cup of coffee when he heard the doorbell.

"Wonder who's coming to call." He got to his feet. Knowing there was some concern about Priam Welby coming to pester Abrianna, Jay made his way from the kitchen to assure himself that all was well.

To his surprise, a woman stood dressed in traveling clothes. Beside her was a younger woman, probably Abrianna's age or less. Both looked rather apprehensive, but Mrs. Madison was there, already putting them at ease.

"You will see for yourself we are a school of the utmost propriety," Miriam Madison declared. "Let me give you a tour."

The older woman motioned them to follow. Jay couldn't help but lock gazes with the new woman. She was beautiful, with sandy brown hair all done up with a smart little hat. She had curled the hair around her face, and the ringlets framed it in such a way that he thought her almost doll-like. She seemed equally captivated by Jay's glance and offered him a tiny smile. He grinned and nodded his head in acknowledgment. Who was she?

He knew it wasn't his place to follow after the trio, but he couldn't help himself. He listened as Mrs. Madison gave a speech about the school and all that they had accomplished over the years. Her desire was to offer practical helps for young ladies of marriageable age who needed to better hone their skills before taking on a household. The school also provided a respectable way for Seattle's young men to meet potential mates.

"Oh, Mr. Cunningham." Mrs. Madison spied him as she turned. "I didn't realize you had joined us."

"I was looking . . . for . . . Miss Poisie." He stole another glance at the lovely stranger.

"Mrs. Snyder, this is Mr. Cunningham. He recently came to help us here. His daughter has been my ward for many years in his absence. Mrs. Snyder and her niece have come from Tacoma to acquaint themselves with our school."

Missus. She was married. The disappointment he felt rather surprised him. He smiled nevertheless as the older woman continued with the introductions.

"This is Miss Flora Ledbetter."

Again Jay nodded. Mrs. Snyder smiled. "I'm afraid in my widowhood I am ill equipped to see Flora finished into a proper young lady, and everyone in Tacoma has heard of this place."

He grinned. She was a widow, and she was making it a point to tell him so. Perhaps that flash of interest he'd seen in her eyes wasn't just wishful thinking.

"It's always a privilege to meet beautiful women." He worried

Mrs. Madison would think him a flirt and hurried to add, "I'm certain Miss Flora will find the Madison Bridal School to be a wonderful experience. Mrs. Madison works wonders with these young ladies, and I am blessed to say she turned out my own daughter to be quite accomplished."

"That is a relief to know," Mrs. Snyder replied.

She continued to gaze into his eyes, leaving Jay feeling little doubt that she found him just as appealing as he did her.

"I believe you will find Poisie in my office." Mrs. Madison broke the magic of the moment.

Jay nodded. "Thank you." He started to leave, then turned back. It would be a crime to waste such an opportunity. "If you need someone to show you around the town, Mrs. Snyder, I would be happy to do so. I should be back later this afternoon."

The woman smiled. "Thank you, Mr. Cunningham. I believe that would be most welcome, provided I can find accommodations."

"You may stay with us," Mrs. Madison said. "We want you to feel certain that this is the place for your niece. We have a guest room that you may use."

"Thank you. I'm more than happy to pay."

"Nonsense. We are glad to have you with us." She looked at Jay, and he saw a hint of amusement in her eyes.

He whistled a tune as he made his way down the hall. The morning had started most promising.

"Abrianna, I wonder if I might speak to you about something?"

Glancing up, Abrianna saw her aunt's determined look. "Of course. Have I done something out of line? God knows I have been searching my heart for any possible faults, although sometimes what others see as faults, I see as a worthy quality. Still, I hope I haven't done something to grieve you."

"Not at all." Aunt Miriam came into the sitting room and took the chair nearest Abrianna. "I hope that you know I'm very happy to see you and Wade find true love with each other. I believe you two will work well together. Has he asked for your hand?"

"Not in so many words," Abrianna replied. "I know it's implied, as he has mentioned our marriage."

"Well, he must do things properly. I will speak to him on this."

Abrianna frowned. "You needn't. I'm sure he'll get around to it."

The older woman frowned. "You sound less than enthusiastic for such a proposal."

Abrianna put aside the book she'd been trying to read. "Aunt Miriam, do you believe that love changes everything?"

"In what way?"

"Well . . . in the way of friendship and everything you've known." She wasn't making sense, and she could see Aunt Miriam's confusion. "Wade and I have been friends for as long as I can remember. Will marriage change that?"

Her aunt seemed to relax. "I believe marriage will change it for the better."

"That's what Lenore said, but I'm less than convinced. It seems to me that people are always talking about change being for the better, but I like things the way they are. I like knowing that Wade is who he is. Marriage will make him someone else."

"It will make him a husband. That much is true. Are you afraid of that?"

"I don't know," Abrianna admitted. How could she explain

all the worries in her heart? Lenore thought her silly, and no doubt Aunt Miriam would, as well.

"Perhaps you are worried about the marital rites between a man and woman. I realize we haven't spoken of such things," Aunt Miriam said without embarrassment. "Those things are better left unsaid until just before the wedding. A physical relationship between a man and woman after marriage can seem rather overwhelming, but I assure you . . . it is . . . well, not without its pleasures."

Abrianna shook her head. "I'm sure I have much to learn about such things, but I wasn't talking about that." She got up and paced a bit. "Wade is my dearest friend. I love him and have for many, many years. Now, however, I find that I am also in love with him romantically. I never looked for such a thing to happen and I . . . I am afraid it will ruin what we have as friends."

"How could that be?"

She stopped and looked at her aunt. "I don't know. I just fear it will."

"You are worrying needlessly, Abrianna. Mr. Madison and I were good friends before we wed. I found that marriage only furthered that relationship. It is a wonderful thing to marry your dearest friend. There is already a foundation of trust established. That foundation is perfect for building a life together."

Abrianna sank down on the floor beside the older woman. Leaning her head on Aunt Miriam's knee, Abrianna was reminded of being a little girl. "If only I could be sure."

Aunt Miriam reached out and stroked Abrianna's free curls. Other times her aunt would have admonished her for leaving her hair down, but this time she said nothing about it. "You should take all of these fears to the Lord. And perhaps to Wade, as well. I suppose it is possible that he might even have some of the same concerns. Whatever you do, don't leave things unspoken. You will only regret it."

Abrianna said nothing. Her aunt's touch was soothing, and Abrianna didn't want to break the mood of the moment. All of her life she had found comfort with Aunt Miriam and the others. She learned so much about the world through their lessons and gentle correction. They had been mother and father, friend and authority, and she loved them.

Aunt Miriam put her finger under Abrianna's chin. Raising her face, Abrianna could see much tenderness in her aunt's eyes. "You have blessed my life, child. Please do not fret. Wade loves you and you love him. Let that be enough for now. The rest will come in time. There will be arguments, just as you have now. There will be laughter, just as now. But above all, you will have each other in a way that you have never had anyone else. It is a precious and mysterious thing how love and marriage make man and woman one of heart and flesh. You will see. And it will fill you with wonder."

Her words were comforting. Perhaps Abrianna had been silly to worry about her friendship with Wade being altered. Surely he would never do anything to hurt her. Not on purpose.

"Thank you, Aunt Miriam. Your words have done much to put my mind at ease. I know I can be rather intolerable at times. It's part of my nature, I'm sure. But I am willing to receive counsel. Especially on this point." She straightened, then rose. "It is hard to put aside my childish ways. I suppose the changes in life—not just the idea of marriage, but becoming a woman of my majority has overwhelmed me. Everything seems to be spinning out of my control."

"Then give that control to God, Abrianna. It will be much better in His hands."

"Yes. I know you are right."

Aunt Miriam stood and smiled. "And while you're at it, I would like you to seek Him on another matter."

"What?"

"Poisie and Selma and I have talked often of how we would like for you to one day run this school." She held up her hand. "Don't say anything, just hear me out. We believe you and Wade would make a perfect team to do so. We'd very much like to be able to take our ease and live out our days quietly. If you were to take the school, we could do so."

"You can do so, anyway," Abrianna replied. "That money you gave me can just as well be returned to care for the three of you long into your years of infirmity."

Aunt Miriam chuckled. "Well, I have no immediate plans for infirmity, but I do thank you for your concern. Your money is not needed. We have invested wisely for ourselves. We have lived frugally and practiced thrift at every turn."

"Then why not simply close the school? We can all remain here. It's a wonderful house, and perhaps Wade would like for us to remain here after we're married. I think we could all be quite happy."

"But I feel the school serves a very good purpose—a ministry. Look at all the couples we have seen joined together over the years. Would you doubt that God has used this school as a ministry for love?"

"No. I just doubt that I should ever run it. I do not feel qualified. You have even posed doubts about my ability to handle a household."

"I suppose I have been rather harsh at times. But Abrianna, please do me—us—the favor of praying about it. Talk to Wade, as well."

Abrianna gave a sigh. "Very well. I will do that, but please do not get your hopes up. I feel confident that my ministry is with the poor of spirit and means, not the poor of heart in search of romantic love."

"Thank you. I will inform the others," Aunt Miriam said. "And I will leave you to your book. Supper will be in one hour, and Wade said he hoped to be home in time to sit down with us. I'm sure you will want to enjoy an evening together, so I will not expect you to help with the meal or cleanup."

"Thank you, Aunt Miriam."

Her aunt gave a curt nod and left the room.

Abrianna thought of Wade, and a delicious shiver ran through her. The memory of his kiss left her with butterflies in her stomach. She loved him. She wanted nothing more than to be with him the rest of her life.

"I am such a ninny," she whispered and hugged her arms around her body. "Growing up is a good thing. Change can be beneficial. And what I feel for Wade is definitely a beautiful thing." Perhaps if she reminded herself of those things often, her fears would diminish and she would find peace.

4

With muscles stretched taut, Wade hoisted another armload of hubs and carried them to his worktable. "I can't say that working from a tent is easy. Every night I have to load my tools and supplies back into the wagon to take home because of all the looting. I know the law is trying to keep things under control, but there are always those who want to help themselves." He looked to his best friend, Thane Patton, and shook his head. "Not only that, but I've made more money working construction for other people than in getting my wainwright business back to where it was."

"Maybe God is leading you in a different direction. Maybe construction is something He wants you to do. I know He's taking me in a different direction."

Wade put down a stack of felloes and gave Thane his full attention. "And what direction is that?"

"Militine and I are leaving Seattle. I wasn't sure how to break the news to you, but I figure you and I both prefer just coming right out with it."

The news took Wade by surprise. "But I thought you liked it here."

"I do, but Militine would be happier if we got farther away from where she grew up. She's always afraid of running into someone who knows her. I figured California might be the place to go. I wrote a letter to the fire chief in San Francisco and applied for a position of full-time fireman. I just got a letter back offering me a job."

"Well, I'll be. I have to say this isn't at all what I expected." He tried not to sound disapproving. "I hope you know what you're doing. Making a big move like that won't be easy."

"It'll be easy enough, since I lost most everything in the fire," Thane said with a shrug. "Militine doesn't have that much, either. We have a little bit of cash set aside from money given to us at the wedding, and with what I've been making working on the rebuilding, I think we'll be just fine."

"I'm sure you will be. You've always been able to take care of yourself. It'll be hard not having you around, however. We've had a lot of years looking out for each other."

Thane laughed. "That's true enough. I know I'd be a lot worse for it if you hadn't come to my rescue a few times."

Wade shook his head with a smile. "As would I. You've kept me out of trouble more than once. It won't be the same here without you."

"Who knows, maybe you and Abrianna will want to relocate one day, as well. It would be great to have you join us there."

"I don't see that happening. Abrianna would fret about her aunts, and there's the fact that her father just came back into her life."

Thane nodded, his expression one of complete understanding. "Do you figure to live at the school after you're married?"

Wade shook his head. "That isn't what I want. I want a house of our own. I'm hoping Abrianna will feel the same way. I don't think it would be all that comfortable to discover life as a married couple with all those folks looking over our shoulder."

Thane laughed. "It hasn't been easy for Militine and me, but we've made do."

"So when do you plan to leave for San Francisco?"

"The end of next week."

Wade pushed back his sweaty hair. "That soon, eh? Well, I suppose it's just as well. You need to get out of here and settled before the weather turns."

"We had hoped to be around when you and Abrianna got married. Have you set a date yet?"

Wade shook his head and went to retrieve another box of goods. "You wanna give me a hand?" Thane immediately came to his aid. Together they hoisted the crate atop the table. "Been so busy I haven't even asked her father for his blessing. Fact is, I feel it's probably more appropriate to ask the old ladies. Either way, I didn't want to break with propriety. Abrianna knows that marriage is what I plan for us."

"I know you'll get their permission, whether it comes from one or all. Militine tells me the old ladies and Mr. Cunningham have had nothing but elated joy when talking about it. Seems they can't think of two people who are more perfectly matched."

Using a pry bar, Wade opened the crate. Inside were some of the tools he'd ordered to replace those lost in the fire. "I'm glad they feel that way." He smiled at Thane and shook his head. "I don't know if it would matter to me if they disapproved. I love her, and I can't get her out of my thoughts."

"I know how you feel. I've felt that way about Militine for a long time now. I remember you once asked me how I could be sure it was love. I suppose you understand the answer to that question now."

Wade remembered the conversation. It seemed to have taken place years ago rather than just months. "I do, but I would be hard-pressed to explain it to anyone else."

Thane laughed. "Exactly."

"Well, I hoped I might find you here," Brother Mitchell, the head elder of the church, announced as he entered Wade's tent. "I've had to ask all over for directions. The city is in such disrepair, what with them widening and replatting the streets."

"Come on in, Brother Mitchell. It's good to see you. What can I do for you? Need a wagon repaired?" Wade put aside the tools he'd been pulling from the box.

"No, nothing wagon related, but there is something I need to talk to you about."

Wade dusted off his hands. He couldn't imagine what the elder wanted with him. "I wish I could offer you some refreshment, but I'm afraid I have nothing."

"Not to worry. I'm here on business. Church business."

As a deacon of the church, Wade often found himself brought into the confidences of the elders regarding church needs. "Is it all right if Thane stays?"

Brother Mitchell looked to Thane and nodded. "Of course. Although I would ask you both to keep this conversation confidential until a formal announcement can be made."

"A formal announcement of what?" Wade asked.

"We elders met on several occasions and have spent a great deal of time in prayer on the matter of finding another pastor. We don't want to feel rushed into a decision, as we did last time. But we have come to a decision. We would like to ask you to be our pastor in the interim while we search."

"Me?" Wade couldn't fathom why they would come to him. "I have no formal training."

"But I have heard you lead the men in prayer and Bible study. I was present at several of your studies with the friendless. I can tell you now that the purpose at that time was for extending a request for you to take a position as elder." He held up his hand, seeming to expect Wade's protest. "I know you feel that being young and unmarried disqualifies you for a position of authority, but we have searched the Scriptures and find that not to be the case. In every situation we have seen only support for your placement. With this new need, we believe you perfect for the job. Besides, others in the congregation have suggested you for the position."

"Me? But why?" This was all news to Wade. He looked to Thane, but he just shrugged.

"Folks liked the way you dealt with Pastor Walker. They felt you were led of the Lord. Not only that, but they know you, know that you're honorable. They feel that God has His hand on you and you need to answer His call."

"I have to say you've taken me by surprise. I have never thought of taking the pulpit as a profession or calling."

"We only ask that you pray on the matter. And speak also to your intended." He smiled. "I know Miss Cunningham's heart for mission work. She has long presented herself as a strong woman of God." His expression changed slightly to one of concern. "Although, I will say she has always been given to speaking first and rushing in to take charge of a matter. I suppose it could be a virtue in a man, but in a woman it oft feels disconcerting."

Wade chuckled. "I'll say. But as for prayer and speaking to Abrianna, I give you my word to do both. If God is directing me to help the church out in this manner, I want to do whatever I can. The church has been good to me, just as it was good to my folks. I owe the congregation that much."

"Wonderful," Brother Mitchell said, his face brightening. "I will tell the elders. We will anxiously await your decision."

Wade shook the man's hand. Once the elder left, Wade turned to Thane. "Well, what do you think of that?"

"Well, Pastor Ackerman," Thane replied with a grin, "I think the Lord works in mysterious ways."

"That He does," Wade replied. Never in his life had he thought of taking on such a position. Never had he felt qualified, but of late he had to admit that God kept putting him in positions of teaching. "Maybe God's taking me in a new direction, just as He has you and Militine."

"What do you think Abrianna will say?"

Wade shrugged. "Who can ever tell what she's going to say? For all the love I hold for her, I can't begin to suppose I know what goes on inside that busy little head of hers."

"Women can be a real mystery."

"That they can." Wade shook his head. "Especially when it comes to my future wife."

Abrianna reached across several new rosebuds to reach one in full bloom. The pink rose gave off a scent so sweet that for a moment all she could do was inhale and enjoy the aroma. She touched the delicate petal, and for some reason her mother came to mind.

"I wish you were here to advise me," she murmured. "I wish I could have known you." Tears blurred her vision. At times, the loss of her mother was a dull ache, and other times it was a piercing pain—as it was now. For a moment Abrianna felt just as she had when she was a little girl awakening from a bad dream. There was a sense of fear and loss that caused her to tremble. Back then, one of her aunts would come and soothe her back to sleep with stories about her mother. But for this moment there was no one who could help her.

She buried her longing and wiped the tears. *I would never want my aunts to think me ungrateful. It seems so ridiculous that I should desire what I cannot have, given the fact that God has blessed me with so much. What a selfish girl I can be.* She glanced heavenward. *Forgive me, Father.*

"You have a lovely garden," a woman said. Abrianna straightened to find Mrs. Snyder walking down the path. "I can't remember seeing anything this nice in Tacoma."

"My aunts are quite enthusiastic about flowers and keeping the grounds beautiful. When we were located downtown we had no opportunity to garden, and it very much vexed them. We haven't been here all that long, but the former owners arranged these lovely gardens. My aunts have great plans for future weddings and parties on the lawn."

"I think one would be quite fortunate to have a wedding here."

Abrianna looked across the garden and nodded. "Yes, I believe I would like to be married here."

"Are you engaged?"

"In a manner," she replied and put the rose in the basket with the other flowers. "We haven't made a formal announcement, but we have declared our love. Although I suppose a declaration of love isn't a true commitment. Still, I feel that my declaration is a commitment and obligates me to put aside any other interests. Oh dear, I suppose obligate makes it sound as if I'm not at all pleased. Loving Wade isn't at all an obligation, so please don't misunderstand me." She drew a breath and could see the woman's confusion. Smiling, Abrianna offered an apology. "You'll have to forgive me. I do tend to prattle on."

"It's not a problem, I assure you. My Flora can be just the same." The woman glanced around the yard, then fixed her gaze back on Abrianna. "You're Mr. Cunningham's daughter, aren't you?"

"Yes. Abrianna Cunningham." She frowned. "We met this morning when you and Flora were introduced to the students. Perhaps your journey here caused you fatigue. Then again, I can't say that I'm the most memorable person. Especially when you came here with thoughts of seeing your niece enrolled. Still, my red hair usually causes folks to recall me without effort."

Mrs. Snyder looked at her with an odd smile. "I am rather poor at keeping track of names and faces. I do recall your beautiful hair, however."

Abrianna smiled at the reference to beauty. "It has been a troublesome burden to me all of my life. Redheaded women are most complicated, in case you didn't know. My aunt Miriam says that we are given to fits of temper and exploits too numerous to list. She said it is as if God made our hair red as a warning to others that mischief was afoot."

Mrs. Snyder smiled. "I can't imagine that is true of you."

"Oh, but you do not know the half of it." Abrianna shrugged. "I am quite strong-willed. I see a matter that needs attending, and rather than seek the advice of others, I simply step in and take care of the need. It's both a curse and a blessing, but I know that it has been a great burden to my aunts. Many has been the time I have overheard them praying for wisdom in how to deal with me, as well as asking the Almighty to keep me from causing harm to myself or others."

"And is your father of that same vein? Does he plunge in to attend a matter regardless of advice?"

Abrianna grew thoughtful. How could she explain to this woman that she was just now getting to know her father? She supposed the truth was best, but of late it seemed the truth only served to stir things up into a frenzy. She couldn't lie, however. That wouldn't be right, what with her new goal to be open and honest, even when it proved difficult.

"In truth, I cannot say that I know whether he is that kind of man or not. You see, he has just come back into my life after being absent for all my growing years."

"Truly? What caused such an absence?"

Abrianna sighed. If she wasn't careful she might very well find herself in tears once again. "He was wrongly accused of a crime he didn't commit." She frowned. "I suppose if you are wrongly accused it goes without saying that you didn't commit the crime, so forgive my unnecessary words. He was imprisoned until the rightful criminal was found and confessed. Unfortunately, that cost my father twenty years of his life and robbed me of his presence in mine."

"My word! What a terrible tragedy." Mrs. Snyder had her hand to her throat and looked very shocked.

"I hope I haven't caused you undue worry. He is a good man and quite kind."

"He strikes me as a very considerate man. Do you know he offered to drive me around Seattle? I'm afraid it didn't work out this afternoon, but we have a plan to do just that tomorrow morning."

Abrianna got the distinct feeling that this woman was interested in her father for more than a tour around the city. There was a glimmer in her eyes that Abrianna had once seen when Lenore first met Kolbein. Goodness, but could Mrs. Snyder be taken with Father?

"At last I've found you," Wade declared, coming from behind them.

Abrianna turned so quick that her skirts caught in the roses, and she started to fall. Wade, ever her hero, caught her in his arms and righted her.

"You must forgive her," he said to Mrs. Snyder. "Abrianna is always throwing herself at me."

The older woman chuckled. "You must be her fiancé. I am Mrs. Snyder. My niece Flora has just arrived to attend the school."

"Wade Ackerman." He didn't let go his hold on Abrianna.

"Well, if you'll excuse me," Mrs. Snyder said, "I will leave you two a moment for yourselves." She left before Abrianna could say a word, for Wade was already turning her in his arms.

"I've thought of nothing but this moment all day long." He kissed her gently and pulled back with a smile. "I think I'm really starting to get the hang of this."

"Oh, Wade." Abrianna nudged him, but he held her fast. "You completely embarrassed me in front of Mrs. Snyder. She'll think I'm positively wanton."

"You're the one who pretended to fall."

"I did not pretend." Abrianna pushed harder this time. "You are insufferable."

Wade laughed and lifted her at the waist. "You may call me anything you like, so long as you tell me that you'll love me forever."

She smiled down at him, feeling much of her worry and fears melt away. "I certainly cannot lie about that matter, for my heart is yours now, as it always has been." She shook her head as he lowered her. Once her feet were firmly on the ground, Abrianna motioned to the pump. "You smell like sweat and ash. I will not bear another of your embraces until you clean up."

Wade made as if he would pull her into his arms again, and Abrianna let out a little squeal and jumped back. "I mean it. You smell something frightful." She took two more steps back.

He walked slowly toward her. Abrianna continued to back up. "Wade Ackerman, I have spoken my piece."

"So you have. You seem to speak quite a few pieces, but I have learned the trick to closing that mouth of yours." His eyes seemed to sparkle in mischievous delight, and his lips were curled in a wicked grin.

Abrianna found his playfulness rather seductive, and for the life of her couldn't remember why she was backing away. She stopped, fully expecting him to take her in his arms and kiss her with the same passion he had on the Fourth of July and more recently. Instead, after crossing the distance between them, he stopped and merely looked down at her. Abrianna lifted her face to make it all the more easy for him to kiss her lips and closed her eyes. She heard him chuckle, and instead of kissing her, he tweaked her nose. Her eyes flashed open as he turned away.

"Perhaps I should wash up, after all. I wouldn't want to offend the other ladies at supper."

She watched him go as a sense of disappointment washed over her. He really didn't smell that bad.

"Oh, by the way," Wade said, turning around in midstep. "The elders have asked me to take over the pulpit until they can find a pastor for the church. What do you think of that?"

"I think it's wonderful." She hesitated before continuing. "Pride goeth before a fall, but I must say I am proud of you. I suppose, however, that pride in someone serving God isn't the same as pride in one's own accomplishments. Therefore, I rest on my previous declaration. I'm proud of you. I believe you'll make a wonderful pastor."

His lips twitched in just a hint of a smile. "Did you ever think you'd be married to a preacher?"

Abrianna shrugged. "I never thought I'd be married, so all of this is pretty new to me."

His smile widened. "Well, you'd better get your mind around it. I intend to talk to your pa as soon as I can find him."

5

Priam Welby paid a boy to watch until all the men of the Madison Bridal School left the grounds. As instructed, the boy hurried back with the news that all three had departed first thing that morning. Priam knew Thane Scott and Wade Ackerman would make their way downtown to work, and as luck would have it Jay Cunningham drove the carriage out, complete with a female passenger. He paid the boy and sent him on his way before climbing into his carriage.

"Take me to the Madison Bridal School," he instructed the driver.

It was a short distance to the estate, but during the ride Priam used the time to plot and plan how he would handle things if the old ladies got in his way. His charms would be lost on them, and threats would be equally useless. He had visions of the old women picking up brooms and umbrellas to beat him back off their porch. He supposed he would just have to do what he could when the time came.

When they arrived at the school, Priam instructed the driver to wait for him as long as it took. The man gave a curt nod and then fixed his gaze forward. He knew better than to counter any request Priam made.

Walking up the porch steps, Priam glanced around to see if any of the women were about. There wasn't a sign of anyone. He hoped the old ladies were busy with their bridal classes and the Chinese maid would give him quick entry to see Abrianna. He knocked and picked lint from his suit coat lapel as he waited.

To his pleasant surprise and relief it was Abrianna herself who came to the door. She stepped back and lost the smile on her face. "Mr. Welby. We weren't expecting you."

He tipped his hat. "Good morning, Miss Cunningham. I do apologize for such an early visit, but I wondered if I might speak to you. We could sit out here on the porch if you like."

Abrianna glanced over her shoulder then nodded. Priam opened the screen door to allow her exit. "You look quite lovely today," he said. The blue and white outfit she wore, along with the way she'd tied her hair back, made her look rather juvenile, but he thought only to put her mind at ease with compliments.

"Thank you. I must say, I really don't know why you're here. I know that Kolbein . . . ah, Mr. Booth was to have settled our business arrangement."

He smiled at her bluntness. "Well, in truth, despite Mr. Booth's delivery of your canceled contract, I find you are all that I can think about."

She frowned. "I am sorry for that, Mr. Welby."

"You're the first person I think of when I awaken and the last one who comes to mind before I sleep. I dream about you. I ponder ways to win your heart." He smiled. "All in all, you are never far from my thoughts."

"That is, I'm sure, most annoying." She looked down as if to study the toe of her shoe. "It would seem that perhaps you could reflect on Scriptures instead. Or perhaps you should read Mr. William Salter's *Ethical Religion*. I am led to understand it has great qualities of interest to the learned reader. Although, I must admit I haven't read this myself and therefore should probably not seek to suggest it, so perhaps you could just forget my mention."

He chuckled and took hold of her arm. "Come sit with me." He pulled her to where there were several chairs positioned close together for easy conversation.

She seemed reluctant, but when he let go of her arm, she squared her shoulders. "For just a few minutes."

Abrianna took her seat. Welby did likewise and drew off his hat. He noted that she seemed most uncomfortable and thought perhaps there was something he could gain by this. Keeping her off balance seemed the most efficient way of handling Abrianna Cunningham.

"I don't suppose you realize that you've broken my heart." She looked at him in disbelief but said nothing. "I know that most people think me heartless and all business, but the truth is, I have fallen quite in love with you."

"Oh dear," she said in a whisper that sounded quite contrite.

"Indeed. I can scarcely think of business or other affairs without you coming to mind. When you sent Mr. Booth to break our contract, I can tell you quite honestly . . . well, I took to my house and hid myself away, neither eating nor drinking for two days." The lie sounded natural enough and given her willingness to believe everyone truthful, Priam felt confident she would buy into his story.

She bit her lower lip. He might have laughed at her anxious expression had he been less determined to get her to reconsider the contract. "You see," he continued, "when you gave me hope that we might have a future together, I was the happiest man alive."

"But I did not give you hope," she protested. "I told you I was certain I would not fall in love with you. Now I know quite well why I was so confident of the matter. My heart belongs to another, even though I didn't realize it at the time."

He sighed. "Then there is no hope for me?"

"There is always hope for each of God's children, but not by courting me," she declared. "You truly must seek another avenue, Mr. Welby, for I am not the means to happiness for you."

He tried to appear thoughtful. "And I can do nothing to convince you otherwise? You did give me your word that you would give me time to woo you."

"I am sorry, Mr. Welby, but to do so would be dishonest. Our contract allowed for either of us to dissolve it should anything arise to cause conflict with the contents. I came to realize that my love for Wade Ackerman was one that would lead us to matrimony. I cannot entertain another gentleman who has thoughts of wooing me when I am all but engaged to another."

"So you aren't formally engaged?" he asked.

She sighed. "It's just a matter of making all the announcements. As far as Wade and I are concerned, we are engaged and preparing for marriage."

He put his hand to his heart. "You have no idea how this grieves me. It pierces my heart as if you'd plunged in a knife."

"Mr. Welby, you have made this matter much more than it ever was or will be," Abrianna began. "I was honest with you from the start, and anything I said or did to otherwise convince you of the possibility that I would fall in love with you is simply a misunderstanding on your part."

Welby worked hard to keep his ire in check. The fact that she told the truth didn't bother him. The fact that she was unwilling to yield to his will was infuriating.

"Perhaps you should speak to Mr. Ackerman about this." Welby fixed her with a most intent but pleading gaze. "Would he truly wish for you to go into the sanctity of marriage having had no other man to consider? What if you are the one mistaken in your feelings? Did that not ever occur? What if what you both are experiencing is just a fleeting summer emotion brought on by the devastation of the city and the urgency of time? You've long been friends. That much is true. But friendship and love are two entirely different matters."

Her brows came together, giving her a rather worried appearance. Welby felt confident he'd gained a tiny bit of ground and pushed on.

"And if that is the case, then not only are you doing your friendship a disservice, but you are denying yourself a chance at happiness with me, as well."

"My friendship with Wade has always been very important to me," she murmured almost as if he wasn't there. "Everyone has told me that friendship is an important foundation for marriage. So even though your counsel is otherwise, I believe that I am better acquainted with the honesty of my friends and family."

"But of course they will tell you that," he said, shaking his head and giving a little *tsk*ing sound. "They are telling you what they believe is best for you. And perhaps they are concerned that . . . well, given your closeness to Mr. Ackerman, other men might believe you have compromised your virtue. Perhaps they are pushing you to marry Mr. Ackerman because they are worried that no other man might have you. However, for me, none of that is important. I love you, Abrianna. If you've made mistakes in the past, I will not hold them against you. I simply plead for you to give me a chance to court you."

"Mr. Welby!"

He'd gone too far. He could see it in her eyes. That tiny spark of fire suggested anger. He stood and put on his hat. "Please know that if I've overstepped my bounds in what I said, I apologize. I didn't mean to allow the conversation to take an indiscreet turn. I will, instead, take my leave." He paused a moment and gave her his saddest look of longing. At least he hoped that's how it played out.

"I shall always regret you. I don't even know how to find the will to go on if you are unwilling to change your mind. I will, however, wait to do anything rash for one week. If after that time you are still of a mind to forget me, then I shall seek the necessary means to put you from my mind."

Abrianna shot up at this. "Grief, Mr. Welby, you are worse at making me feel guilty than Aunt Miriam, and she's quite accomplished. You mustn't allow yourself to think such dire thoughts. I would advise you to get spiritual counsel. I realize our little church is currently without a pastor, but there are the elders and of course other churches with strong men of God."

"Oh, there you are, Abrianna," Flora Ledbetter called out but came up short as she spied Mr. Welby. "Excuse me. I didn't know you had company."

"It's quite all right." Abrianna looked at him and then to Flora. "Miss Ledbetter, this is Mr. Priam Welby." She turned back to Welby. "This is Miss Ledbetter. She is a new student to the school. Perhaps you might get to know her better when you attend the monthly receptions. Although my aunts will have her behind the refreshment tables for some months to come, you might actually be able to strike up a conversation across the punch bowl."

"Miss Ledbetter, I'm charmed to meet you." Priam gave a little bow. "However, I don't believe I will be attending any more receptions." He tried his best to sound utterly hopeless and defeated. "I bid you both . . . good-bye." He paused for measure and added, "I mean good day."

Abrianna wasn't at all sure if Mr. Welby was serious in his thoughts of ending it all, at least that was the implication she'd assumed. He didn't come right out and say he would kill himself over her, but he did speak of delaying rash action.

"Is he a friend of yours?" Flora asked.

"Goodness, no. He was to have courted me, but that was prior to my realizing that I was in love with Wade." She watched Welby's carriage leave the grounds and go slowly down the street. Turning away, she shook her head. "What a perfectly complicated man."

"He has rather large ears," Flora said.

Abrianna looked at her as if finally finding a kindred soul. "Exactly my observation. I've said that on many occasions, and while I would not refuse a gentleman merely because of the size of his ears, they are a terrible distraction. That along with his dark eyes. They seem to be set apart rather far."

Flora nodded. "I agree. He dresses nicely, however."

"Oh yes. Mr. Welby is a most fashionable gentleman." Abrianna tried to forget the scene that had just played out. Surely he wouldn't go so far as to end his life over her. Perhaps she should consult her aunts on the matter.

"Mrs. Madison sent me away," Flora said, as if Abrianna had

asked about her sudden appearance. "She was annoyed with me, I think. I kept telling her about the way we did things in Montana. I don't think she much cared about that."

Abrianna motioned the younger woman to sit. "No. She is very fixed in how she believes things should go. You will do better to keep that in mind. I know from personal experience that even information obtained by books and magazines is of little interest to my aunts. They all have their opinions of how certain things should be managed, and that is that. I remember once when *Godey's*, no, it was *Peterson's Ladies National Magazine* gave a recipe on making mutton pie. It did not meet my aunts' standards. It had something to do with an inordinate amount of rosemary in the recipe. But from that point on they avoided *Peterson's* all together."

"I hope I didn't ruin my chances here." Flora seemed quite contrite, and Abrianna felt sorry for her. "Even my roommate Elizabeth seems to despise my enthusiasm."

"My aunts may be fixed in their ways, but they are also most generous with their forgiveness when it comes to students. As for Elizabeth, perhaps she just doesn't appreciate your fire for living. If you like, I will have my aunt move you to share my room. I'd rather like having a roommate like you."

"Oh, that would be so grand," Flora said, holding her hands to her breast. "I cannot imagine anything that would make me happier. How can I repay you?"

"I would love to hear something of Montana. Tell me about your life there. I heard you say you grew up on a ranch."

"Yes," she replied, nodding with great enthusiasm. "My mother and father owned the ranch, and my older brother Dusty"—she leaned forward as if to share a great secret—"his real name is Zedekiah, but he won't let anyone use it."

"How odd. It's a perfectly good Bible name," Abrianna countered.

She nodded. "He wouldn't even go by Zed. Mama told me that when Dusty was six years old, he came home from school with a blackened eye and bruised face. He declared then and there that he would no longer be Zedekiah Ledbetter, but Dusty Ledbetter."

"That is most peculiar. Where do you suppose he got a name like that?"

"Mama thought it was something he dreamed up after riding herd with Papa. No matter the origin, he refused to answer to anything else."

"Where is he now?"

"He has the ranch. When Papa died, Dusty was grown and took over the place. Mama was very grieved over losing Papa, and she stayed mostly to herself for a long time. In the meantime, I busied myself by going to school and doing some of the cooking chores. Dusty was gone a lot and I gave it no mind, but then one day he shows up with a bride—Mrs. Lorelei Ledbetter, formerly Miss Lorelei Vandercamp. She was a most tedious woman who resented having to live with her mother-in-law. I suppose she resented me as well, but her worst attitude was directed at Mama."

"Goodness, that hardly seems right."

"It was truly a nightmare. Lorelei didn't like Mama and me. She used to nag Dusty something fierce to send us elsewhere. Why she figured she had the right to throw us out of our own home, I'll never know. Just meanspirited, I guess."

"It would appear so," Abrianna replied, getting caught up in the story. "Do you suppose she was lacking in spiritual qualities? Or perhaps she had suffered an injury as a child and was unable to think clearly?"

"I don't know what she suffered, but she sure made the rest of us suffer." Flora shook her head. "Made Mama downright sick. She would take to her bed rather than have to deal with Lorelei. After a while she truly took sick, and the doctor said there was no hope of her recovery. That was when Mama made me pen a letter to Aunt Eloise. She knew Lorelei would be mean to me, and Dusty would never believe it, so she wanted my aunt to raise me. I was just fourteen when mama died."

"What a tragedy, and one I know well." Sadness washed over Abrianna. She hadn't wanted to stir thoughts of her mother, but it was impossible to change the conversation now. "I lost my mother when I was barely first walking. Had these three gracious ladies not cared for her and promised to care for me, I might have been thrown into the streets. Instead, I have lived a most beneficial life."

"I've enjoyed living with Aunt Eloise, but she says I'm much too wild for her. I worry her into states of panic and excessive headaches. I think it's because she's old. Once a person grows older than thirty, they seem to lose their ability to enjoy life." Flora shrugged. "I never gave Mama headaches."

Abrianna drew a deep breath and dug her nails into the palms of her hands. Pain of the flesh was better than pain of the heart. "I felt you were a kindred spirit when you first arrived. I have always been too wild for my aunts. They would prefer I be demure and quiet, but no matter how I try, it just never seems I can be that way for long. Inevitably, I will see something that needs to be attended and no one else willing to take on the matter, so I jump in to see it through."

"I am that way, as well," Flora agreed. "When I saw the upstairs windows at Aunt Eloise's house were in need of a good cleaning and the servants were much too fearful to climb out onto the roof and tend to the matter, I did so myself. It seemed perfectly logical to me. The windows were dirty, and I wasn't afraid of heights."

Abrianna felt the sorrow lift at the idea of Flora's deeds. "I can definitely agree with your thinking. It would seem that older people are less capable of understanding our motives. They are always complicating matters with detailed planning. I would rather plunge straight ahead and get the thing done."

"We are kindred spirits, you and I," Flora agreed. "It is a shame we didn't know each other sooner in life. Perhaps we might have helped each other."

Abrianna nodded. She'd often wished for a friend who thought just as she did. She'd expressed that on one occasion to Wade, and he had merely laughed and said everyone was thankful that there weren't two of her, otherwise the worries would be twice as many.

"Do you think you would want to return to Montana one day?"

A frown crossed Flora's thoughtful expression. "No. I don't think so. Montana isn't big enough for Lorelei and me. I still hold her a grudge for what she did to Mama. I blame her for Mama getting sick and dying. After all, it was hard on her when Papa died, and had Lorelei been a friend, Mama might have gotten through it. Instead, Lorelei was cruel and manipulating. If I ever go back to Montana, it'll be to punch Lorelei in the nose."

Abrianna thought on that for a moment. "I can definitely understand why you would feel that way. I have felt that way myself." She lifted her gaze to Flora. "Not regarding your sister-in-law, you understand. But there are folks here in Seattle who have given me cause to think that way. Although it's not the fault of Seattle. I wouldn't want to besmirch the good name of this city. I have quite enjoyed growing up here. There are a great many good people here, and I hope you come to enjoy Seattle as I have. I find there is always some diversion and someone in need of help."

"Do you have opportunity to help very many people?"

"As many as I am able. Before the fire I ran a food house for the poor and friendless. Of course, I did not do this on my own. Wade and Thane were a part of that, as well as my dear friend Militine. They were very generous to donate much time in that noble task. There were about fifty men who came each day to eat there. They were mostly sailors and old loggers who could no longer work. Some were layabouts, but most were honorable, and layabouts can be just as hungry as those who attempt to work." She sighed but hurried on to explain.

"The fire destroyed our building, but right now there are services available for all the homeless. However, I heard that the shelters and food kitchens are soon to be dissolved, and my friends will once again need me. That has been uppermost on my mind, and I believe I shall have to buy land and build a place of my own if I'm to see those poor souls cared for."

Flora gave a gasp. "I am completely in awe of your accomplishments. What a marvelous way to extend the love of God to your fellowman in need. Pardon me for asking, but however did you talk your aunts into letting you do this? They seem most strict."

Abrianna glanced heavenward and smiled. "I found in life that the best way to get my way was to move forward without seeking permission. I suppose that was wrong of me, however, as I said before, I am a woman who likes to get things done. I was already sneaking around, giving out food to this one and that. I think having an organized structure with Wade gave my aunts the assurance that I would be safer and better watched. And, as I mentioned, Thane and Militine were also there. They're married now."

"I met Militine," Flora admitted. "She is quite a beauty. I envy her that dark hair. My blond hair seems much less dramatic, and I do so long for the dramatic in my life."

"It is funny how we all wish our hair were something other than what the Good Lord gave us." Abrianna pondered for only a moment whether hair color might be one of those things that the Devil had interfered with. The Bible said God had numbered the hairs on her head, but had He also colored them, or were mischievous spirits at work on those matters?

"The food house sounds wonderful. Do you suppose I might help you?"

Flora's question brought Abrianna back to focus. "Well, as soon as I can figure out how to revive it. I was to get help for another place by means of Mr. Welby, but that is no longer possible. I have just come into an inheritance, so my thoughts are to speak with a property broker and purchase a place of my own."

"How positively daring! Such modern thinking. I'm all for that."

Her enthusiasm gave Abrianna reason to believe that the idea must be right. "I will see what I can come up with and keep you apprised. However, we should probably say nothing to the others."

"Oh, but this will be exciting. We will plot and plan it all as our great conspiracy." Flora clapped her hands. "I wish I had grown up with a sister like you. What fun we would have had. No doubt we could have sent Miss Lorelei Vandercamp packing before the nuptials were read."

Abrianna laughed. The young woman made her spirits much lighter. "No doubt. Oh look. There's my father and your aunt." Abrianna looked at Flora with an impish grin. "Perhaps there is a wee bit we might conspire with there, as well."

Flora looked off to the approaching carriage, then turned with a knowing look and a nod. "I do believe you might be right. I think I'm beginning to enjoy being forced to attend bridal training. At least so long as I don't get married off. I really see no need to tie myself to yet another person who will just boss me around."

"The trick"—Abrianna lowered her voice so that no one could overhear—"is to prove yourself very unskilled and slow to learn. That way, you needn't worry about having to present yourself to potential suitors."

Flora nodded in a most serious manner. "You shall be my most trusted advisor, and I your most ardent pupil."

6

You look to have a great deal on your mind, Abrianna."
Wade watched her with growing apprehension. "When
that happens, I usually find I'm required to rescue you from a
burning building or help you down from a tall tree. What are
you up to?"

"I'm not up to anything. Why must you always believe the
worst of me?"

They had received permission to take a walk to the neighbor-
hood park where a band concert was to be given that evening.
Wade had taken special care with his grooming and clothes, as
he intended to formally ask Abrianna for her hand in marriage.
He even had his grandmother's wedding ring to offer her as a
seal to their engagement, but he found he couldn't concentrate
on that plan. She was plotting something or at the very least
contemplating a plot. He could feel it.

He entwined his arm with hers. "I don't believe the worst of
you. I just know you, and when you are quiet, it means you're
up to something. That always turns out to be either very dangerous for you or more work for me."

She stopped, and because he held tightly to her arm, it pulled him back. He raised a brow as he met her determined expression.

"Wade Ackerman, if you are going to insist on berating me for something I haven't even done, then I am going back to the house."

He grinned. "Abrianna, I'm hardly berating you. I just know you well enough to know that you're contemplating something. You might as well just tell me what's on your mind."

A heavy sigh escaped her. "I want to find a place to set up another food house. I know that you are also trying to figure out where you should rebuild your business. Perhaps we could incorporate them together. I have plenty of money we could use, and surely you would worry less about my exploits if we were working in the same place."

"First of all, you need to understand something right now. Your money is yours. I don't intend to use it for our life together. I will make a good income and support the both of us and anyone else who comes along."

"But the money will be ours if we marry."

"If?" He looked at her a moment. "If we marry?"

"Well, it's not exactly like you've asked for my hand. Besides that, now that I know you plan to be so very pigheaded about money . . . well, it gives me some concern. Many a relationship has been dissolved over financial issues."

He laughed. "I'm pigheaded? Abrianna, you have but to look in the mirror to see someone who epitomizes that title."

She tried to pull away, but he was prepared for this and held her fast to his side. "As for proposing, well, I plan to do that tonight. I have the ring in my pocket and all the words memorized. I've thought of little else since asking your father for your hand. However, if you're going to call me names . . ." He let the rest go unspoken just to see her reaction.

Abrianna met his gaze. "Sometimes I wonder if we're suited at all. Even Mr. Welby pointed out that we may well be experiencing nothing more than a moment spurred on by the urgency of life, due to the fire."

"Mr. Welby?" Wade dropped his hold. "When did you see him?"

"He stopped by the house earlier today. Apparently I'm tormenting his thoughts."

"I'm going to torment him right in the nose if he doesn't mind his manners." Wade shook his head. "How dare he try to come between you and me?"

"I don't think his actions were due to a desire to come between us. Not in the sense that he wanted to hurt you, but rather he was trying to assuage his own misery. I told him I had no interest in him. He said he would give me a week to think on it before he . . . well . . . he said he might be given over to do something rash to end his anguish."

"He threatened to kill himself if you didn't yield and allow him to pursue you?"

"Not in so many words, but that was implied."

"Of all the low-down unreasonable things to do to someone. I hope you told him to leave."

Abrianna looked away. "I told him I was uninterested. I pray he will not resort to anything desperate. I do not wish him harm, and selfishly, I'm not sure I could live with myself if he were to take his own life." She turned back to meet Wade's eyes. "Sometimes I really don't like being of age or being a woman."

Wade felt sorry for her. No doubt she truly believed Welby besot with her and willing to end his life at her refusal, but Wade felt confident it was nothing more than a game. Given all that he'd heard about Welby, especially his business deals after the fire, Wade believed the only person Priam Welby loved was Priam Welby. Even so, he didn't want Abrianna dwelling on the man.

He reached out and took hold of her arm again to continue their walk. "I, for one, am very happy that you are a woman. However, I know that sometimes it is hard to be grown up and face the ugliness of the world head on. That's why marriage is good. Two can face it together. You and I have already faced a great deal over the years. Wouldn't you agree that we are well-suited to deal with the trials of life together?"

She nodded, causing the ribbons of her summer hat to flutter across her face. She pushed them back in annoyance. "I cannot in all honesty imagine my life without you. I suppose that is why I am both worried about marrying you and equally troubled at the thought of losing you."

"How can you even contemplate the latter?" he asked. "You will never lose me. I love you and you love me. I want you to be my wife."

Again she stopped. "Sometimes . . . I know it's silly, but I suppose . . . well, what if I'm not the wife you hope I'll be? I mean, there's so very little I know about being a wife, despite my aunts' attempts to teach me. Grief, you would think growing up in a bridal school would prepare one for all the necessities of such a role, but honestly, Wade, I feel very worried that I'll disappoint you."

He chuckled, and despite the very public setting, he pulled her behind the nearest tree and drew her into his arms. "You will never disappoint me. And besides, I know very little about being a husband. We're both bound to make mistakes, but we've made them before, and we'll learn to work through them."

"Do you really think so? I mean, will it be that simple?" She looked up at him with such hope in her expression.

"Abrianna, it's been my experience that nothing with you is simple. But, that doesn't mean it isn't worth pursuing. My pa used to say that the best things in life were worth fighting for. I'm willing to do whatever I can to be a good mate to you. Don't you think you could promise to do the same for me?"

She nodded. "I suppose I do. But I have to be honest, Wade, though I promise you I will try very hard to do so . . ." She paused a moment but kept her gaze on his face. "I'm afraid."

"Of me?"

She frowned, looking confused. "I don't think it's you. I can't really say what it is. I think it's more of not knowing what to expect."

He smiled and kissed her very gently on the lips. "There's nothing to be afraid of if we have each other." He kissed her more passionately this time and felt her tension ease. His longing for her was unlike anything he'd ever known. He knew he would have to be careful of moments like this. He pulled away and produced his grandmother's ring. A solitary emerald with a small diamond on either side had been his grandmother's pride and joy. She had given it to his mother as an inheritance to give to him when he found a bride.

"Will you marry me, Abrianna?"

She nodded and let him slip the ring onto her finger. It was just a bit snug but otherwise looked as if it had been made for her small hand. She held it up for a moment, and then Wade noticed the tears in her eyes. He produced a handkerchief and extended it without a word. When she had composed herself, he once again offered her his arm.

"There's something else I want to discuss with you." He began to walk once again in the direction of the concert.

"All right."

Her lack of words amused him. He had teased her about his kisses being able to shut her up when he couldn't otherwise get a word in, and once again it seemed to prove itself true. "As you know, the elders have asked me to take the pulpit at church until they can find a permanent minister. We haven't had much of a chance to discuss what this might mean."

"What it might mean? It will mean our little church will finally have a decent man in the pulpit. After we lost dear Pastor Klingle and that awful . . . goodness, I can't even bring myself to call him a pastor. Mr. Walker created such havoc that we have needed a solid man of God. You are clearly such a man, despite also being a wainwright. I see no reason the two can't coincide. After all, you are able to lead a Bible study and work a job. And wasn't the apostle Paul a tentmaker or some sort of thing? And Peter was a fisherman. Why not preach a sermon and make wagons?"

"But that wasn't exactly what I meant, Abrianna." He steered away from a large gathering of people to a more private area where they might sit. There was a nice stone bench that would suit them nicely, and Wade helped Abrianna to sit before doing the same.

"We have no way of knowing how long I will be needed. I suppose you realize that the money I make as a wainwright and carpenter are much more than I will make as a pastor. I won't have as much time to do other duties while serving God. The elders have informed me that they will expect me to make home visits to the elderly and sick. Which brings up another issue. It would be nice to have you at my side for such visits."

"But of course I will be at your side if you want me there." Abrianna once again battled with her ribbons. "I wish I'd never worn this hat, but I suppose I would scandalize everyone if I took it off. And now, given that I am to be a pastor's wife, I suppose I shall forever be wearing them. That will be the most vexing part of this venture."

"Truly? You think the wearing of a hat will be your biggest dilemma?" He gave a chuckle. "Oh, Abrianna, you do look at life in a different way than the rest of us do."

She looked at him with an odd expression. For a moment Wade worried that he'd offended her, but then she gave a little shrug and folded her hands in her lap. "I'm just coming to realize that for myself. I cannot tell you how many times I have displeased my aunts because I couldn't understand their point of view. However, I yield to your thoughts on the matter. A hat is hardly a weighty topic of discussion.

"I am quite happy that you have been asked to preach, Wade. I think God has put a calling on your heart. When we were much younger, you were always a good example to your friends, and you've always worked hard to help when you were needed in the church. I think you will make a wonderful minister, although I cannot say for certain that I will be the perfect minister's wife. But you have my word that I will try to the best of my ability. I see it as my greatest challenge."

"I think, dear girl, you will be an amazing minister's wife. Your love of people will outshine any supposed flaws. I will tell Brother Mitchell that I accept. Your thoughts were all that remained a concern to me."

Lenore poured Abrianna a cup of tea before retaking her seat. "It is a lovely ring and how special that it belonged to his grandmother."

"Yes, I thought so, too. Wade's grandfather was a very

successful wainwright, as was his father before him. When his grandfather married, Wade said it was the event of the year. People came from as far away as fifty miles. I think most were folks he'd built wagons for, but nevertheless it was a huge wedding. Wade said they were very happy, and his grandmother specifically bequeathed the ring to him in hopes it would bring him as much love and happiness as it had brought to her and his grandfather." She took a sip of the tea and then put the cup and saucer on the table beside her. Some of Abrianna's favorite times were in private moments like this with Lenore. She relaxed in the comfortable chair, unworried that Lenore would correct her less than rigid posture. It wasn't that Lenore didn't believe in the requirements put upon women, but she had yielded to the fact that Abrianna had little interest in them.

"So do you plan a huge wedding, as well? No doubt there are a great many people who would like to attend. Have you set the date for the wedding? Oh, and did you tell Wade that I wished to stand up with you and would have to wait until after the baby is born?"

"Goodness, you are full of questions. We didn't really talk much about the date, but I prefer a simple wedding. I'd just as soon have a very private affair with just my friends and family," she admitted. "However, we didn't speak on it. We sort of moved on to discuss his taking the pastorate at our church."

Lenore nodded. "Kolbein told me about that. I was delighted. I know Wade to be a solid man of God. He will do a good job."

"I think so. Sometimes I have wondered what ministries God might lead us to as husband and wife. I never dreamed it might be this, but I have to admit it pleases me. I even imagine one day when we have another shelter for the friendless and poor, Wade might be able to hold services for them."

"So you're planning another food house?"

"I am. I plan to speak to someone about property that might be available downtown. Since the fire some of the business owners want to sell out and leave. I thought it would be the perfect time to purchase land and build a place to my own specifications."

"And what does Wade think?"

Abrianna shrugged. "He thinks that my money should be mine alone. He doesn't want to use it for our life together, so I can't see why he would mind my spending it on a shelter. I've never in my life known him to be more pigheaded and stubborn. Well, I suppose those two descriptions are really one and the same. I don't mean to repeat myself, but I am very agitated when it comes to this matter. I do not understand why it should matter whose money it starts out. By law, once we're married everything belongs to the man anyway."

"You must understand that some men are very prideful about providing for their families. Wade would never want others to think he was marrying you for your fortune."

"Wade certainly has never cared about such things, but I did hope he would allow me to benefit our lives in whatever way I could. It seems silly to have that money just sitting in a bank while we struggle to make a life for ourselves. It's rather like that article in the newspaper a couple of years ago about that old woman back east. She was thought to be very poor, as she lived in a tiny cottage. Do you remember?"

Lenore shook her head. "I don't believe I do."

"Well," Abrianna continued, "people were always helping her out. They would bring her food and hand-me-down clothes. They even went together to rebuild her picket fence when hoodlums vandalized her property. When she died, the entire town was shocked to learn she had over one million dollars in the bank. She bequeathed it to the city in order to build a library and a home for the poor. I don't want to struggle along in life, only to die and leave large sums in the bank. I'd rather build a library and shelter while I'm alive."

"Do you really suppose you will struggle? Wade is quite industrious, and there is more than enough work. I think you might be surprised at his abilities. I know for a fact he's already spoken to Kolbein about several properties nearby that might suit for the two of you."

Abrianna hadn't realized this, but it didn't surprise her. "And what advice did Kolbein offer?"

Lenore laughed. "To buy a big place so that you will have ample space to raise a family."

A family. Abrianna felt almost embarrassed to ask but knew the question would plague her if she didn't. "What is that like? To have a child growing inside you?"

Lenore blushed and put her hand to her waist. "I have to admit it is still a wonder to me. I never knew what to expect. My mother wasn't very forthright in speaking to me about such matters. She still isn't. But I am quite delighted to become a mother, and Kolbein all but bust his vest buttons off when he heard he was to be a father. I can scarcely wait for you and Wade to have children. I know that you will love being a mother, Abrianna."

"But it's happened so quickly, and children are very demanding of attention."

"They certainly can be," she admitted. "Even so, I'm very pleased and hope to bear Kolbein many children. What of you? Do you and Wade want a large family?"

"I don't know. We haven't talked about it. And frankly, I don't know how I can do all that I want to do in serving God and have babies at the same time. Aunt Miriam always said that a husband and children were a woman's first and most important ministry, and while I can see the benefits of serving in such a capacity, it seems that a great many other works would have to be put aside."

"And that troubles you?"

"It does. I have always felt called to help people—people beyond just my family. What if I have a great many children and can't work with the poor? What if Wade won't allow for me to do anything but keep house and tend to our children?"

"You make setting up house sound like a very disagreeable thing, but I think time and circumstances will change your mind and put your heart at ease." She smiled and lifted her teacup. "In life's complications, God has a way of working out all the details. At least that's what you once told me."

"It was easy to believe that back then." Even a year ago it had been so much easier to imagine and understand her future, but now as soon as she began to comprehend one aspect of her life, ten other pieces seemed to fall apart in confusion. Now she was to be married and perhaps become a mother and then what? She wasn't even certain she'd make a good wife, much less a good mother. What if she failed miserably? What if she was a terrible mother who had no understanding of her offspring? What if she burned all of their meals and scorched their clothes? Goodness, what if her children turned out to be as headstrong as she was?

7

I wonder if I could have everyone's attention," Wade said to the crowd gathered around the large dining room table at the Madison Bridal School. A few continued to scrape their dessert plates at the conclusion of supper. Wade didn't blame them; the chocolate cake was the best he'd ever had. But now seemed the right time to speak, before the students scattered to clear the table and do other chores. And he wanted everyone to hear the news. Wade looked to Mr. Cunningham and then to the three old ladies who ran the school. "Abrianna and I have an announcement."

Miss Poisie clapped her hands. "Oh, I have so longed for this moment. It's just like a fairy tale. Mmm." Her eyes were closed and the dreamy look on her face made Wade smile. Ah, Miss Poisie—the great romantic of the group.

"I've longed for it, too." Wade smiled as the woman opened her eyes and nodded. "Anyway, Abrianna has agreed to marry me."

Cheers and comments of approval erupted around the table. Wade glanced at Thane, who lifted his glass in a toasting manner from across the table. Wade smiled and raised his own glass.

"I am quite delighted to hear this news," Mrs. Madison declared. Her normally grim expression softened. "We have always felt you were a part of the family, Wade, and now you will truly have a permanent place." She motioned to the students. "You all know your duties. After cleanup, you are free to spend the evening as you wish. Wade and Abrianna, won't you join us in the parlor?" She looked to her sister and Mrs. Gibson before turning to Abrianna's father. "You are most welcome to accompany us, as well."

Jay Cunningham exchanged a look with Flora's aunt. The woman was to leave in a day or two, and Wade could clearly see the man's desire to remain in her company. "I'm sure there will be plenty of time for us to celebrate together. I have a feeling you might have other things to tend to."

Abrianna seemed to take notice and nodded with great enthusiasm. "Of course we can celebrate later. We'll be celebrating for years to come. I think you and Mrs. Snyder should enjoy the lovely evening together. I do think the two of you make a charming couple."

Her father leaned down and whispered something, but Wade couldn't hear. He supposed the way Abrianna giggled that it had something to do with her obvious matchmaking.

Wade assisted Abrianna from her chair and offered her his arm. He liked having her so close. Sometimes he found himself almost afraid that if he let her out of his sight for long, she might very well disappear. For all her ambitions and schemes, Abrianna wasn't always given to planning things out very well, and common sense was often avoided altogether. Perhaps she would never be overly cautious in life, but he prayed she might practice some restraint once they were married.

They followed the trio of older women into the small sitting room. The intimacy of the room was generally reserved for the family, yet Wade had often taken his meetings with Mrs. Madison here. The way they treated him, Wade always felt a part of the family, just as Mrs. Madison suggested.

The ladies took their seats, leaving Wade and Abrianna to share the settee. Sitting this close, Wade could smell the delicate scent of rosewater that Abrianna used to wash her hair. It was funny how he was only now beginning to notice those kinds of things about her. The softness of her skin. The blue of her eyes.

"Of course we anticipated this announcement," Mrs. Madison began, "and we are quite delighted at the news."

"Oh, indeed." Miss Poisie beamed. "I am ever the romantic at heart. My dear departed Captain Jonathan . . ."

Mrs. Gibson leaned forward with a nod. "God rest his soul."

"Amen," they all answered in unison, including Wade.

"He often said I was terribly romantic. He would tease me and say that perhaps Cupid was an ancestor of mine." Miss Poisie gave a girlish giggle. "I told him I wouldn't be at all surprised."

Mrs. Madison's expression suggested this was nonsense, and her words seemed to affirm as much. "Since Cupid is a mythological creature, we must allow that he has no ancestors. Be that as it may, we are pleased by your announcement, Wade. I know I speak for the others in saying that we could not imagine a better man for our Abrianna."

"Thank you." Wade wondered exactly where the conversation was headed. These old ladies were well known for their management and opinions. He could only hope their thoughts didn't lean toward a long engagement.

"Have you a thought as to the date of your wedding?" Mrs. Madison's question hung on the air.

Wade looked at Abrianna, wondering if she had given the matter any consideration. She shook her head, and he in turn looked back at the women. "No, I guess we haven't."

"Oh, do let it be soon," Miss Poisie declared.

"But not too soon," Mrs. Gibson added. "We wouldn't want folks thinking that the marriage was necessary. There would be great shame in that, especially now that you have agreed to take the church."

Mrs. Madison appeared to consider this for a moment. "Certainly that would create conflict. We mustn't have scandal brought down on either of you."

"I think you should marry just after the first of the year." Miss Poisie's tone was quite animated. "I don't think it's wise to be married in an odd-numbered year. Especially given all the misfortune of 1889, what with the fire in Seattle and that terrible flood in Johnstown. You wouldn't want your anniversary to ever be marked with memories of such things."

"Poppycock." This came from Mrs. Gibson as she gave a brief shake of her index finger. "We will not be given over to superstitious notions, Poisie. The year 1889 is a perfectly acceptable year. However, there are only four months left to it."

"Four months is plenty time enough to plan a wedding," Miss Poisie countered. "Why, I heard that when the Princess Beatrice married, the wedding was planned out in a very short time."

"But remember, Sister, the accomplishments of royalty are not necessarily the same that can be had for commoners." Mrs. Madison fixed Wade and Abrianna with a stern expression. "We must be practical. Don't you agree?"

"Yes, most assuredly. Lenore is to be my matron of honor." Abrianna looked to Wade as if for support. "She cannot stand up with me until after the baby is born, and that will be in December."

Miss Poisie smiled as if she'd just gotten her way. Wade might have laughed at the little woman's delight, but he knew such matters could be quite serious amongst the trio. There was no sense in adding to the issue.

"We want to help, no matter," Mrs. Madison continued. "We would like to host your wedding here in the gardens if you like, so that would suggest a spring or summer wedding."

Wade didn't like that thought. Now that he realized his love for Abrianna and she for him, he could see no sense in waiting that long. Just being this near to her made him have unruly thoughts of hoisting her over his shoulder and eloping. He didn't think he was patient enough to wait until spring.

"Thane would like to be my best man." Wade tilted his head, then shrugged. "But they are leaving day after tomorrow, so that would be much too quick to plan a wedding." He half hoped they might contradict his comment, but no one did.

Mrs. Madison rose. "You have a little time to think about it. We simply want to help in whatever way we can."

"Goodness, yes." Miss Poisie bobbed her head. "This is so very exciting. A wedding for our very own Abrianna. When I think of all the other brides we have helped to prepare, it positively inspires my senses to plan a wedding for her."

"Have you any thoughts at all on what kind of a wedding you would like?" Mrs. Gibson asked.

Wade knew such questions were usually the bride's responsibility, but he felt it only fair that he have a say. "I would like to be married before the year is out, so I suppose a simple wedding would be best."

Abrianna remained silent. He hoped she wasn't having second thoughts, what with all her fears. Surely having apprehensions about marriage was normal. He didn't doubt her love for him, and he'd never known her to back away from a challenge, so he had no reason to suspect she would back away from marrying him. Still, she had her fears, and he wanted to be mindful of her needs. They caused him to want to protect her all the more.

"I believe a winter wedding could be quite lovely," Mrs. Madison said after several moments. "Is that your desire, Abrianna?"

She looked startled, then nodded. "I think the end of December could be good. However, it's also possible that Lenore will not be delivered by then."

"It's true," Mrs. Gibson nodded. "Some babies are given to arriving late. Perhaps we should consider the end of January."

"And then she could be married in an even-numbered year," Miss Poisie said with a smile of satisfaction.

January seemed like forever to Wade, but he would do whatever the others decided. The last thing he wanted was to impose himself on the situation. This was a decision for the ladies to make—Abrianna in particular.

"We could have Mr. Cunningham build us a hothouse." Mrs. Gibson looked to Mrs. Madison as if for approval. "That way we could still have a great many flowers."

Miss Poisie clapped in delight. "Oh, I do like flowers at a wedding. Wouldn't that be a perfect solution, Sister?"

"We have talked often enough about a greenhouse being added. I suppose it could suit this purpose quite nicely."

Mrs. Gibson looked quite pleased that her suggestion was met with such approval. "And maybe by January the constant noise of all that new city construction will be diminished. I don't know why such affairs have to be so noisy."

"It's true," Miss Poisie said. "Yesterday there was a constant pounding that carried on the stillness of the day. I counted over one hundred strikes, although I have no idea what was being hit. It was most upsetting to my nerves, and I found it necessary to seek a tonic."

Wade did his best not to smile. The ladies were always opinionated about one thing or another. No doubt Abrianna came to it by example.

"I had hoped that with the required use of bricks we might not have such noise," Mrs. Madison added. "I suppose, however, there are wooden interiors to arrange."

"You would think that perhaps there might be a way to cushion the blows so that the noise would be lessened, Sister." Poisie looked momentarily thoughtful, as if trying to conjure a plan. Then she gave a little shrug. "But surely by January it will be better."

Abrianna finally seemed to regain her ability to command the situation. "I think I would like to ponder the exact date for a short time. Wade and I have a great many things to consider, and it would be wise for us to discuss those issues prior to setting the day." She looked at Wade. "I'm sure you understand. We haven't had a chance to really discuss the future in detail."

He could see a pleading in her eyes. "Of course." He hoped she wouldn't want to delay the wedding even more, but at this point he didn't want to cause her any problems in front of her aunts. "I figure weddings are more for the bride than the groom, anyway. Most men would just as soon elope." He smiled at the older women. "But fear not. I wouldn't dream of depriving you the joy of wedding preparations for the one you have so long loved and cared for. Abrianna is worth waiting for."

He felt Abrianna relax at his side. A part of him longed to reassure her that their marriage would be a good one, while another part wanted to shake the apprehension right out of her and tell her to stop acting like a scared schoolgirl. He sighed.

"I appreciate your agreeing to walk with me," Eloise Snyder said in her soft alluring way.

Jay found himself completely besot with the young widow. He felt a small sense of guilt for having left his daughter's side just after the big announcement. Still, Abrianna seemed as eager for him to be alone with Eloise as he. Eloise also appeared quite pleased. She was all smiles and charm and yet personable and full of information. Jay thought her a perfect companion and hoped he might yet persuade her to consider him the same.

"I was glad for the opportunity. I'm also glad that you can see the good things here at the school. I think the old ladies will surprise you."

She nodded. "I think so, too. When I told Mrs. Madison that I would be leaving on the day after tomorrow, she encouraged me to return in several weeks to see for myself how things were going."

"And will you return soon?"

"I would like to."

He smiled. "I'd like that, too. You're good company."

"I fear I've done nothing but rattle on and on about myself." She smiled and met his gaze. "But you have a way of putting me at ease. I feel I can speak to you about most anything. I haven't known that freedom since losing my husband."

"For all the talking you've done, you haven't said much about him."

She looked away and seemed to consider that a moment. "Darius was a good Christian man. As a husband he was considerate and generous. As a physician he was compassionate and driven. I always blamed the latter for his having caught tuberculosis. He so longed to find a cure. I fear it caused him to spend more and more time at the sanitarium." She paused and her countenance took on a sad expression.

"I suppose after losing our sons, Darius found home to be a painful place. I know I did. It was almost unbearable at times."

"I am so sorry. I know something of losing those you love."

"Yes, I know." She paused in their walk to face him. "Your daughter told me about your false imprisonment. I find it abominable that such an error should rob a man of so many years. I am amazed that you aren't bitter and angry."

"Neither would change what happened. Besides, I'm quite content to be here now. I figure the past is dead and gone. Don't do much good to dwell on it."

"Yes," she nodded. "I, too, look at it that way. I was married for ten mostly good years, but I can't live in the grave. Flora helped me to see that. She's a remarkable young woman. So very much like your daughter."

"I've noticed that. Both lean a little to the unmanageable side, but both are smart as whips."

"Yes. I fear Flora has always been much more adventurous than I ever was. I suppose growing up in the wilds of Montana on a ranch did much to encourage that."

"Some folks are just spirited." Jay wondered how he might turn the conversation back to her return without sounding obvious in his desire to see her again. "But I'm thinking that you'll see a good change in her. These old ladies have a way about them. They are good teachers. I'm sure if you were to return in just a couple of weeks you'd find Flora a different girl."

"Do you think just a few weeks would be time enough? I've tried for four years to tame that child."

He chuckled. "I think Mrs. Madison can accomplish a great

deal in a very short time. Why not make a plan to return and see for yourself?" He stopped walking. "I'm sure it would be worth your trouble."

She smiled at him, and it took years off her worried face. "I suppose it bears consideration."

Jay finally decided to just be honest with the woman. If she spurned him he would count the loss and move on. But if he said nothing and her feelings matched his own, then he would miss a most valuable opportunity.

"I'd like it very much if you would consider something else." He swallowed the lump in his throat. "I think you know that I enjoy our conversations. The time I've had getting to know you has given me reason to think we might work well together. I know that sounds rather bold, but I'd like for you to think on that."

She shook her head and for a moment he thought she would refuse him. "I don't need to think on it, Mr. Cunningham. I've very much enjoyed our time together. I think you may be right. Perhaps we might work well together."

He let out the breath he'd been holding and smiled. "Well, I'm glad that's behind us." He linked his arm with hers and turned back toward the school. "I've never been all that good with words. Guess I haven't had much practice."

"I thought your words were just fine, Mr. Cunningham."

"Please don't call me that. Just call me Jay or even James."

"I will do so only if you will call me Eloise," she replied.

"I'd be delighted, Eloise."

She smiled up at him. "Thank you, Jay. You've given me a reason to look forward rather than behind."

8

Abrianna hugged Militine close. "I feel positively desolate at your departure." She pulled back. "Not that I want you to feel guilty. I know you aren't truly abandoning me, although I shall suffer the loss greatly."

"I will, as well," Militine replied. "But, it'll give me better peace of mind to be farther from my old life. Thane was the one to suggest it, and what a blessing it is to know he understands."

Abrianna nodded. "It is. I know this is best for you, dear friend, but I will miss you so deeply. I was reading *Northanger Abbey* by Jane Austen just yesterday and came across something one of the characters said and thought of you leaving. She said, 'There is nothing I would not do for those who are really my friends. I have no notion of loving people by halves, it is not my nature.' That is how I feel. I cannot love by halves, and so knowing this is best for you, I can say good-bye. I can let you leave me with a glad spirit, realizing this is something of a gift that I can give back to you. I do pray, however, you will write to me."

"You know I'm not very good at such things. My education

was very limited, and my speech only improved because of Mrs. Madison's efforts, as well as the others."

"I know, but I also know that Thane will help you, should you need. Even the fewest of words will let me know you are doing well and haven't forgotten me."

Militine laughed. "Abrianna, after all we've been through, it would be impossible to forget you. Some of my fondest and most terrifying moments were spent in your company." She sobered. "I do wish we could be here for your wedding. That is my biggest regret in leaving."

"Well, maybe they can make a wedding trip to San Francisco to see us." Thane put his arm around Militine's shoulders.

Wade came alongside Abrianna and looked down at her. "That might be a fun adventure. I'll see what I can do to put aside some money, but we have a great many other expenses just now."

"Well, there is my . . ." Abrianna fell silent at the disapproving look that crossed Wade's face. He was determined her money not be used for their needs. It frustrated Abrianna to no end, but she held her tongue—something that did not come easily.

"I hope you will try." Militine seemed to notice the tension. She smiled at Abrianna and took hold of her hands once again. "Please tell your aunts that I said thank-you for taking a chance on me. I know they broke all of their rules when they allowed me to come without references or any letter of introduction. It was all God's doing. I see that now. Thanks to you."

"I didn't do anything."

"You never gave up on helping me to see that God truly loved me. No one else showed such concern. You dogged me about it every step of the way, and in looking back I can see that I needed that persistence. So while I know we had some difficult times over such matters, I thank you for being willing to remain strong in your faith and to love me enough to offer steady witness."

Abrianna wiped away tears with the back of her hand. "Oh, Militine, I do love you so very much. I pray you will have a wonderful life." She looked to Thane. "You, as well. You have been such a good friend both to Wade and to me. Farewells are never easy, and losing the two of you to such a great distance will definitely leave a void in our lives."

"Yes, but we will all see each other again," Wade said. "I feel certain of that."

"I do, too," Thane replied. "Now, we must go aboard our ship, or we will certainly be left behind."

The two women exchanged kisses on the cheek. Abrianna turned to Thane and gave him a brief embrace. "Take care of her and yourself."

Thane nodded as she stepped back. "I will." He turned to Wade. "You going to be all right taking care of our Abrianna on your own?"

Wade laughed and gave his friend a slap on the back. "You know it will be a challenge, but I have great hope that God will aid me in the matter."

"Oh, stuff and nonsense." Abrianna rolled her eyes heavenward. "Must I forever bear up under such harsh judgment?"

The two men embraced, laughing. Thane shook his head and whispered something to Wade. It was no doubt further comments on dealing with her difficult nature. Abrianna might have said something had it not been the occasion of Militine and Thane's departure. After all, she didn't want to mar their good-byes with a reprimand.

Thane picked up the small valise at Militine's feet. "Are you ready, my love?"

She smiled. "I am."

Abrianna watched them walk up the gangplank and bit her lower lip to keep from crying. It was a good thing for Militine to leave Seattle. She knew the fear that her friend had suffered in worries as to whether her most abusive father might one day find her again. That, coupled by the dread that even if he didn't, some of his cronies might, caused Militine no end of discomfort.

"They'll be fine, you know." Wade put his arm around her shoulder.

Abrianna was surprised at this public display but was grateful. She leaned against him, feeling so safe and comforted. He was truly the dearest friend of all. "What did Thane say to you just now?"

Wade chuckled. "He told me that he and Militine had left us a wedding present in their old room. A wooden mantel clock."

"How kind. I do wish they could have been here for the wedding."

"I do, too. However, since they are doing what's best for them, I think we should do likewise. While we're down here, I want to show you something."

She looked at Wade, most curious as to what he had in mind. "I would like that very much. Anything to take my mind off this sorrowful moment. I've always found the best way to deal with sadness is to focus one's thoughts elsewhere."

He looped his arm with hers and drew her back away from the dock and the bustle of the men who were working to load last minute supplies on the ship. Abrianna looked out across the bay. The sky had a few wispy clouds, but otherwise remained a brilliant blue. Even so, there was a definite hint of change in the weather. The temperatures were lower now, and the rains were finally starting to come with some regularity. Before long, it would be autumn.

The noise and bustle of the area soon drew her attention away from thoughts of anything but the rebuilding of the city. The workers had made great strides in clearing away the rubble and resetting foundations. Basements were being dug for businesses where possible, and already the foundations had been set in place for others. Even so, there was still relatively little in the way of actual buildings.

"It's all so strange, so different."

"As you can see, most of the businesses down here are still operating out of tents." Wade shook his head. "So many of the folks, myself included, didn't have any kind of fire insurance, and rebuilding is difficult and riddled with expenses."

"I've read much about it in the paper. I have wanted to speak to you about it several times, but there always seemed to be someone around."

He led her to a small tent in the same area where his shop used to be. He untied the flaps and threw them back to allow the sunlight to filter in. "I have a small supply of wood and wagon materials here. I usually take my tools back and forth, so as to not encourage theft. Most won't bother with the rest of the stuff."

"They probably have no idea what to do with it. Not everyone is as brilliant as you are. I've always admired that about you. Still, this is a very small space, and you deserve more. Your old shop was so well organized and supplied." Abrianna felt a sense of sorrow at the minimal workspace. Wade had always prided himself on his previous shop. He and his father had worked it together, and she knew there were a great many memories for Wade here.

"Part of the reason I wanted to bring you here was to say that I'm thinking perhaps this isn't the place for me to rebuild. I had an offer on the land, and I think it might be wise to take it. It'll give me a nice sum of money to use in getting us a little home, where I might also be able to work."

"Wade," she took hold of his arm, "can you not see yourself giving in to use at least a little of the money I inherited? I know you are a prideful man, and Lenore explained all about how men like to be in charge of providing for their families, although I will say that utilizing perfectly good money that is available to them seems like a sensible thing to do. Even so, I am trying my best to understand. God knows I have tried to bear up under your pride for years, but remember what the Bible says about pride going before a fall."

He chuckled. "I had no idea you were working so hard to bear up."

"I know you think it quite amusing, but it's true. You have been most vexing at times. You really should pray about this matter."

He turned and touched her face. "I have. I've prayed about our marriage and about our finances. I've prayed about whether to sell, and if so, where to relocate. I'm not given to making rash decisions. You know me better than that."

"I do. But I thought I knew you well enough to believe you wouldn't let money come between us. Money has never been an issue before now, but I suppose, given my inheritance, we shall begin fighting about it all the time, and that plagues me."

"And that's what you think I'm doing? Letting money come between us?"

"Well, it seems that way to me. I have money sitting in the bank or at least in investments, and you are in need. We are in need."

"Our needs are not so great, Abrianna. Like I said, if I sell this lot, then I will have a good amount of money to put elsewhere. I might have lost my tools when the horse and wagon disappeared in the fire, but I managed to keep my savings, and that, along with the money from selling the land, will give us a good start."

She opened her mouth to comment, but Wade put his finger to her lips and smiled. "Don't make me kiss you."

The thought didn't seem like much of a threat, and she pushed his hand aside. "I understand that you desire to be the kind of man who is solely responsible for his wife, but Wade, I wish you wouldn't be such a ninny about it all."

"A ninny? Now I'm being a ninny? The other day you called me pigheaded." He took hold of her face and leaned forward as if to kiss her. "You didn't used to call me names."

"Oh, I did. Just not to your face."

He laughed. "You are quite the prize, Abrianna." He gave her a rather brief and chaste kiss.

"You were the one who made me pledge honesty."

"I thought that was God. Wasn't He the one who commanded us to be truthful?"

"Indeed." Abrianna cocked her head to one side. "But His forgiveness always seemed easier to come by than yours."

"Oh, Abrianna. I've never withheld forgiveness from you. You are most dear to me and always have been. Don't you see? I just want to take care of you and love you."

"But you don't want me to love and care for you in return."

He frowned. "Why would you ever think such a thing? Of course I want you to love and care for me."

"But not if it involves my money. Money that I'm quite willing to call 'ours.'"

He dropped his hold. "We aren't going to argue about it, Abrianna. I refuse. Your aunts gave you an inheritance and meant for you to use it for your benefit."

She put her hands on her hips. "And you are too blind to see that it would benefit me to benefit you. Honestly, I don't see how marrying you will ever work out if you refuse to let me help in whatever way I can. You know that my cooking skills are minimal. Oh, I can most definitely make soup and cookies, as I did for the homeless, but I'm not good at creating full meals. And my sewing is atrocious, and I can't play the piano very well. It would seem that my money is one thing I can actually bring to benefit our marriage, and I shan't go into a marriage where I feel useless."

Abrianna turned to walk away, but Wade grabbed hold of her and swung her back into his arms. "You will never be useless to me. I want you to share my life and work alongside me. All I am asking is that you allow me to be the man of the house. I realize you haven't ever had that in your life. You've grown up with three spirited and self-sufficient women. I know that you see yourself taking on that role, but I want to take care of you. I want to make a good life for you. Can't you see? That's part of showing you how much I love you."

She hadn't considered it that way. She supposed, given the silliest notions men were given over to, perhaps she would do better to just agree and work on helping him to see her way another time. Abrianna sighed. Why did men have to be so difficult?

"I suppose I have no other choice," she said, not trying to disguise the disappointment in her voice. "I love you and suppose that love will always come with its sacrifices."

He shook his head. "Is it such a sacrifice to yield this one thing to me? Will we always argue about such matters?"

She wondered in that moment if Wade, like most men, simply wanted a wife who would smile and agree with everything he said. The thought troubled her.

"Wade, you do know that I have never been one for sitting around being idle. You know that I am very poor at taking direction, even though I work at it. Sometimes I just see that there are more important things to be done and feel that it's my job to take care of those things."

He chuckled. "Of course I know all of that."

"And you know, too, that I've never been one to seek approval. Not yours or anyone else's. Save God's, of course. I really do want His approval. But I fear that I will disappoint you in my lack of obedience. I'm not at all good with such things when I perceive something else to be God's will. Life with me will not be easy."

Wade looked at her with great tenderness in his expression. "I love you, Abrianna. With all your quirks and notions. I've never looked for the easy way in life, just for the way that I feel God is leading me. So long as you are doing that, as well, we are certain to be on the same path."

But while his words sounded convincing, Abrianna had her doubts. After all, didn't the Bible say that some were called to one gift and responsibility and some to another?

"You seem troubled, Daughter." Jay Cunningham eyed Abrianna with concern. That morning at breakfast she'd only toyed with her food and then did the same thing at lunch. He figured, as her father, he should at least attempt to get to the bottom of it and had followed her out to the far reaches of the expansive lawn to where she sat under a tree.

Abrianna glanced up and smiled. "I'm fine. I didn't mean to give you cause for worry."

He sat down beside her and plucked a blade of grass. "You don't look fine. You barely ate anything at breakfast and nothing at lunch. You've been in a mood since your return from seeing your friends off. Is that what's bothering you?"

"I will miss them." She looked away. "Militine is a dear friend. Thane, too. It won't be the same without them, but I know they have prayed about it and feel God is guiding them to San Francisco." She sighed, as if she held the weight of the world.

Jay frowned and tried to figure out how to get her to talk. He knew so little about this young woman, but he was her father and felt it his duty to try. "If you aren't worried about them, then what? Do you have concerns about getting married?"

Her expression seemed to become a mask. She looked at him oddly. "Why would I have worries about marriage? It is what men and women do. It's expected for a woman to marry so that she'll have a man to take care of her."

"I thought folks were supposed to marry for love these days. It's not the dark ages anymore." He smiled, but Abrianna remained expressionless. This was unlike anything he'd ever seen in her before. Had something happened between her and Wade? He hesitated to ask. She might refuse to answer or feel he wasn't entitled to know. A thought came to him.

"You know, when I married your mama, I was dumbstruck by love." He gave a chuckle. "She was the prettiest little thing. She worked at a little restaurant, and when she came to pour me a cup of coffee and smiled . . . well, I just lost my heart."

Abrianna said nothing, but he felt certain she was listening.

Jay continued. "I was determined from the start to win her. What I didn't know until later was that she had set her cap for me, too. We led each other on a merry chase and could have avoided a lot of conflict had we just talked it over. I think she was worried I'd think less of her if she declared her love first, and I was rather fearful of her rejecting me."

"But she didn't. She gave in and obviously felt marriage was purposed for the two of you." Abrianna sounded sad and resigned.

"Are you having doubts that it's the right step for you and Wade?"

She looked at him, and a tiny flash of pain crossed her face. "Why would you ask such a thing? Wade and I have been good friends for a very long time. He loves me and I love him. Isn't that enough?"

"Is it?"

Abrianna looked away. "Did you allow my mother to help with your needs?"

"In what way?" He felt he was finally making some progress.

"Did she use her own money to help with expenses?"

"She didn't have much more than I did. We rarely had much more than what would pay the rent and put food on the table."

"Did she continue to wait tables after you married, or did you forbid her to do so?"

"Somehow I get the feeling this conversation isn't really about me and your mama. So why don't you tell me what Wade has said or done to make you feel out of sorts."

She shook her head. "I doubt it would matter, although I am most perplexed. However, you are a man, and men are a complete mystery to me. You think and feel things in ways that differ from the female gender. I doubt there is a woman alive who understands what you are really about."

Jay laughed. "Ain't a man who don't feel the same way about women."

She turned to him. "But how can that be? We're very easy to understand. We want to be useful. We want to know that our lives count for something. We want to serve God and make the world a better place. Is that so hard to comprehend?"

He chose his words carefully, hoping she wouldn't clam up again. "I suppose you're worried that marriage will keep you from helping the poor like you used to."

She shrugged. "That and much more."

"I know I haven't been here for your growing up, but I do love you, Abrianna. I want to help you if I can, but it is obvious that you're pretty caught up in your fretting."

"Oh, I suppose I am." She sighed, and he felt the walls collapse around her. "So much is changing, and I feel that I'm changing with it. But I don't want to. I always thought God had a specific plan of work for me, work that I would do for the poor. Work that would be done either with or without a husband."

"Has Wade decided you can't help the poor anymore?"

"Wade doesn't want me helping anyone with anything, apparently."

"Did he say that?"

She shook her head. "No. He said he doesn't want any of my money to help us get our start in life. He won't use my inheritance to buy us a place or to benefit his business. He would probably even complain if I bought him a gift with it. I don't see why he should be so pigheaded, and I even told him so. But he is a most complex man. I think he probably even challenges God. I suppose that is going too far. I do have difficulty with making exaggerations to prove my point."

Finally Jay could see the problem. "A man wants to know he

can take care of his family, Abrianna. It was always a worry of mine. It was the reason I was away from you and your mother. I was looking for work. I wanted to be able to give you both a good life, and that meant I had to make a better living."

"And just see where that kind of thinking led. Goodness, but it seems to me that if God intended man to go it on his own, He wouldn't have said that it wasn't good for you to be alone. Sometimes I think the entire world has gone mad, and I'm the only one left in it that understands the truth."

"Maybe your kind of truth."

"And just what do you mean by that?" Her question sounded like a challenge.

"I mean that you've decided how the world should be, and when it doesn't cooperate, you get your feathers all ruffled up. Maybe you got this way because I wasn't around to help advise you. Maybe it's because you lost your mama and me and got yourself raised by someone else. But I will say that you've got a stubborn streak in you that runs a mile wide and ten miles long." He grinned. "That, you get from me."

She looked at him for a long moment, and as she did, the anger seemed to fade and tears formed in her eyes. "I can't be what I'm not. Why can't people just accept me for who I am?"

"And what is it Wade won't accept?"

"That I am capable of helping him. That I want to share what I have with him. Not just my heart or even my body." She blushed. "Excuse my boldness. I want to share my intelligence, my blessings. My aunts gave me an inheritance, and I want to share that, as well."

"But Wade doesn't want your money?"

"I don't think Wade wants me. Not really. I think he wants me to be someone else, and I don't think I can do that."

"Did you talk to him about this?"

"I tried. Oh, stuff and nonsense." She sniffed and her voice faltered. "I don't even feel like I can control my emotions. I've spent most of my life not being given to tears, and it seems of late they are all too present in my life."

Jay could see the tears slide down her cheeks. He wanted to comfort her, to reach out and pull her close and hold her, as he might have when she was a little girl. Unfortunately, the years of separation came back to haunt him. He had no right to impose himself in her life, but that didn't stop him from wanting to be her father in full.

"Abrianna, I know we don't really know each other very well. I hope that will change in time and you will come to know me and know my love for you. I only want the very best for you. I wanted that for your mama, too. Sometimes a man has to do things that seem odd to a woman. It's not just about pride. You need to understand that. It's more about the way God made us."

"God told us to share one another's burdens," Abrianna said, not bothering to wipe away her tears. "He told us to consider others as better than ourselves. He said to give generously to one another. Why don't those things matter?"

"They do. You know they do." He reached out and took hold of her hand, hoping and praying she wouldn't refuse him. She didn't. "A man needs to be the protector and the provider for his family. It fulfills his sense of who he is. It's something God puts into us, Abrianna. Don't try to take that away from Wade. It's who he is and probably one of the things you love best about him, if you really think about it."

"But what about the way God made me? What about what Wade's taking away from me?"

"And what is it he's taking? I thought a minute ago you

were accusing him of not being willing to receive anything from you."

Abrianna opened her mouth, then closed it again. She looked perplexed and shook her head. After several minutes of silence she finally spoke. "I don't know. My head is spinning, and I can't think clear at all. Up feels like down and right feels left. I'm most perplexed, and that vexes me." She got to her feet. "I hate being an adult. I thought much clearer when I was a child. I knew what I wanted. I felt I understood what God wanted. Now I just feel lost and confused. I'm not even sure God is listening, because He certainly isn't giving me any answers."

Jay got to his feet slowly. He offered Abrianna a smile. "You kind of have to stop talking in order to hear what He has to say. Just like you have to stop fretting and fussing about what you think Wade is saying and really listen to hear what he's actually talking about."

Her shoulders slumped, and he could see the defeat in her eyes. "I am quite hopeless. All of my life people have sought to change me. I bore their criticism and direction and did truly endeavor to change. Now I'm not at all sure I've accomplished anything at all. Just when I think I have a grasp on what I'm supposed to do, it seems like everything changes again, and everyone wants something different."

Jay took a chance and stepped forward. He opened his arms to Abrianna and prayed she would know the love he felt for her. She hesitated a moment, searching his face as if for understanding. Then, without a word, she stepped into his embrace and put her head on his shoulder. A great heavy sob escaped her lips, and her entire body shook as she cried in his arms.

Swallowing hard, Jay glanced heavenward and prayed. *Help me to help her, Lord. I don't know what to do but love her, and that just don't seem enough.*

9

Abrianna listened to Wade conclude his sermon and couldn't help but smile. Her fiancé loved God and was a gifted speaker, even without formal training or seminary schooling. He took the Bible, studied it, and sought answers when he didn't fully understand. But most importantly, he listened to God's direction for putting the teaching into practice. Who could want more from their pastor?

"I will read once again those verses from Second Corinthians chapter five. 'Therefore if any man be in Christ, he is a new creature: old things are passed away; behold, all things are become new. And all things are of God, who hath reconciled us to himself by Jesus Christ, and hath given to us the ministry of reconciliation; To wit, that God was in Christ, reconciling the world unto himself, not imputing their trespasses unto them; and hath committed unto us the word of reconciliation. Now then we are ambassadors for Christ, as though God did beseech you by us: we pray you in Christ's stead, be ye reconciled to God. For he hath made him to be sin for us, who knew no sin; that we might be made the righteousness of God in him.'" Wade looked up as he closed the Bible.

"The old debris of our city is being put aside, carried away, or plowed under for the purpose of rebuilding. The old is being passed away and all things are to become new. There is a new life to be had, a new city to be born. But in order to allow for it, we must rid ourselves of the old. The same is true of our own lives. We have an old nature that must give way to allow for the new reconciliation we have through Christ. We cannot be renewed unless we are willing to set aside the old. Let's pray."

Abrianna bowed her head. All the Scriptures Wade used that morning flowed through her mind. She wanted to pray, but her heart was burdened. She had to find a way to ease her fears. Wade was a good man, and God had given him a wondrous gift to teach the Word. Wade was a good man, and God had given him the ability to love. Wade was a *good* man . . . why, then, should she struggle so much with her feelings?

"Amen."

Wade's deep voice brought her head up, and she realized she'd not prayed at all but had simply mulled over the same old thoughts she'd wrestled with all week. She gathered her things and then stepped to one side of the sanctuary to watch people greet Wade. They were all smiles. Encouraging him with their comments and approval. It warmed her heart to see their acceptance of the man she loved.

"I must say, he gives a good sermon."

Abrianna looked to her right and found Priam Welby standing there. "He does." She tried to think of something to say without bringing up his threats to do himself harm. "I'm glad you could be here."

"I am, too. I hoped we might have a word."

"To what purpose?"

He smiled. "I believe you know what purpose."

"Mr. Welby, please do not put me in this most difficult position." Abrianna clutched her Bible to her breast. "I cannot court you. I am engaged to be married." She held out her left hand as if to offer proof.

"It's lovely. Although I would give you something much grander."

"I think it's perfect. Just as I know Wade is the man I'm to marry."

"I think in time you will change your mind."

She shook her head. "Then you do not know me very well. Even if I were to dissolve my engagement with Mr. Ackerman, I would not court you. You see, I believe God has some very important work for me to do. At this point I'm not even sure it can be accomplished in marriage."

His expression grew quizzical. "So you are thinking of remaining single? Are you planning to end your engagement?"

"I'm trying my best to leave all of my plans in God's hands." She hadn't meant to give him the impression that she might not marry Wade, but concern about it was ever uppermost in her mind these last few days.

"Abrianna," he said in a hushed voice, "you know how I feel about your work for God. I would never dream of interfering and would, in fact, be most beneficial. I would still help you to rebuild a new facility for the needy. We could reinstitute our contract, and you would see just how much it could help all those people you care so much about."

Glancing across the sanctuary, Abrianna shook her head. "Mr. Welby, I appreciate your thoughts and your support of my calling." She paused and gave him a smile. "But I cannot." She started to leave, but he took hold of her arm.

"I'm not a very patient man, Abrianna." His tone sent a chill through her. "I'm used to having what I want, and I want you."

She looked at him for a moment and shook her head. "I am sorry, Mr. Welby. I am not for sale."

"Everyone has their price, Abrianna. I think in time we shall learn yours."

His eyes darkened, and the look he gave left Abrianna in a state of unease. A chill skittered through her limbs as she contemplated what lengths he might go to force his hand. Were the stories Wade and Kolbein had heard about Mr. Welby true? Had she truly misjudged him and given him the benefit of the doubt when she should have been suspect all along? This was more complicated than she ever thought possible. She narrowed her eyes and straightened her back. "Good day, Mr. Welby."

Abrianna hurried to the back of the church where Wade was speaking to the last of the parishioners. She didn't wait to talk to him but slipped out behind the older couple and hurried to where her father stood with the other ladies of the Madison Bridal School.

"Your Wade did a mighty fine job today." Her father beamed.

"He did." She let out a long breath, feeling that with her father and the others, Mr. Welby would not risk making another scene. "I've always thought he would make a wonderful preacher, and now I see that I was right."

"I saw you speaking to Mr. Welby," Aunt Poisie came alongside Abrianna. "I do hope he was not causing you grief. The world often talks of the revenge of women scorned, but I believe men can be just as dangerous."

"I do, too, Aunt Poisie, but I am fine. Mr. Welby was merely commenting on Wade's sermon."

"Oh, it was grand, wasn't it?" Aunt Poisie clasped her gloved hands together. "It was as if the apostle Paul were right there in the pulpit, although I'm sure he never had a fine black suit." She looked most thoughtful. "But I cannot imagine Wade in robes. Even so, I've never heard the Scriptures recited with more reverence and feeling."

Abrianna nodded, but her mind was still on Welby's threatening tone. At least he was no longer talking about causing himself harm. She supposed she should be glad about that. Brother Mitchell and Wade came to join the group, causing her to let go of further contemplation.

"I'd say our young man here did an exceptional job today," Brother Mitchell declared.

"He did indeed," Aunt Poisie replied before anyone else could speak. "I was just telling Abrianna that it was almost like having the apostle Paul himself in the pulpit. I have never heard the Word spoken with more feeling and understanding." She put her hand over her heart. "It moved me."

"As it did me" came a feminine voice.

Abrianna turned to find Clara, one of the bridal school students, batting her eyes at Wade. She leaned forward and took hold of his arm. "I was truly blessed. I hope maybe later we can further discuss some of the teaching you shared. I'm afraid I don't understand everything, but I'd like to."

A twinge of jealousy rose up in Abrianna. The girl was throwing herself at Wade. His next words helped to put her at ease, however, as he pulled his arm from Clara's touch. "I know Abrianna can expand on it and would love to help you understand. She's studied the Bible with great interest."

"But I find men to speak with more clarity and authority." Clara had the audacity to touch him again. "Do say you'll help me. I'm certain to understand if you will but spend a few moments with me alone. Those Scriptures are vexing me."

"Clara, I believe you need to join the other girls in the omnibus," Aunt Miriam said, coming from behind to give Clara a push toward the awaiting transport. "You and I will spend the afternoon going over those Scriptures that seem to vex you."

Abrianna would have giggled had Clara not fixed her with a fierce glare. Abrianna watched as Aunt Miriam led the younger woman away and could only imagine how tormenting the afternoon would be for Clara. Aunt Miriam was quite tedious in her Bible teaching.

She turned to say something to Wade, but he was already busy talking to another parishioner. So instead, Abrianna tucked her Bible under one arm and made her way to the carriage. Without assistance she climbed up and plopped down in a most unladylike way. She said nothing, but it still troubled her that Clara could be so openly disrespectful of her engagement to Wade.

"I know that look."

Aunt Miriam stood beside the carriage. Abrianna waited as her father helped the older woman up. Once Aunt Miriam was seated, she fixed Abrianna with a stern gaze.

"Something has irritated you."

"I suppose it has." Abrianna tried to arrange her skirts then gave up. Even though no one was around to overhear, she leaned forward and whispered. "I do not like the way Clara flirts with Wade. It's unbecoming and uncalled for since she knows we are engaged."

"I thought it might be something like that," Aunt Miriam replied. "I will deal with her this afternoon. However, you might as well get used to such things. Men of the cloth seem particularly vulnerable to the wiles of women. Often a woman of questionable conscience will put a pastor in a difficult position. Some women do it to feel important, and others act thusly because it's their sinful nature. My point, however, is that if Wade continues to take on the role of pastor, this is something you will face."

"I find it appalling." Abrianna crossed her arms, hugging the Bible close.

"As do I. But you must credit Wade for handling the matter in good order. You will need to figure out a way to deal with it and help Wade, as well. Perhaps after you are married, you could make calls with him when he goes to visit the congregation. I know the elders never called upon people unless all three were able to go. If a woman comes alone seeking help, you might make certain that you remain with Wade as he speaks to her or prays with her."

"I doubt he'd want my help. He's a very independent man." Abrianna knew her words sounded harsh and Aunt Miriam would confront her if she didn't explain. Giving her aunt a smile, Abrianna hurried on. "But he can have my help whenever he wants it. I am determined to be helpful in whatever way possible. I suppose I shouldn't allow my thoughts to turn to jealousy, but you know how I can be. Grief, but it seems I always have something to repent of. I know you must weary of trying to teach me. You have always been so very patient with me."

Aunt Miriam eyed her with a look that made it clear to Abrianna she wasn't convincing the older woman of anything. Just then, Aunt Selma and Aunt Poisie came to the carriage and, with the help of Abrianna's father, climbed in to take their seats.

"Wasn't Wade amazing?" Aunt Poisie began.

Abrianna settled back in her seat and fixed her attention on the church's graveyard. She could only pray that Aunt Miriam would let the matter go. Abrianna would just have to figure out how to deal with her feelings of jealousy, as well as her doubts.

"If you ladies are ready," Wade said, taking the driver's seat, "I'll take us home."

"Drive on, Wade. We are properly assembled," Aunt Miriam declared.

Abrianna looked to where her father was taking his place to drive the omnibus back to the school. Wade had made the large enclosed vehicle to transport as many as ten passengers. Her aunts had instructed him as to the size, the window locations, and even the paint colors of red and yellow. He really was a very talented builder and a wonderful friend.

She bit her lower lip, as she was wont to do when worrying over a matter. Losing him would be the worst thing she could imagine. Outside of her faith in God, it was her love—their shared love—that had given her life meaning.

But if I don't change, I will lose him.

The thought settled hard on her spirit. But love was about sacrifice. Jesus showed His love by sacrificing His very life. Should she do less in her love for Wade? What if sacrificing her own desires and plans for the future was what God was calling her to? A sort of laying down her life for her friend, just as the Bible spoke about when defining the greatest love.

Sunday dinner offered little relief. Abrianna watched as Clara continued to tease and flirt with Wade and wondered if there was something she should say or do. *If I make a scene, it will only let Clara know that her actions are a bother to me. I will sound accusing and petty. But it's not petty. She's clearly being unkind toward me and loose with Wade. That's uncalled for.*

Aunt Miriam rose as dinner concluded. "Ladies, let us be about our duties so that we might enjoy a long afternoon of rest. Today, Abrianna, you and Flora will handle washing and drying the dishes. The rest will be responsible for clearing the table and putting away any remaining food." Several of the girls jumped up and began to take the empty plates. Aunt Miriam then turned to Clara, who continued to giggle and speak in hushed whispers to Wade. "Clara, you will be excused from helping with the cleanup."

The girl looked quite smug. "Why, thank you, Mrs. Madison."

"It's quite all right. You and I have studies to see to. I will expect you momentarily in my office. Oh, and bring your Bible." The girl's expression fell. She could not possibly have looked more miserable and left the room near to tears.

Abrianna breathed a sigh of relief and was surprised when Wade gave her a wink and got to his feet. "I believe I'll see my way to a Sunday nap. The week promises to be a busy one."

Aunt Miriam nodded and waved him off. "Yes, do go rest. I must tend to business and help Clara to better understand the Bible." A hint of a smile caused her lips to lift at the corners.

Aunt Selma rose and gave her friend a pat on the back. "I hope that should you tire in helping our Clara to understand, you will send for me. I will be most happy to reprieve you and further the lesson."

Abrianna breathed a sigh of relief. She might not understand Wade's mind and reasoning, but she could not possibly misunderstand that of her aunts. They loved her, pure and simple, and they weren't about to allow Clara's flirtatious nature to cause Abrianna and Wade even the slightest bit of grief.

Wade joined the old ladies and Abrianna later that evening in the small sitting room. In spite of a short nap, the day had worn him out, and he was more than ready to head off to bed, but he had hoped to have a word or two with Abrianna beforehand. He knew she had been pleased with his preaching. Several times he had looked down from the pulpit to find her looking up at him with an expression of pure joy. Even so, he knew she was still troubled over his insistence that they not use her inheritance for their future together. He felt he'd done a poor job of explaining it. He'd come across as demanding and dictatorial, and he, above all others, knew that was no way to get Abrianna to understand a matter.

"It's hard to believe that today is the first of September." Mrs. Madison shook her head. "I find the older I get, the faster time seems to pass."

"It's true," Mrs. Gibson said. "I'm sure men of a scientific nature would declare it all having to do with evolution or some other equally insipid matter. It never fails to amaze me the way such things are determined. I heard that the university recently hosted a lecturer who spoke of the moon's effect on the earth. Utter nonsense, if you ask me."

Wade smiled. "I suppose time just has the appearance of passing quicker as we get older because we have so much to do."

"I agree." Miss Poisie bobbed her head. "There just never seems enough time to accomplish everything. I find myself at great odds with myself, like yesterday. I was faced with several tasks that each seemed of equal importance and felt most perplexed."

"And how did you resolve the situation, Miss Poisie?" Wade asked.

She seemed pleased to be the focus of conversation and straightened in a most regal manner. "Well, of course I first prayed for direction, and then it seemed that everything just fell into place, and I was no longer vexed with many duties. You see, I had ironing to do, as well as cleaning in my room. But I also had dried herbs that I needed to bottle." She gave a quick glance around. Wade knew she was used to her sister putting her in check. This time there was nothing said, and Miss Poisie hurried to continue.

"I decided I would first iron my laundry. Then after hanging it in the wardrobe, I would be free to spread out my dried herbs and bottle them. After that, I was better able to assemble my room in proper order. For, you see, had I attempted to do it first, I might have had remnants of herbs to clean up. No matter how neatly I try to work with them, they are wont to get away from me. To have to clean the rug twice would have vexed me to no end, and I would have been most disagreeable."

Wade nodded, ever amazed at the things that seemed to upset the older ladies.

"Mr. Cunningham has agreed to build us a greenhouse, and he has found a man to come and plow up part of our acreage." Mrs. Madison changed the subject. "He will come and plow it after the first frost and then work up the soil for planting next spring."

"I do hope we can plant pumpkins." Miss Poisie grew quite thoughtful. "Pumpkins can be so very useful. I find few vegetables to be as worthy of my praise. Of course potatoes are very worthwhile, as well. I suppose if I were to rank them in order of importance, a potato might rise above that of a pumpkin. However, I simply prefer pumpkins. Do you like pumpkin, Wade?"

"I do." He smiled and added, "Especially in pie."

"We would do well to grow beans and corn." Mrs. Gibson picked up Mr. Masterson—a gray tomcat with smudge of black under his nose that imitated a mustache. She stroked the animal thoughtfully. "I don't know that either will take to this soil and climate. I suppose we should consult the *Farmers' Almanac*."

"We might even speak to local farmers," Mrs. Madison added. "I'm sure they can advise on what plants might work best for our ground."

Wade listened as the older women continued discussing various ideas they had for the garden. There was some conversation about adding additional animals to their small collection, but everyone eventually agreed that animals were a great deal of work.

Then just as he thought to call it a night, Wade was surprised when the conversation turned in another direction.

"I don't know if Abrianna has mentioned it to you or not, but we three are hoping that you and Abrianna might consider taking over the school after you wed."

Wade looked to Abrianna. She gave him a little smile and shrug. "I haven't exactly had time to talk to him about it, Aunt Miriam. We've been very busy with other things."

"Speaking of which," Aunt Miriam took the conversation in yet another direction, "have you set the date for the wedding? There is a great deal to prepare, and we mustn't let time get away from us."

"It's true," Aunt Poisie added. "Though I've not ever married, I was once engaged, and the preparations were quite extensive to consider."

"I'm open to whatever date Abrianna would like." Wade, too, hoped to pin down the date, but Abrianna had been less than forthcoming in a choice.

Everyone fixed their gaze on Abrianna. She smiled. "I'm still contemplating the matter."

"Well, even so, we can begin work on your wedding gown."

Mrs. Madison seemed to have already given the matter consideration. "I'm certain your friend Lenore will be giving you additional gowns, so we needn't worry about creating a new wardrobe, but a wedding dress is something special and will take time to put together."

Abrianna actually seemed to perk up at this. "I have in mind exactly what I would like."

This surprised Wade. She'd said nothing to him on the matter. Of course, he knew she was still rather hurt at his refusal to use her inheritance. He had hoped to ease her worries by letting her know about the large price he'd been offered for his property. Apparently once word got out that he was willing to entertain the idea of selling out, several buyers became interested enough to fight over the piece.

"I must discuss it with Wade first." Abrianna turned to him. "We will need his approval."

Mrs. Gibson gave a *harrumph*. "A groom seldom has anything to say on the matter of the wedding gown."

"Well, it's come to my attention," Abrianna countered, "that such things are of concern to Wade. He is very particular in how money is spent, and I wouldn't want to offend him in making a decision without his approval."

Wade felt the intense gaze of the older women. They appeared almost accusing in their expressions. He shrugged. "I figure a bride should have the kind of dress she wants."

Mrs. Madison rose. "I believe it would be good to give them time to discuss the details of this matter. Come, ladies. Let us make our rounds and see to it that the house is readied for the night."

They filed from the room and closed the door, leaving Wade and Abrianna alone. Wade turned to Abrianna and narrowed his eyes. Confusion and a bit of irritation mingled in his thoughts.

"Do you want to explain?"

"I just want to do whatever it takes to please you. I've come to realize that I know very little about the workings of a man's mind and pride. It's been brought to my attention more than once that you need to feel that you are in charge of everything, and I thought this would be one way to give you that control."

"I'm not seeking to control everything. You make me sound like an ogre. I thought for a moment your aunts might very well dip me in tar and feathers."

Abrianna smiled. "I am sorry about that. I'm sorry, too, that I've been difficult of late, but I am attempting to work on my heart. I was quite torn at first. You know that I can be very opinionated."

He relaxed and chuckled. "No, I hadn't realized."

"Don't lie," she admonished. "I know I've been difficult. The changes going on around me are quite challenging. However, I also realize that a woman is to be obedient and mindful of her husband's desires. Your desires are to be in charge of our future, so I am trying my best to yield." She held up her hand as Wade started to speak.

"This isn't easy for me. I have tried to understand why you feel as you do. I've spoken to my father and Aunt Miriam, and I have come to the conclusion that what you desire in me is a yielding of my will. Therefore, I am attempting to do just that. I cannot promise that it will be easy for me. Nor can I promise the outcome. I fear it will be my most arduous task to date, but I am determined to do whatever I can to satisfy your requirements, and you must correct me when I am in error."

He frowned. "Is that what you think I want from you? To be your master?"

She looked at him for a moment. "I suppose that does seem

to be a difficult word, but the Bible makes it clear that I am to be submissive to you."

"Abrianna, I love you. I want you to be my wife, my friend, my love. I'm not asking you to change who you are. I love who you are."

She looked perplexed. "But you told me how you wanted things to be. My father said that you men need to have this position of authority, so if I am to marry you, I must give you that position. Is that wrong?"

Wade drew in a breath and held it a moment. "This is about the money, correct?"

"It's about our marriage," she said frankly. "I don't know how to be a wife, but I am seeking advice and trying to learn. My father pointed out that I hadn't been raised with male authority, and therefore it was most foreign to me. However, it is biblical, and I am seeking to make my heart over to better understand what it is you expect of me—what God expects. I don't necessarily like the change, but then I didn't like taking a purgative when it was needed."

"You're comparing our life together to a purgative?" He couldn't help but smile. Sometimes Abrianna did make the silliest references.

"You know what I mean," she replied. "Wade, I've battled with myself until I was miserable. I've sought counsel, and I've tried my best to understand your heart and mind on matters of money and obedience." Tears came to her eyes. "Oh, stuff and nonsense. Here I am all teary again. Just ignore me." She wiped her eyes with the back of her sleeve. "I'm willing to change if I can. I'm just not sure I can, and I don't want to be unfair to you."

Wade got to his feet and went to where she sat. Kneeling

beside her, he took hold of her hands. "I don't want you to change who you are. I love you, Abrianna. Always remember that. I figure there are places where we can both work together to make things better as a married couple. I don't want you to think that you have to reorder the entire world to make me happy. Maybe I've been too prideful as you once suggested. Maybe I need to pray about that and figure a way to compromise."

"I'm really trying." A tear slipped down her cheek. "It just seems all the joy between us is gone. Now it's all grown-up thinking and making plans. It makes me sad to think that we will never have any fun together."

He grinned and got to his feet and pulled Abrianna up. "We will have a lifetime of fun, I promise you. I can hardly imagine anything else with you in the picture. You have worried and fretted way too much, and now I want you to put it aside. This doesn't have to be so hard. We fell in love with each other with all our failings and oddities, and we will go on loving each other with them. I'm sorry I made you feel that you had to change. That wasn't my desire."

He wiped the tear from her cheek. "Do you forgive me for making you feel bad?"

"I made myself feel bad, Wade. All day long I've made myself quite miserable, especially when I saw Clara flirting with you. I knew I was being difficult and there was nothing pleasant about me. But even so, I wanted to pull her chair out from under her."

He couldn't help but laugh. "You were jealous?"

Abrianna nodded. "I suppose that's the only word for it. As I said, I've been quite overcome by one feeling or another. Another of my shortcomings, I'm sure."

Wade leaned down without touching her and kissed her on the nose. "Silly girl. You never need to be jealous of any other woman. My heart has belonged to you for longer than I can even remember, and it will always be yours."

Abrianna reached up and drew his face down to meet hers. It was the first time she'd initiated a kiss, and Wade didn't want to do anything to discourage her. Gently he encircled her with his arms.

"I love you so dearly," she whispered, pressed her lips to his, then eased away. But changing her mind, she pulled him close again and kissed him with more passion. She sighed and let him go.

"January tenth seems a perfectly nice day for a wedding. It's a Friday, and we could have a lovely morning service here at the house with just our friends and family."

He smiled and felt a charge rush through him. "That sounds good to me."

Abrianna met his gaze and smiled in return. "Just remember, you promised me we would have fun."

Laughing, Wade nodded. "Indeed, I did."

10

Priam Welby pressed the tips of his steepled fingers together as he sat at his desk and considered a plan to force Abrianna Cunningham into marriage. That young woman was complex, to be sure. Where most women could be cowed or forced, Abrianna was unmoved. Even so, she had her vulnerabilities, and Welby knew those at least in part. Her family was uppermost in importance to her, as well as that Ackerman fellow. Given this knowledge, Welby felt he had a good start on a plan. If he threatened the well-being of the people she loved, Abrianna Cunningham would yield to save them.

He smiled. It was really too simple. He could affect a few accidents that threatened the lives of those dottering old ladies, perhaps even claim the lives of one or two to get his point across. Or he could cause her father to be arrested. After all, the old man had quite a history. Welby had put a man on investigating Cunningham's existence prior to coming to Seattle. It hadn't been difficult, even though the man went by the name Jay Bowes for a time. Cunningham had a history of brawling and letting his fists settle disputes. He also spent most of his adult life in prison. And while the punishment had been for a crime Cunningham hadn't committed, Welby knew he could use all of this to his advantage.

The key to his plan was to start first with observation and follow up with action. It was no different from the plans he'd used to rob his father. He'd started with observation, learned whom his father trusted and how his businesses were handled, and then systematically Welby bought off each and every man. They were his puppets now, and his father was completely clueless that he was about to fall over a cliff of financial ruin.

Welby leaned back in his chair. It was most satisfying to imagine the day when he would announce to his father and all of his cronies that the supposedly worthless son of Vernon Welby had become quite rich and powerful. So powerful that he ruined his father's social standing and living. The desire for that moment was like a palatable taste in his mouth. The urgency for satisfaction drove him forward day after day, and no matter the problems at hand, Welby always knew that this one goal would see him through any problem. Some thought him crazy, but few said so to his face. And those who had weren't going to ever say anything ever again. Welby smiled. Power was intoxicating.

"Boss, here are those plans you've been waiting for. I have to say you were right about using the fire to your advantage. There have been some choice pieces of property we've managed to buy. You're gonna be the most powerful man in Seattle."

Welby smiled. "What do you mean going to be? I already am."

His lackey, Carl, nodded with a laugh. "You sure are. Folks know better than to mess with you."

"So what else can you tell me?"

"Well, we have all the permits, and the first supply of bricks are on the dock waiting for delivery." He handed Welby the papers and waited for instruction.

"Perfect. You know what to do." Welby looked over the final drawings of what would become Seattle's finest brothel. "No matter what else happens, we must keep my identity from being known. I'm building a powerful reputation as a law-abiding, albeit cunning, businessman." He looked up with a grin. "This lovely . . . hotel must remain the property of one Mr. Peter Bishop, wealthy investor from New York City."

Carl smiled and nodded. "Sure thing, boss. Ain't nobody gonna know you're really the owner. We got 'em eatin' outta your hands."

Welby put the drawings aside. "Now report to me about Miss Cunningham."

The younger man's lip curled in a suggestive sneer. "Always did enjoy that piece of work."

"Watch what you say," Welby replied in a rather cold manner. "That piece of work is soon to be my wife."

"Sorry, boss." Carl looked momentarily uncomfortable. "Didn't mean to offend."

Welby nodded. "Do go on. Tell me what you've learned."

"Well, she sticks pretty close to home these days. She does go for walks down to the Booth place and sometimes takes walks to the park with that Ackerman fellow. She likes to get away to the farthest spot on the estate to just sit by herself. I've seen her out there several times."

"And what of the others?"

"Well, Ackerman and her father live in the carriage house, as best I can tell. Used to be another fellow and his wife lived in the house, but they're not there anymore. The old ladies live on the second floor. That's where most of the bedrooms are, but there are also some on the third floor off the ballroom. Storage is up there, as well."

"And how did you learn all of this?"

"I did what you suggested. I snuck in after they all left for church. I nearly got caught. They have a pretty little Chinese maid who doesn't go out at all. She was busy in the kitchen, so I had to be real quiet. Weren't a problem though."

"Very well. Keep watch on Abrianna. If she does anything unusual, or if anything in particular seems of interest to her, I want to know about it right away."

"Happy to oblige," Carl said. He left Welby, humming to himself.

Priam knew the man had an eye for the females and he would have to make certain Carl knew better than to tamper with Abrianna. He wouldn't see her handled by anyone save himself. Of course there was no way of knowing what had already gone on between her and Mr. Ackerman. Those two spent an awful lot of time together, and now they were for all purposes under one roof. He figured those aunts of hers kept a pretty tight rein on the girl, but Abrianna was seemingly untamable. He was going to enjoy breaking her in.

Abrianna handed Flora several books. "These are some of my all-time favorites. I think you'll enjoy them, as well."

"I love to read. Especially romantic stories." Flora's dreamy smile accentuated the point. "I suppose I'm rather daffy when it comes to them."

Abrianna grew thoughtful. "I don't know what to think of that word. Daffy. It makes me think of daft, so I suppose it works. Mercy, but have you noticed all the new slang words that have come into our everyday language? Aunt Miriam positively had a fit the other day when Kolbein commented on how he and Lenore learned to play a Japanese card game that was quite a 'corker.' 'Corker' was not at all an acceptable term, to Aunt Miriam's way of thinking."

"I suppose it depends on the card game. What was it?"

"Something called Hanafuda. Cards alone are enough to put Aunt Miriam on her guard. She never has allowed for any kind of card game, but Kolbein— Mr. Booth—pointed out that this game was not a card game of numbers for the purpose of gambling. Apparently these are cards printed on mulberry tree bark, of all things, and they are painted with various images. I really know very little other than the fact that Mr. Booth said the man responsible was in the process of incorporating his company and planned to sell cards in America. The company is called Nin-ten-do something or other. Oh yes, Nintendo Koppai. I thought it a very pretty name. Aunt Poisie thought Nintendo would be a good name for a cat. She would like us to get another, since Buddy ran away."

"How interesting. How is it that Mr. Booth knows about such things? Has he been to Japan?"

"Apparently his law offices have some connection to the man and his business. I know little else. The game sounded quite interesting, but don't let Aunt Miriam hear you call it a corker."

Flora giggled. "I won't, and I won't use the word *daffy* around her either."

"It's better that way," Abrianna admitted.

"Do you think Miss Poisie will really name a cat Nintendo?"

Abrianna sighed and began pulling pins from her messy coif. "If she does, I don't know if Aunt Miriam will ever agree to it."

"Maybe she could call the cat . . . Corker."

Abrianna laughed at this. "Perhaps." Her cinnamon curls fell down to her waist. The long sunny days of summer had kissed her hair with golden streaks that shimmered when caught in the lamplight. "I swear I have more trouble with my hair. Nothing ever wants to stay where it's supposed to be. And look, it's only just past noon. I can't even make it through the day."

"Let me help. You have to learn to use your curls to your advantage," Flora said, coming to Abrianna's aid. She began pulling and twisting until she had Abrianna's hair neatly piled atop her head once again. "My hair isn't curly like yours, but it does have a strong wave. Mama taught me first thing that I could use this to assist in dressing my hair. There. Now you are perfectly respectable."

"It's a good thing you've come to share my room." Abrianna smiled at her image in the mirror. "Not only have you been good company, but now you benefit me with this."

A knock sounded on the bedroom door. Abrianna rose. "At least I'm presentable, thanks to you, dear Flora." She opened the door to find Liang's smiling face.

"Missy Lenore is here to see you."

"Thank you, Liang. Is she in the parlor?"

"Yes. I bring tea?"

Abrianna nodded. "That would be fine." She cast a glance back at Flora. "I suppose Aunt Miriam has something for you to be about, otherwise I would ask you to join us."

Flora sighed and nodded. "I'm supposed to learn to quilt. Something was said about learning to stitch in the ditch, but I haven't a clue what that means."

"It means you cannot take tea with me. I will pray for you instead. Quilting was never my strong suit." Abrianna frowned. "Actually there is very little related to housekeeping and such that was my strong suit. I fear poor Wade will suffer once he's married to me."

With a frown, Flora squared her shoulders and preceded Abrianna out the door. "It is such a trial to be a woman training to be a bride. Do you suppose men ever have such ordeals to go through?"

Abrianna followed her down the hall. "I don't believe they do. I am convinced they have no idea of what it takes to keep a household. Most probably think it like the cobbler's shoes, that elves come at night and set everything right."

Flora paused at the top of the stairs. "I wouldn't be surprised at all if that was exactly how they thought."

Making her way downstairs, Abrianna put aside her sympathies for Flora and thought instead of Lenore. She made her way to the parlor where Lenore was already seated. Her pregnancy was becoming more evident, especially given the new fashions she had taken to wearing. Abrianna could clearly see the changes in her friend's body.

"You look so lovely." Abrianna stopped to stare at her friend. "I do believe this state becomes you." Lenore was dressed immaculately in a silver-blue walking suit trimmed in black edging and completed with a lacy white blouse. She sported a matching hat that had an arrangement of white ostrich feathers.

"I do, as well." Lenore put her hand to her side. "Although I walked here much too quickly and now have a stitch in my side."

"Aunt Selma says there's nothing that helps a body like apple cider vinegar. Would you like me to get some?"

"No. I'm sure it will pass."

Abrianna took a seat across from Lenore. "I asked Liang to bring tea. That might help to relax you."

Lenore nodded. "I am already much better." She smiled. "So have you been giving more thought to your wedding?"

"I have. Although there have been many things to interrupt my thoughts."

"Such as?"

Abrianna shook her head. "Where to begin? Well, Aunt Miriam is arranging a greenhouse to be built for the purpose of growing hothouse flowers for my January wedding. My father seems to have a growing interest in Mrs. Snyder, Flora Ledbetter's aunt. Oh, and Mr. Welby says he will do something drastic if I don't relent and agree to court him."

"Those sound like very interesting complications. We should probably start with Mr. Welby. Did he threaten you?"

"No. I believe the implication was that he would harm himself. Goodness, but I have no idea why he would act in such a way. I've done nothing but rebuff that man. A woman shouldn't have to say no more than once, should they? Perhaps it's because of those silly traditions where you aren't supposed to say yes right away, lest a man think you are wanton. But I simply find that annoying. I have a great deal to tend to in life, and I haven't got time for such games."

"I'm certain with your many interests in life, you can't be bothered with social edicts. However, I'm certain Mr. Welby will get over his infatuation with you. You mentioned your father being taken with Mrs. Snyder. Do you suppose anything can come of it?"

"I do hope so. I don't know my father very well, but he seems rather lonely. Mrs. Snyder also seems lonely, and Flora declares her to be so. I think they might find some comfort in their aging years if they were to marry."

"Mrs. Snyder can't be much older than Kolbein. Hardly her aging years. And your father isn't that old. He's not yet ready for a rocking chair." She smiled. "But you are right. I think they might be perfectly matched. We shall pray about it. By the way, I love your hair. You have fashioned it quite perfectly."

Abrianna nodded and touched her hand to her hair to make sure it was all still in order. "Flora did it for me. She has hidden talents."

"She seems a very pleasant sort of girl."

Shifting to ease back into the chair, Abrianna sighed. "She is. She is very much like me."

"Oh, that could be trouble."

She saw the smile on Lenore's face and knew her friend was teasing. "It could be, I suppose. Although I am much older."

"Hardly that," Lenore replied. "I heard your aunt say Miss Ledbetter is eighteen. You are but twenty-one. That's not so great a span of years."

"Perhaps not, but with all my new responsibilities, I feel old."

Lenore started to speak but instead gasped and clutched her stomach. "Oh, I think something is wrong. I feel quite overcome."

"Is it the baby?"

She shook her head and got to her feet. "I don't know. I suppose I should return home." She stood and pressed her hands to her rounded abdomen.

"I'll get my father to drive you."

"Maybe you should get Mrs. Madison. I'm not certain I can make it home. I feel . . . oh . . . dear . . ." She sat back down. "Hurry, Abrianna."

Abrianna shot from the room, calling for her aunt at the top of her lungs. She knew Aunt Miriam would normally be instructing girls in the kitchen, so that was where she went first. Thankfully, her aunt was there.

"Good grief, Abrianna, you needn't shout. You've startled everyone with your bellowing."

"Aunt Miriam, hurry. Lenore is having pain, and she doesn't feel good."

Her aunt immediately nodded. "Girls, I want you to practice making pie crust. Get to work." She pulled off her apron and followed Abrianna.

Lenore was doubled over and crying by the time they reached the parlor. Aunt Miriam assessed the situation and commanded Abrianna to get her father to run for the doctor. She would see Lenore was made comfortable.

With a look of terror, Lenore reached out for Abrianna. "Please pray. Pray for my baby. I cannot lose him. It would break my heart."

It seemed like it took forever, but the doctor finally arrived. In the meantime, Aunt Miriam sent Abrianna's father to find Kolbein at his office. Abrianna continued to pray for God's intercession. How awful to be so happy one minute and completely devastated the next. It was also quite disturbing to even contemplate Lenore losing the baby.

She paced the hall outside the parlor, where Aunt Miriam had created a makeshift bed for Lenore, using the fainting couch. Lenore was such a tiny person that it made a perfect examination table for the doctor.

When the door finally opened, the doctor was instructing Aunt Miriam. "I will take her in my buggy and go straightaway to the hospital. I will need help to get her settled in."

"I will assist you," Abrianna offered. "I'm quite strong."

The doctor nodded. "We must hurry."

"Is it the baby?" Abrianna couldn't help but ask.

Shaking his head, the doctor handed his bag to Aunt Miriam. "It's her appendix, and I'm afraid it may have ruptured. We must get her to the hospital where I can operate. Otherwise we will lose both mother and child."

11

The hospital's sterile quiet was too much for Abrianna's nerves. She did her best to comfort Kolbein and to pray, but once Wade appeared to join them, all she could do was chatter on and on.

"I believe Lenore will be perfectly fine," Abrianna told Kolbein. "She's young and strong. She's one of the strongest women I know, and she's always been quite healthy. Once, when we were younger, Lenore and I suffered influenza. Lenore overcame it much faster than I did. She just seems to have a healthy constitution."

Kolbein's expression was set in a grim intensity that left Abrianna uncertain he'd heard a single word. Wade reached out to pat her hand, but Abrianna felt little comfort. The doctor had been working on Lenore for nearly an hour. Did surgery always take so long?

She bowed her head to pray again, pleading with God to spare Lenore and her unborn child. Abrianna couldn't imagine life without her dear friend. They had found solace in each other for so long now that to have Lenore suddenly taken would completely disorder Abrianna's world.

Oh, Lord, I don't mean to be so selfish in this, but I cannot bear the thought of losing her.

Time passed in painful slowness until finally a white-clad nurse appeared. "The surgery is complete. The doctor will come to speak with you shortly."

Kolbein jumped to his feet. "Is she . . . is my wife all right?"

The nurse gave him what seemed to be a look of disapproval. "I am not at liberty to speak on the matter. The doctor will be here shortly." With that, she turned and left them to wait and wonder.

Kolbein's jaw clenched, and Abrianna could see he was near to reaching his breaking point. She got to her feet and took hold of his arm. "I'm certain she's fine, Kolbein. Let's just wait for the doctor."

"It's just not right. She shouldn't have to bear this." Kolbein ran his hand through his hair. "I don't know what I will do if she . . . if she . . ."

"Look, there's the doctor now," Abrianna interrupted. Kolbein pulled away and hurried to the man.

The doctor's smile was encouraging. "She's come through the surgery just fine. The baby, too."

Kolbein exhaled, and Abrianna thought he might well collapse to the floor. Instead, he stumbled back to a chair and sat down hard. "I was so afraid." Abrianna took the chair beside him.

"You needn't fear now, son." The doctor put his hand on Kolbein's shoulder. "The appendix hadn't yet ruptured, so I do not believe it will be a difficult recovery. She will remain here for two weeks, and after that I will release her to go home. She should have only minimal activity for the weeks that follow."

"I'll put her to bed until the baby comes," Kolbein said. "She won't have to lift a finger."

"Now, now. You needn't go that far," the doctor replied with a chuckle. "I believe your wife will fully recover. She's young and strong."

"That's exactly what I told him." Abrianna nodded. Still, hearing the doctor speak the same words gave her great comfort. "When can we see her?"

"Yes." Kolbein stood again. "When can I see her?"

The doctor stepped back and glanced down the hall as if to ascertain the answer. "I will allow just you to look in on her for a moment. She's sleeping and won't know you're there," the doctor told Kolbein. "You may visit her tomorrow. I would suggest you go home and get a good night's sleep. You look quite exhausted."

Kolbein nodded. "I am." He looked to Wade and Abrianna. "But I'll be all right. You two go on home and let the others know that she and the baby have come through without harm. After I leave here, I'll go let her folks know. I couldn't see alarming them until we knew one way or another, what with her father's weak heart."

"That was wise." Abrianna shifted in a restless manner. "Lenore's mother can be such a fuss. She would have made you quite nervous."

Wade looked at his watch. "It's nearly six. You could come back to the house and have supper first. I'm sure Mrs. Madison would want you to know you were welcome."

"Absolutely." Abrianna reached out to touch his hand. "You do need to eat to keep up your strength. Lenore would never forgive me if I failed to care for you in her absence."

"That's all right. Lenore's mother and father usually sit down to eat at six-thirty. I will impose upon them."

Abrianna could see that all he wanted was to see Lenore.

"You should go ahead, then. Wade and I need to get back before everyone begins to fret and think the worst."

The doctor led the way, Kolbein close on his heels. They disappeared around a corner, and Abrianna rose and took hold of Wade's arm. "I've never been so afraid. What a relief to have it done with."

Wade smiled down at her. "You held up very well. I'm sure it was a comfort to Kolbein that you were here." He started with her toward the door. "I'm sorry I wasn't there when Lenore took sick."

"It was a terrible thing to watch. There was nothing I could do. I felt so helpless. I hope never to see anyone in that much pain again."

Outside, the evening air was cool and damp. It had rained while they'd been inside, and the streetlamp's glow was reflected in the puddles that dotted the road. Wade directed Abrianna to the carriage and helped her up to the driver's seat.

"No sense you sitting back there by yourself." He climbed up and sat down beside her. "Besides, this is much cozier. I like the feel of you beside me."

"Do you worry about me dying?"

A puzzled look came over Wade's face. "Why? Do you have something planned?"

"Of course not. What a foolish question."

He grinned. "I thought the same of yours. I don't worry about death at all. Although I would hate to lose you . . . even to the Lord."

Abrianna frowned. "I never thought about it before, but now it vexes me. I don't want to imagine life without you. As I sat there thinking about how awful it would be if Lenore died, I couldn't even bring myself to consider losing you."

"Well, that's good, because I intend to be around for a long, long time."

"Be serious, Wade. Death is something that none of us can avoid."

He sobered. "I know that. But if you expect me to get all morose about it, think again. I know that God commands my life and my death. I know, too, that one day we who believe in Jesus and have confessed our sins to Him will be with Him. Death doesn't scare me."

"My death doesn't scare me, either." Abrianna looked away. "But yours terrifies me."

Wade pulled the carriage to the side of the road and stopped. "Abrianna, don't let this day cause you to worry. If something happens to either of us, we know God will provide us with His comfort and hope. Life is fragile, but our eternity is sure."

"I know that, but I can't imagine a world without you in it." She looked up and momentarily lost herself in his intense gaze. "You've always been here for me. I've come to count on seeing you each day. If you were gone, I don't know how I would manage to go on."

"Stop it now. You know better than to let your thoughts get wrapped around *ifs*. I'm not planning to die anytime soon."

"So you wouldn't be sad if I died?"

"Of course I'd be sad. It would be devastating. But worse still is if I give my thoughts over to that idea, I'd waste the time we do have. Don't you see? We can live in the dread of what might come and make ourselves so miserable that life isn't worth living. Or, we can rest in the Lord and cherish the days we have and make them worthwhile."

Abrianna felt her mind clear. "You are, of course, right." She felt a small peace settle over her heart. "I suppose it's silly to let such thoughts get out of control. Seeing Lenore so near death and how hard it was on Kolbein, I suppose I couldn't help myself."

Wade smiled. "Life is temporary. Everybody is going to die. You. Me. Them. That's why we have to do what we can to be good to each other and live a life pleasing to God."

"Time is very fleeting." She heard the words echo in her head and without thought spoke again. "I'm going to use some of my inheritance to build a food house and shelter." She looked at him. "If you approve. And if you don't . . . well . . . I may do it anyway."

He laughed and slapped the reins on the horse's back. "Now wouldn't that be a surprise."

"Surely you can't think to disapprove. You said it was my money to do with as I pleased."

"And I meant it. I also think it's a wonderful idea. It will help a great many people."

"Will you help me?"

He laughed. "Don't I always?"

"I know you have the church to consider now, as well as rebuilding your shop and finding us a place to live. Oh, Wade, I just want very much to help people, and I know you feel the same way." The urgency of the day's events stirred her unlike anything had in weeks. "I just know that this is of the Lord, and I have to do it."

"Then of course I will help, and we will see it through. Do you have any thought as to where you would like to build this food house?"

"No, but I plan to see a property seller about it. If you have time to go with me, that would be wonderful. Otherwise, I'll see if my father can accompany me. I know you wouldn't be happy to have me doing it on my own. I might have asked Kolbein to look for a place, but he will be very busy with Lenore, and I don't want to take him from her side."

"I doubt you could. I won't be able to get away very soon, but I think your father would be a good one to have at your side. Just don't sign anything until you can consult me or Kolbein. There are a lot of folks out there doing what they can to make money on our tragedy. Some folks even claim to have property for sale when they don't. Practice caution this one time. All right?"

She looked at him in surprise. "I always practice caution."

"Like when you crawled down the coal chute to rescue those Chinese girls? Or what about that night you decided to confront the would-be murderer of those men at the Madison Building?"

"I was cautious both times."

Wade gave a hearty laugh and shook his head. Abrianna had no idea why it amused him so much. She always practiced great caution in whatever she did. Maybe it wasn't the same kind of attention someone else would give, but it was still great caution for her.

"Abrianna, you are a corker."

She looked at him in surprise. "And you, sir, are quite daffy."

Two nights later Wade related the conversation to Abrianna's father and Flora's Aunt Eloise as he and Abrianna shared supper with them at a newly opened restaurant. Although set in a tent, the food was quite good and the company even better.

"She does know it's a sin to lie?" Abrianna's father asked.

Abrianna folded her hands across her chest. "I did not lie. Perhaps my definition of caution is different from yours. However, I gave deep thought to my actions on each of those occasions."

"She's right." Wade looked at her for a moment. She always seemed to bring out the orneriness in him. "On the night she confronted the man in the alleyway, she had a boning knife strapped to her calf."

Her father nearly choked on the sip he'd just taken. Eloise Snyder looked at him with concern, but the older man quickly regained his composure. "A knife? And just what did you think you'd do with that?" He looked to his daughter and shook his head. "You're hardly big enough to stand up to a boy, how would you have managed with a killer?"

"That was my question." Wade looked at her with a raised brow. "I'd even showed her prior to that just how easy it was to take that knife away, but apparently that didn't concern her."

"I'll have you know that I also had a fireplace poker. Besides that, I had the Good Lord watching over me." Abrianna didn't appear at all amused.

"That must surely be a tiresome job," her father said. "Good thing for you that Wade doesn't scare easy."

Eloise put her hand atop Abrianna's. "Don't let them trouble you, my dear. Men always make themselves feel better when they can cast aspersions on someone else's weakness."

Abrianna looked grateful for Eloise's support. Wade smiled and took hold of Abrianna's free hand. He drew it to his lips and kissed her palm. "Forgive me for teasing you. I couldn't quite help myself."

"Especially when she gives you such wonderful material to use against her," Abrianna's father countered. "Oh, but I wish I could have watched you growing up."

Abrianna shook her head. "It's better that you didn't. I am sure to have worried you into constant headaches, just as I did my poor aunts. I seem to have that effect wherever I go."

The trio chuckled, but Wade knew the truth of it. Abrianna's fearlessness was a never-ending worry, for sure.

Later that evening Wade bid Abrianna good-night on the porch outside the school. Her father and Eloise had already gone inside because Eloise planned to leave in the morning for Tacoma. It was clear, however, that they were very close to an understanding that would keep her in Seattle permanently.

Abrianna seemed uncharacteristically quiet, and Wade feared that his earlier jesting might have offended her. He reached out and drew her close.

"You do know, don't you, that I'm very proud of you. I even admire your fearlessness, although it gives me cause for worry, as well." He touched her cheek and marveled at the softness. "I've always been amazed by the way you never let anything scare you away from your duties. I suppose that's why I was so surprised when you were afraid of getting married."

"I wasn't afraid of marriage. I just didn't want to lose what I already had for the promise of something that might never be," she said. "It's like the bird in hand phrase. Having one in hand is better than the promise of two in the bush."

"Whatever would you do with two husbands?"

She looked momentarily confused and then nodded. "You thought I was implying that two birds equaled two husbands, but I assure you, I wasn't. It's merely a metaphor to express the benefit of sticking with what you know."

"I realize that. I just wanted to make you smile."

Abrianna looked at him for a moment. "I don't suppose men concern themselves with such things as losing friendships, but we women do. It's important to us to—"

Wade had heard enough. He pressed his lips to hers and kissed her for a very long time. If only the moment could just go on and on. He longed for the day they would be married, and no one could ever separate them again. His hand trailed down her back to pull her closer. She gave him no resistance, but his mind did. This was more than a little dangerous.

He dropped his hold and stepped back rather abruptly. "Good night, sweetheart."

She looked at him with the same wide-eyed expression that she always had after he kissed her. He smiled, then jumped the porch rail and made his way to the carriage house. It was obvious she enjoyed their intimate moments as much as he did, and that made it all the more important to keep their behavior in check.

"So do you think they will marry?" Flora asked Abrianna after she returned later that night.

"I do." Abrianna had seen the way her father and Eloise looked at each other. She felt certain that it would just be a matter of time before they announced their engagement.

"Oh, I hope so. I know it will be just perfect."

"Your aunt mentioned being ready to move here to Seattle. She said there really was nothing left in Tacoma for her. I think it was her way of telling my father that she was ready to make a commitment to him."

Flora clapped her hands. "How romantic. It's just like a fairy tale." She plopped down on her bed. "I think this will change everything for Aunt Eloise. She'll be able to let go of the past and all the deaths."

"Love has a way of healing all wounds, that's to be sure." Abrianna unfastened the neck of her gown, and Flora jumped back up. "Here, let me help you." She quickly undid the back buttons. Abrianna slipped from the bodice. "I think I'm starting to get used to dressing up. I know Lenore will be glad to hear that."

"How is she?" Flora made her way back to the bed, but this time she didn't sit. "I know you were quite worried."

"She's doing better. She'll remain at the hospital until the end of the two weeks. I plan to go see her tomorrow. Maybe you'd like to come with me?"

Flora rolled her eyes and sank to the mattress. "I wish I could. Mrs. Madison said that I must learn to make better bread."

"Oh dear. I remember how miserably I failed at such endeavors. I think Aunt Miriam came to realize that it would be my fate to buy bread rather than bake it for myself." Abrianna finished undressing and pulled on a white cotton lawn nightgown. Going to the vanity table, she added, "I shall probably never bake bread, although I can do rather well with cookies, so long as I don't forget them in the oven. Sometimes I find my mind so otherwise occupied that I cannot focus on baking. Baking seems quite trivial when there are matters of the world to resolve."

"I find it all so tedious. My mother tried to teach me. I remember when I was little. She would put me on a crate and have me knead a tiny lump of dough." She smiled. "That is a rather pleasant memory. Perhaps if I think of her when I'm taking instruction from Mrs. Madison, it will pass the time faster."

"That's a wonderful idea." Abrianna sat down and began to pull the pins from her hair. "I wish I had such memories. Of course, my aunts have been wonderful, and I have pleasant memories of working with them. My favorites are when we would study the events of the world or history. I do love history." She smiled. "It's quite amazing the things that come to mind from our childhood."

"You and Wade have known each other since you were children, haven't you?"

"Oh yes. We met through church events. He's nearly six years older than me. When I was very young, I thought he was amazing. He would teach me things like how to throw a knife and how to carve wood." She hadn't thought of those things for a very long time. "He was always around, just like an older brother."

"My older brother could be very annoying. He was always ordering me around and doing his best to keep me from having any fun at all."

Abrianna nodded. "Yes. Wade was guilty of that, too. I suppose he was just endeavoring to keep me safe."

"Dusty said as much. He said that little girls were full of mischief and Mama and Papa had told him when I was born that it would be his obligation, as well as theirs, to keep me out of harm's way. Seems an awful lot of responsibility for a young boy. When we were older, it was just plain annoying."

"Yes. I agree. When I was fifteen—goodness that was just six years ago—Wade caught me sneaking out of our building downtown. Apparently Aunt Miriam had grown wise to what she called my escapades. Wade was a grown man of course, so no one was ordering him around like they were me."

"Where were you going?"

"To take food to one of my old sailors."

"At fifteen? Were you never accosted?"

Abrianna laughed. "No one would have dared. All of those old men looked out for me. I started slipping food and coin to the poor sailors and homeless when I was just ten. Usually it was at the bake sales we held in the park. Everyone was so busy, they didn't have time to worry too much about me." She took up her brush and began to work it through her hair. "One day I saw there were some old men sitting a ways from the sale and went over to strike up a conversation. I asked why they didn't come buy some sweet rolls, and they told me they had no money. I went back to the table and took two of the rolls and delivered them to the men." She frowned and turned to look at Flora. "They were so hungry they very nearly ate them in one bite. After that, I knew it was my duty to see that such people had food."

"How wonderful to know your calling at such a young age. I still don't know what God would have me do. Unless it's to help you."

Abrianna gave up trying to brush her hair. She quickly braided the mass into a single plait and tied it with a ribbon. "I am happy to have your help. Militine was good to assist me, but since she left, I've had no one else who showed even the slightest interest. Most of the young ladies here are quite afraid."

"Of helping?"

"Of the old men. Of the young ones, too." Abrianna rose and made her way to her bed. "I don't know why. They are just the same as other people, only poorer and hungrier." She pulled back the covers. "I suppose, however, fear comes in many forms."

Flora nodded and crawled under her own quilt. "I suppose so. But just so you know, I'm not afraid. I think your cause may very well be what I need. Life without a purpose can wear hard on a soul, and I've long been without one." She sat up rather abruptly. "Purpose, that is. My soul will ever be with me, as you well know."

Abrianna settled into bed and yawned. "Everyone needs to know they have a purpose or a calling. I find it amazing that callings can change, but I have seen how God has remade mine several times over. Thankfully, it remains that I am to help the poor. If He were to give me another task, such as singing in the choir or—"

"Making bread?"

"Yes. If God gave me a calling to bake bread, I would fail miserably." She leaned over and blew out the lamp before adding, "But because God knows all things and knows how big a mess I would make of it, He doesn't call me to bake bread. He is, after all, a God of mercy."

12

I'm glad you agreed to go with me." Abrianna gripped her father's arm as he drove the wagon. The gray skies and chill to the air couldn't keep her from looking at available property. She had taken moderate care to her appearance, not wishing to look too juvenile in her fashion. The real estate broker needed to understand she was a woman of means, a woman who understood what was needed and expected him to pay heed to her wishes.

"I sure couldn't have you going alone. Wade told me about your plans and told me that if I didn't go along, you'd just find a way to tend to business by yourself. You really should consider the worry you give other folks."

Abrianna grew thoughtful. "I do consider it. That's why I asked you to go with me. I try not to worry people, but at times it seems the only way to ensure that is to sit and do nothing. If you knew me . . . well, I believe you are getting to know me quite well, but for those who have known me for a lifetime, they should understand this by now."

"Understand what? That you're bound and determined to have your own way at any cost?"

"That is hardly fair. I am not determined to have my own way. Rather, I choose to make choices that will benefit others more than myself."

She looked ahead at the view afforded her and changed the subject. The city was coming back to life, to be sure. "I am completely astonished at how quickly buildings can be remade. I never expected to see anything in place until the new year."

"These folks are properly motivated, I'd say. Business being business, they need to make a living or lose their homes and comfort. Rebuilding and doing so quickly is to everyone's benefit." He pulled the buckboard to one side. "I see this is the address you gave me. Looks respectable enough."

"I should hope it would be, although Wade says there are a great many schemers." She climbed down unassisted. "I'll go on ahead. Join me as soon as you can."

He nodded. "I'll get the wagon parked up ahead and be right in."

Abrianna made her way up the brick walk. The building stood just outside of the destroyed sections of downtown on the east side of Seattle. She read the words painted on the glass. "Guyland Greene, Real Estate Broker."

She opened the door and glanced around the small office. A portly, older man with a thick gray mustache looked up. "If you're from the Ladies' Aide Society, I've already given as much as I'm going to give."

"Excuse me? I'm not with the Ladies' Aide Society, but if I were I would find your demeanor to be somewhat uncalled for. Are you in business here or not?"

He eyed her suspiciously and stood up. "I am. I am quite busy at the moment, so whatever you are about, I am not interested."

"I am about the task of purchasing property."

"You're a woman."

Abrianna cocked her head to one side. "And you, sir, are rude. I hope not to hold that against you and would suggest you do likewise toward my gender. Now that we've established that, I would like to know about the properties available near the northern docks. Although I'm uncertain now as to whether I want to conduct business with you."

"That is quite all right," the man replied. "I do not do business with addlebrained women. Go home and let your husband handle such affairs."

"I'm not married."

The man scoffed. "I'm not surprised. I can't imagine any man taking such an unruly wife."

Abrianna frowned and shifted her reticule to her left wrist. "I'll have you know that I am a woman of means, and I don't need a man to handle the task of picking out a property for the charitable organization I intend to build. However, if I'd known that you would be as abominably offensive as you are, I wouldn't have bothered to come here at all."

"Then do us both a favor and depart. As I said, I have a great deal of business to take care of, and I do not need this distraction." He retook his seat and picked up his papers.

Abrianna stared at his bent bald head and fumed. She'd never been treated so unfairly in all of her life. Just then the door opened. The man looked up and smiled. "Good day, sir. How might I assist you?"

Abrianna replied before her father could speak. "You won't be able to assist him. This is my father, and I'm hoping that perhaps he can help you to get your thoughts straightened out."

"Is there a problem?" her father asked.

"There most certainly is." Abrianna pointed her gloved finger at the heavyset man. "This very rude man has refused to work with me because I am a woman and therefore of no consequence in his mind."

Jay Cunningham narrowed his eyes as he looked at the man behind the desk. "That true?"

"It is, and if you were any kind of man you would have known better than to allow your daughter to make such a foolish trip. Women have no place in business." He looked at Abrianna with a sneer. "If you are insistent upon purchasing property, you should have the decency to allow your father to handle the matter for you."

"I am quite confident my daughter is capable of handling the matter for herself," her father replied. "I do believe, however, that you may need a lesson in common decency."

The portly man stood. "Whom do I have the displeasure of addressing?"

"Name's James Cunningham. This is my daughter Abrianna—Miss Cunningham, to you."

Abrianna hoped that they might be making some headway. She no longer planned to utilize this man's services, but she wanted him to come to the place where he offered to do so, just so she could refuse.

"Well, Mr. Cunningham, Miss Cunningham, I will give you to the count of ten to remove yourselves from my office. If you aren't gone by then, I will feel the need to call for the police. They are always nearby, and I doubt we will have any trouble rectifying this situation."

Abrianna's father tensed. She could see he was assessing the man in a most determined manner. "Daughter, go to the wagon."

She thought to protest, but the tone of her father's voice made it clear to her that it would be best to leave. Without a word, she turned and left the office, hoping with all her heart that the situation wouldn't get out of hand. She saw the wagon parked just a little way from where her father had let her off and made her way there.

For several long moments she wondered if she'd done the right thing in leaving. Her father had admitted many times to having a temper. She frowned and climbed up to take her seat. If she went back, she would only prove to the property broker that she was disrespectful of her father's instruction. Yet . . . She glanced back over her shoulder and sighed in relief at the sight of her father leaving the office.

He joined her in the wagon and, without a word, let go the brake and urged the horses forward. Abrianna said nothing, but her gaze fell on his scuffed knuckle. They were nearly home before she had the courage to ask.

"Did you . . . did the two of you come to blows?"

"I came to blows. He simply received." Her father was very matter-of-fact in his comment.

"I'm sorry. I never meant to put you in such a position."

"It's of no importance. The man was rude and out of line to treat you the way he did. Some of the things coming out of his mouth were uncalled for, and I decided to educate him."

Abrianna frowned, uncertain if she should say anything more. On one hand, she understood her father's actions and even felt a bit of pride that he would defend her. On the other, she was worried that the consequences would be dire.

Was it wrong to hit the slimy real estate broker? Jay shook his head. No. The man deserved it for his derogatory comments in regard to Abrianna. It couldn't go unchecked. While Jay would never repeat what the man said, and even though the man had promised legal action, Jay knew he would have done it all over again if need be.

A man can hardly stand by and allow his daughter to be defamed. I might have missed out on being there for Abrianna all those years, but now that I'm here, I won't let the likes of that pompous windbag call her names.

There might still be legal repercussions, though. Folks around here are operating on a shortage of patience for lawbreakers. After years spent in prison, Jay had no desire to return. He stood contemplating the whole scenario and rubbing down the horse when Wade sauntered into the stable.

"I heard you had a little trouble today."

Jay nodded. "Not near as much as the other fella." He finished with the horse and led him to the stall. "I suppose Abrianna told you all about it."

"She did. She's all fired up and wants to go back and give the man a piece of her mind, but I've convinced her it would be best for us all to lie low. Maybe the man will just let it be."

"I doubt that." Jay secured the stall gate. "That Greene fella wasn't very congenial. I have no doubt he'll talk to the authorities just like he threatened."

"Even so, maybe the law will overlook it given the situation."

He shook his head. "The law hasn't overlooked anything where I'm concerned. I don't expect they'll offer any favors this time around."

"Well," Wade looked quite concerned, "perhaps Abrianna can relate what happened."

"She wasn't there. Not when I hit him. I made her go to the wagon. I knew I planned to give the man a piece of my mind." He shook his head again. "I didn't intend to hit him at that point, but the man was vile. I've never heard such language come out of the mouth of a man who calls himself a gentleman. The things he called Abrianna . . . well . . . I won't repeat them."

Wade's expression changed to anger. "All because she wanted to know about a piece of property? I know Abrianna can be forceful, but that's no call to be lewd."

"Exactly." Jay dusted off his trousers. "I figure I need to go speak with Eloise. I know she's going to be upset, and I want her to hear it from me in case the authorities do have a mind to cause me grief."

"I can understand that. I have a meeting at the church with the elders." Wade kicked at the straw on the floor. "But I should be back by eight. Maybe we can figure something out. Could be Kolbein might have some idea of how to handle this."

Jay felt a bit of his tension ease. "Maybe he would at that. I'll be here when you get back. Just find me, and we can figure out what to do next."

"I will." Wade went to the door that led upstairs to the carriage apartment. "I've got to clean up a bit before I take off. I told Abrianna to save me some supper, but she was madder than a wet cat. You might remind her."

Jay chuckled. "I will. It's probably best that I sent her to the wagon. No telling what kind of fight that girl has in her."

"It's just good that she didn't have a fireplace poker handy." His eyes seemed to twinkle in delight.

Jay watched him go. *That man's going to make a wonderful husband for my daughter.*

Wade found Jay in the carriage house later that evening. The man looked no less worried than he had before. Wade pulled off his boots and went to the small stove where he found a warm plate covered by a dish towel.

"I see you brought my supper."

"Abrianna did. She also came to check up on me." Jay put aside the paper he'd been looking over.

"Looks like things stayed quiet." Wade picked up the plate

and uncovered it. He could almost taste the roast beef and potatoes that awaited him.

"So far. Abrianna said if you want dessert, you'll find it in the kitchen."

Wade picked up a fork and settled down at the table opposite Jay. "I swung by Kolbein's on the way home. He wasn't back from the hospital, but I told his butler to have him get in touch with us." He ate several bites and savored the enticing flavor. He hadn't realized how hungry he'd been.

"You get church business settled?"

Wade swallowed and nodded. "I did. The elders said we needed to be thinking about the holidays to come. Thanksgiving time we usually have a church dinner. Christmas, there's Advent, a program the kids put on, and usually cookies and punch afterwards. Oh, and the church puts together sacks of goodies for the poor children and orphans. I guess there's a lot of planning to do."

"I suppose so." Jay yawned and pushed one boot off with the toe of the other. "Think I'll probably just go to bed early. Don't imagine Booth will come by tonight."

"No, I suppose not. I was of a mind to talk to you a minute. If you're not too spent."

Jay shook his head. "I'm always willing to lend an ear. What's on your mind?"

"Well, you know about Abrianna's inheritance."

"I do. She's also told me that you won't allow for her to share it with you in regards to setting up house or restarting your business."

Wade laughed. "I'm sure she did. Fact is, I'm getting a really good price for my land downtown. I have enough to turn around and buy a place outright. If I find the right place. Nothing too fancy." He took another mouthful of the roast and chewed it as he considered what he would say next.

Jay got up and poured two cups of coffee and brought one to Wade and took the other for himself. He sat down and waited with what seemed infinite patience for Wade to get to the point. The problem was, now that Wade had brought up the subject, he felt almost embarrassed to continue.

"Abrianna has it in her mind that I'm being pigheaded because I won't let her contribute the money to our life together, but I think it's important that she keep it in her control. However, she did get the idea to use it for a food house and ministry to the poor. I definitely commend her on that idea, and I've promised to help as much as I can."

"So what's got you all worried?"

"It's not so much a worry," Wade admitted. "I guess I'm just weighing my future with her. I want us to work together—especially in ministry. We both feel called to serve God, and I've always been open to whatever job God sends my way. Being a wainwright was always something I took pride in because my father taught the business to me and his father taught him. I like working with my hands.

"I like serving the church and leading folks in learning about the Bible, too," Wade continued. "I believe Abrianna's love for the poor is a beautiful outpouring of God's love and the love she's capable of sharing. I've never known anyone to care so deeply or be so loyal."

"I can see that for myself." Jay scratched his chin. "Wish I could have been around for her growing up. But then, maybe she wouldn't be like this. Go on. What is it you're getting at?"

"I'm not exactly sure. After meeting tonight with the elders it got me to wondering if maybe the two ministries couldn't be somehow combined. I'd like to see the church take a part in ministering to the poor. But I am just the temporary pastor. A new man might not feel that way, so I'd hate to suggest Abrianna go with me to the elders in regard to tying the two together when there might be a risk that the next pastor would put an end to it and use the money given for another purpose. That would never sit well with Abrianna."

"Don't think it would probably sit well with God if the money were marked for one thing and the word of the elders was given. But I do see your point. I guess like you're always telling me, we ought to pray about it."

Wade nodded. "I know. That's what my heart tells me, as well. I guess I just needed to talk it out with someone I respect."

Jay looked at him oddly, then shook his head slowly. "I never had anyone say that they respected me. Not in all my years. Not many folks will respect a convict or a man who leaves his family high and dry to fend for themselves."

"But you didn't do it on purpose. You had in mind to find work to support them. You were honorable in your intentions."

"Yeah, but you know what they say about good intentions," Jay said. "Hell's roads are paved with 'em."

Wade heard regret in the older man's voice. There was no way to reclaim the years. He could only look to the present and the future. "Well, I for one admire what you did to try to put bread on the table for your family. I'm sure it wasn't easy to leave your wife and daughter to seek employment. It took courage, and that's admirable. No matter the result, your heart was right, and the Bible says that the heart is what God sees."

Jay finished his coffee, then surprised Wade with a grin. "I hope God wasn't looking this afternoon. I'm afraid my heart wasn't all that pure when I punched old Mr. Greene in the eye."

13

I'm glad you're feeling better." Abrianna sat beside Lenore's hospital bed and patted her hand. "I felt complete terror when you fell ill. I was quite beside myself."

"I didn't mean to give everyone such a fright," Lenore replied. "I was glad Kolbein didn't tell Mother or Father until after I was recovering. With Father's weak heart, the shock might have compromised him."

"Have they come to see you?"

"Oh yes. They sent me flowers and then came to see me. The hospital nurse was quite put out at the size of the bouquet. It was very large. The nurse said flowers had no purpose in a hospital, given their ability to transport insects and such." She gave a soft giggle. "Kolbein arrived an hour later, and she demanded he take them home. He asked why he should do that—they weren't his. Oh, but that only sent her into another round of complaints. I tell you, that husband of mine can be quite ornery when he wants to be. He did, however, take them to the house."

"Kolbein has a great sense of humor, but most men are known to be capable of mischief. At least that's how I find them to be.

Did I tell you that my father came to blows with the property broker I went to see?"

"Yes, you did mention that."

"I can't say that I blame him. I wanted to hit the man myself." Abrianna sighed. "But let us not ponder such unpleasant things. I apologize for even bringing it up. I'm so glad to see your color has returned. And what of the baby?" Abrianna frowned. "I don't mean to inquire as to whether the baby's color has returned. Rather, is all well with the baby?"

"The doctor assures me that the baby is fine. I believe it's a boy and say so at every turn, but the doctor admonished me for that. I assured him I could love either equally, but given the amount of movement, I feel confident it's a boy."

"Could be a girl like me." Abrianna contemplated what that might be like. "I would not wish that on anyone. As we both know, I am given over to causing a great deal of consternation. And I would never wish red hair on anyone."

"There are no redheads in my family, so I doubt the baby will have red hair. However, if this should prove to be a little girl and she is like you—I shall love her all the more. Of course I'll need to arrange round-the-clock nannies to keep an eye on her."

"And have you picked out names?"

Lenore smoothed her bed covering. "Kolbein and I were just discussing that last night. If it's a girl we want to name her Rachel after his mother."

"Rachel is a good biblical name. I think that would be most appropriate."

"For a middle name we thought Abrianna would be appropriate. After all, were it not for you, Kolbein and I might never have met."

Abrianna thought she might cry. She put her hand to her

heart. "I'm deeply touched. I cannot begin to tell you how thoughtful that is. I have known many kindnesses and compliments throughout my life, but this is by far and away the most precious. Now I find myself hoping it's a girl."

"Well, if this is a boy, we will simply save the name for another time," Lenore assured. "If it's a boy, we plan to name him Daniel after Kolbein's father. Daniel Kolbein Booth."

"That's a perfectly inspiring name." Abrianna leaned closer. "At least you didn't pick John. Aunt Selma would have been positively beside herself if you'd even hinted at a reminder of John Wilkes Booth. I swear for all the forgiving my aunts have taught me, apparently Mr. J. W. Booth is not deserving of such mercy."

"Well, I have never given it much thought one way or the other. You and I are really too young to remember such things. I don't see it important to eliminate using a name, just because another misused it. And I do like the name John—it's strong and simple. But upon reflection, I would avoid it for the very reason you mentioned."

"It's best that way."

"Oh!" Lenore put her hand to her stomach. "He's kicking up a storm. Would you like to feel?" She took hold of Abrianna's hand without waiting for her answer.

Abrianna's mouth dropped open at the movement beneath her hand. "That's the baby?"

"It is. I believe he must surely be dancing a jig. Goodness." Lenore let go Abrianna's hand and smiled. "I can hardly wait to hold him in my arms."

Abrianna shook her head in awe. It was difficult to pull her hand away and settle back in her chair. "What a wonder."

"It truly is," Lenore agreed. "I marvel at it constantly. I do hope you and Wade will have children right away."

"Your friend will have to leave," a stern-faced nurse announced, coming from behind a framed partition. "Your parents are here to see you, and you cannot fill this ward with visitors. There are other sick folk who need peace and quiet."

Abrianna got to her feet. "That's quite all right. My father is waiting for me downstairs." She leaned over and kissed Lenore on the forehead. "I love you, my dear friend. I will look forward to your return home."

Taking her leave, Abrianna found Lenore's parents waiting just outside in the hall. "Hello, Mr. Fulcher. Mrs. Fulcher. Lenore seems much improved, I'm happy to say."

"We were so grateful that you were with her through this," Mrs. Fulcher declared. "You have always been a most encouraging friend to her. I'm afraid I haven't always appreciated that."

Abrianna couldn't help but smile at this compliment. The Fulchers had not always thought her influence a positive one. "I was glad to be there for her, and I will be more than happy to be at her side when she returns home." She bid them farewell and made her way outside to where her father waited.

"How's Miss Lenore today?"

"She's much improved, I'm happy to say. I'm going to sit up on the driver's seat with you, if you don't mind."

"Of course not." he smiled. "I would be proud to have you there." He helped Abrianna up. "'Course your aunts might not like it."

"Oh, they will understand. I've done far worse things, and should any of their friends spy me, they will simply murmur to themselves that it's that rapscallion Cunningham girl." She grinned and settled her skirts.

Father laughed and joined her on the seat. "No doubt."

"Lenore gave me the most pleasant news. She said that if she has a baby girl, they have decided to call her Rachel Abrianna Booth. Isn't that marvelous? I was quite honored and thought I might cry. But then, these days I often seem given to tears. I've never known such an upheaval of emotions. I do hope it won't go on this way all of my adult years."

"Oh, daughter, you are a wonder to be sure. The things you worry about are amazing to me."

"I can't help it," Abrianna replied. "I have a great many things on my mind. It seems to be my lot in life. I ponder and ponder, and yet there always seems to be more to consider, whether it's regarding the plight of the Chinese or how to make a proper loaf of bread when your talents don't lie in that direction."

He fixed her with a smile as he snapped the reins. "That's probably why everyone loves you so much. You take the worry for us."

She nodded, weighing the matter seriously. "I do try."

Priam Welby hadn't wanted to attend tonight's dinner party, but given the fact the councilman hosting it was to play a vital role in one of Priam's new schemes, he didn't want to miss an opportunity to make his presence known.

The meal had been good but nothing overly extravagant. Now the men were congregated in the library, sharing brandy and cigars while the ladies were off visiting elsewhere. Priam watched each man with decided interest. Most had secrets that Priam used to his advantage. None seemed overly glad to have him present, but they were all too afraid to act on that feeling. He determined to keep it that way.

Edging through the gathering, Priam overheard the mention of the name Cunningham. He integrated himself into the group of men who were discussing some mishap that had befallen one of their friends.

"He would have been here tonight, but Cunningham beat him. The poor man's eye is black and swollen," his host said in a hushed tone.

"Did Mr. Greene say why this brute hit him?" another asked.

Welby took a sip of brandy as the host answered. "The conflict had something to do with the man's daughter."

He all but choked on the fiery liquid and would have laughed out loud had he not had his wits about him. No doubt the Cunningham they discussed had to be Abrianna's father.

"I've heard about her," one of the men said, then glanced up at Priam. "Weren't you two something of an item for a time?"

Welby smiled in an indulgent manner. "If you are referring to Miss Abrianna Cunningham, then yes. She is quite dear to me. In fact, we have an understanding of sorts."

The councilman looked surprised. "I presume by understanding you mean that you two intend to wed. If that is the case, I find it surprising that you would allow your betrothed to venture out to run her own affairs. Guyland said that she had actually come there to buy property to build some sort of charity."

Priam nodded. "She wishes to set up a permanent charity to help the poor and needy. It is something I fully support."

The men fell silent for a moment, nursing their brandy. Priam could tell they were uncertain how much to say or whether he would take offense at what they'd already mentioned. He shook his head. There wasn't a strong man among them. He waited for them to comment further, but instead, the group broke apart, and most of the men ventured elsewhere. The imbeciles bored him, but they could also be useful. A thought came to mind, and he took hold of his host's arm.

"So do I understand that Mr. Cunningham, Abrianna's father, took umbrage with Mr. Greene and the results were a physical altercation?"

"You do," his host replied. "I was appalled."

"Will Greene press charges?" Welby could already see a great plan coming together.

"I don't know. He did mention the possibility of speaking to the police."

"He should," Welby replied. "Abrianna, Miss Cunningham, has long been humiliated by her father. It was the reason he was so long out of her life. That and the fact that he was serving time for murder."

"Murder?" his host exclaimed.

"Do say!" another man declared, coming to join them. He'd apparently overheard enough to be intrigued. "Are you certain?" he asked, as if Welby had addressed his comments directly toward the man.

"It's all quite true." Welby remained as nonchalant as if he'd just told them it was raining outside. "He is not a man to be trifled with. He belongs back in jail, if you ask me. I believe Mr. Greene should press charges immediately."

"I will instruct him to do so," the councilman replied.

"I wouldn't wait long. Cunningham has a way about getting back at people who offend him."

"I will send him a letter this very moment."

Welby noted another man joined them. This one was another of the councilmen. Rather than dwell on the topic of Abrianna's father, Welby changed the subject. "I understand the railroad has agreed to some additional free freighting as a means to aid the city."

The conversation turned to the rebuilding and generosity of

many from all over the country. Money had poured in immediately after the fire, with additional pledges of free goods and other helps. It was the perfect topic with which to busy these men. Priam listened for a time, then excused himself and made his way across the room to speak for a moment with one of the local bank owners. By the time the ladies rejoined them, Welby was more than satisfied with the turn of events. The evening hadn't been wasted after all.

Reaching his home, Welby wasn't surprised to find Carl there waiting to speak with him. He gave his report about Abrianna's activities that day.

"It would seem"—Welby poured himself a scotch and offered Carl one, as well—"that Abrianna's father has been up to a little fighting. Apparently her visit to the property agent did not go well. The man managed to do something that upset the dear girl. Her father apparently beat the man."

"Well, like I told you, he did join her in the office, and then she came out alone and waited at the wagon for him. It would definitely have given the man time to start a fight."

Carl took the drink, tossed it back, and put the glass on the table. Welby grinned, then took only a sip of his drink. "I believe," he continued, quite pleased, "we can use this. I encouraged the man's friends to get him to file charges. We'll get Mr. Cunningham thrown into jail and create a bit of a crisis for Abrianna."

"But, boss, that ain't gonna amount to much. There's folks scamming and lynchin', thieving and killing. No one is gonna pay much attention to a poke in the face. They'll fine Cunningham and turn him loose."

"I suppose that is true. We'll have to up the stakes, then. I'll speak to a friend of mine and see to it that Cunningham fits the description of several other crimes. We'll keep him tied up for a while. Meantime, I have to figure out how to get Wade Ackerman in even hotter water."

Carl laughed. "Too bad he wasn't the one who beat that man."

Welby turned to Carl. "That's a wonderful idea. Only why stop at a beating? Our Mr. Ackerman seems like the type to defend his beloved's honor. Perhaps we can further this matter to our benefit. I have an idea."

"I want a very simple dress." Abrianna showed Aunt Miriam the style she'd settled on. "See, the front would be very flat. The bodice would be shaped with a sort of V draping. It will have tulle and lace to the neck. The sleeves will be long and slightly puffed at the shoulder but then belled at just above the wrist. The undersleeve would be of the same tulle and lace that trims the bodice. The skirt of the gown would be very simple, but the hem would be trimmed with pleated tulle."

"And what of the train and bustle?" her aunt asked.

"I don't wish for either, but I suppose it is rather difficult to eliminate the bustle. I still fail to understand why that has become so fashionable. It would seem to me that the silhouette is all wrong. I find nothing stylish or appealing about bustles. But, of course, no one in fashion has sought out my opinion."

Her aunt's lips hinted at amusement. "Dear Abrianna, I'm certain that if they knew of your distaste, they would be most concerned."

"Oh, don't tease me, Auntie." Abrianna sat back from the drawing. "I found the proper pattern, and with the tiniest of alterations it will be the exact gown I want. There will be plenty of time to create it, but Lenore suggests I get right to it. She even had her mother bring me twenty yards of satin and another dozen of tulle, with the promise of the lace to be expedited from a place she knows in New York. It's her wedding gift to me."

"It is a most generous gift. I had heard that Mrs. Fulcher came for a brief visit and brought you that. I appreciate Lenore's determination, and I believe her advice in order. One can never tell what events might combine to interfere with the best-laid plans. If you would allow, Selma and Poisie and I would be honored to help in the creation. We could begin cutting out the gown in the morning."

"I would love it. To have you three involved will make it all the more special." Abrianna leaned over to give her aunt a kiss on the cheek. "Not only that, but you know what a poor seamstress I am. Goodness, Wade will have neither mended clothes nor freshly baked bread." A loud banging on the front door caused Abrianna to jump back, nearly knocking one of Aunt Miriam's prized vases to the floor. She managed to catch it at the last minute.

Liang arrived just as Abrianna put the vase to rights. She looked ashen faced and frightened. "The police here now."

Abrianna bit her lip while Aunt Miriam rose gracefully and moved to the vestibule. Abrianna already knew they had come to speak to her father. She slipped out the side door and hurriedly made her way through the house to the back door. It was dark outside, and the only real light afforded her was that given off from the windows of her home and the carriage house.

It didn't matter, however. Abrianna hiked her skirts and all but ran to find her father. She didn't have far to go. He was in the stable securing the horses for the night.

"The police," she said gasping. "The police are here."

"For me?" He looked at her with a most grave expression. "Say nothing. I'll handle it." He went to a bucket of water and washed his hands.

Abrianna could see the worry in his eyes, and it frightened her. She wished that Wade were there, but he'd gone with Kolbein to pick up a large bureau from Lenore's parents. They were to have sent the servants with it in the morning, but Kolbein wanted to manage the matter himself.

When her father finished drying his hands, he squared his shoulders. "Shall we?"

Abrianna nodded and followed him. She prayed, or at least tried to pray. Her mind was a muddle of thoughts and fears, and it made finding any peace in communing with God impossible. Once back in the house she reached out to stop her father.

"Maybe it's not about you. Maybe you should go . . . go get help at Kolbein's house. Surely they've returned by now."

Her father gave her hand an affectionate pat. "I know what you're doing, and you don't need to worry. It'll all be fine. I did wrong and I have to account for it. I know that. Like I said before . . . just keep quiet and I'll handle it."

She nodded, but even as she did Abrianna had a feeling that things were about to take a turn for the worse.

An hour later Wade finally came home. Abrianna didn't give him a chance to get to the carriage house, however. She'd waited and watched and the moment she heard him coming up the graveled drive, she hurried to greet him.

"Oh, Wade, it's terrible!" She burst into tears, unable to think of anything but the sight of her father being led away to jail. "The police have taken my father." She threw herself into his arms. "You have to help him, Wade. I just know they aren't going to treat him fairly. They were already treating him quite rough."

"Wait. What happened? Is this about him hitting the property broker?"

She nodded. She couldn't see his face very well. "Come to the kitchen so we can talk. I need to see your face. I take such comfort in it, and right now I desperately need to calm my spirit. I am in such a state."

He held her close and kissed her forehead. "All right."

Abrianna pulled him along, regaining control of her tears. "They just came storming in and demanded he come with them. They weren't at all kind. They treated him like he was responsible for setting Seattle on fire rather than just punching an obnoxious man in the eye. Grief, but they didn't even want to hear him tell what had happened. I tried to tell them, but nobody wanted to hear me, either. They simply dragged him from the house and hauled him off. It was terrible. I don't know where he's been taken, and I don't know whether he's all right."

She opened the back door and hurried into the lamp-lit kitchen. Turning, she could see that tender expression she'd grown to love. "Oh, Wade, what are we to do?"

"I don't know, but I would imagine it's too late to find out tonight." He shook his head. "Your father was afraid this would happen. He told me he knew he'd have to account for what he'd done. We even prayed it might go easy on him."

"I know. He said the same thing to me about accounting for it, but I don't understand why the police were so cruel. They even hit him at one point and told him to cooperate. But, Wade, he wasn't being uncooperative. They were just being mean." She felt her emotions change from grief to anger. "If I'd been a man, I would have thrown them out."

174

Wade blew out a long breath. "And they would have thrown you into jail. There's a lot of crime going on. Has been ever since the fire. Maybe they were just expecting trouble and acted out of line. It's possible your father will return tonight, so don't get too worked up."

She let her breathing even and her fears abate. Wade's presence calmed her and gave her hope. "I suppose you're right. He's only been gone an hour or so. It's just that it was so late when they came for him, and now it's nearly ten. I'm sorry I acted the way I did."

Wade reached out and brushed back a loose curl. "You never need apologize to me for being afraid. I will always take care of you, and if it's in my power to do so, I will keep you from ever being afraid again."

"I do love you so." She allowed him to take her in his arms. Aunt Miriam and the others would be scandalized, but Abri-anna eagerly yielded to him for a long passionate kiss. How she wished they were already married and could just remain in each other's arms throughout the night. She feared this comfort would leave her the moment he went his way and she went hers. It was times like this that she wished they'd eloped, as Wade had suggested.

14

When Abrianna's father didn't come home that night, Wade took it upon himself the next morning to see what he could learn. He dressed in his work clothes, hoping that once the matter was resolved, he might head off to his duties. Abrianna was inconsolable.

"I just know they have locked him up somewhere without regard to his welfare," she told him.

"Well, since the jail burned down and they're using the armory to keep law and order, I would imagine he's there with the other prisoners. Try not to fret. I'll see to getting to the bottom of this. He's bound to have bail set by now. Maybe they've even processed the matter for dealing with it quickly. I've heard that in some of these lesser cases, that's the way it's done."

"Do get word to me as soon as possible," she said as he finished loading his tools in the buckboard.

"I promise I will." He turned before climbing up. "How about a kiss for luck?"

She frowned. "We neither one believe in luck, so kissing for it seems completely uncalled for. I would have expected—"

Wade drew her into his arms and kissed her into silence.

"There," he said and pulled away, "that was a kiss for love—and silence. I've got to go now." He climbed up into the wagon. "I'll send word." He took up the reins and gave them a snap.

The road system was still in upheaval, although the city made a little more progress each day. The obstacles of debris were gone for the most part, although here and there they had been piled up for removal. The newspaper said that a good portion would be used to fill in and level up the low-lying parts of the city.

There was plenty of activity when Wade arrived at the armory. An increase in looting, pickpockets, and scam dealers kept the police force busy, despite over two hundred men having been added to the force. After looking at his pocket watch for the tenth time in as many minutes, Wade was relieved to hear his name called.

"I'm here to see about James Cunningham," he told a uniformed officer who acted as clerk.

The man looked through a stack of papers. "I don't see him here."

"He was just brought in last night. He never came home, and we're quite worried about him."

The man nodded. "That would account for it. I haven't yet received that information. I can have you taken to where we keep the new prisoners, and you can see if he's there." He motioned for an older officer. "Sergeant Clemont will take you to the new prisoner holding area." He looked to the sergeant. "This man is seeking a James Cunningham. Know anything about him? He would have come in last night."

"I weren't here through the night. Just came on this morning." The man's gruff response made it clear that he thought this all a great annoyance. "But I'll take him."

He led the way past the front office and down a long corridor. The older man said nothing as he unlocked a door and ushered Wade inside. Two other officers were there guarding the prisoners.

"This fella is looking for a James Cunningham. Would've come in last night."

The men exchanged a look. "That's the troublemaker we have set out by himself. You can have five minutes, nothing more. And we'll need to search you before you see him. He's a dangerous one. They didn't even set bail for him."

Wade thought surely they had the wrong man, but he said nothing. Holding out his arms he submitted to the search, and when they found nothing amiss, he remained in place until they directed him where to go. He didn't want to give them any reason to believe he was anything other than cooperative. From what Abrianna said of the men who'd come the night before, it very well might be that the entirety of Seattle's police force were more than a little anxious.

One of the officers motioned Wade to follow. They moved past several rooms and finally came to a door. The man took out a set of keys and unlocked it. "I'll be back for you in five minutes."

Wade nodded.

The man opened the door and all but pushed Wade into the dimly lit room. He slammed the door behind him and relocked the door. "Five minutes. No more."

The only light provided emanated from the narrow rectangular window over the door. "Jay, you here?" He waited for his eyes to adjust, then saw something stirring on the floor. It appeared to be a man.

He went closer to inspect. "Jay?"

"Wade?" The word came out muffled as if the man had cotton in his mouth.

"What's happened to you?" Wade tried to help Jay to a sitting position, but the man let out a moan of pain, and he stopped. "Are you hurt?"

"They . . . they beat me bad, Wade." He could barely speak. "Said . . . I wasn't cooperating with . . . the officers. But . . . I swear I was." He slumped against the wall.

Wade knelt beside him. "This is uncalled for. Just because you punched Greene in the eye, this doesn't make sense."

"They said they . . . were gonna . . . keep me for some . . . some other things, too. Wade, I ain't done anything . . . else."

"I know that, Jay. Look, I've only got a couple of minutes. They won't give me longer. I'll go right away and talk to Kolbein. I have a feeling you're going to need a lawyer to get out of this."

"Don't . . . don't tell Abrianna about . . . the . . . beatin'. She'll . . . she'll just worry."

"I'll not share the details with her, but she is already worried. When you didn't come home last night, she insisted I find out where they'd taken you. I don't think any of us expected to find you like this."

"I know. Me either."

Wade reached out and gently touched the older man's shoulder. "Why don't we pray?"

"I'd like that. Been . . . been doing just that."

Wade bowed his head. "Father, we don't know why this has happened or how your purpose will be served, but we put our trust in you and ask for guidance. Help us to know the direction we're to take and help Jay to heal from his wounds. Amen."

"Amen."

As if the guard had been listening outside, the door opened. "Time's up."

Wade rose, and as the light spilled across the room, he could see Jay's battered face. The brutality had been fierce, and it was little wonder the man could barely speak. "I'll take care of this, Jay. Even if I have to go see that Mr. Greene myself."

He left the crumpled man and turned to the officer. "What are you holding him on?"

"Attempted murder," the man said matter-of-factly.

"Attempted murder? Because he punched someone in the eye? That's ridiculous. I demand to see your superior. Better yet, take me to the chief of police."

The man looked at Wade and shrugged. "I'll take you there, but don't expect to be seen. The chief is a busy man and don't brook interruption well, especially these days."

"I don't care. That man has been gravely injured and needs a doctor's care." Again the man shrugged but this time said nothing.

Wade was led back toward the front of the building where he'd entered and then directed to the office of the chief of police. A uniformed clerk looked up at Wade's approach. "What is it you need?"

"I want to see the man in charge."

"You have an appointment?" The man narrowed his eyes. "He doesn't have time to see you if you aren't here by appointment."

"I don't have an appointment, but he will see me." Wade moved past the man's desk and headed straight for the door. He opened it to find an older man behind a large mahogany desk.

"Who are you? What's the meaning of this?" the man demanded.

"The name's Ackerman. You have my . . . soon to be father-in-law, James Cunningham, locked up."

The younger man followed behind Wade. "Sorry, sir. He just burst through. I told him he couldn't come here."

"Get back to work. I'll take care of this," The chief frowned. Fixing Wade with a hard look, the man rose. "I have a great many prisoners here. You need to see the clerk for posting bail."

"I was told bail wasn't set, as the man is being charged with attempted murder. Apparently your people believe him to be quite dangerous and beat him nearly to death. I demand you get a doctor to look him over—right away. I plan to go see a lawyer about it in the meanwhile. He'd better have had some medical attention by the time I get back."

"You presume too much by ordering me around. Now get out of here before I have you arrested."

Wade knew the threat was genuine and figured he'd be of no good to Jay if he got thrown in with the other prisoners. He left without another word and headed away from the armory. Kolbein had told him of his law office setting up business in one of the Denny Hill homes, but he couldn't remember exactly where. The only thing he could do was make his way to the hospital. Kolbein said Lenore was to go home early and had hoped the doctor would release her today. With any luck at all Kolbein would be there.

However, on the way to the hospital, Wade realized that Greene's real estate office was just one street over. He decided it wouldn't hurt to take a moment to speak to the man. It was possible he could be reasoned with. Perhaps the entire thing had just gotten out of hand and the man exaggerated the seriousness of his encounter with Cunningham. No matter, Wade hoped to persuade him to see reason and drop the attempted murder charge. He turned the gelding to the east and made a right at the next corner. The office was just ahead.

Wade parked the wagon and made his way up to the small house. A sign encouraged clients to come in, so he did. Pausing just inside the door, Wade peered across a vestibule. In the room beyond, a rather rotund man sat behind a desk. When the man looked up Wade could clearly see his bruised and swollen eye. "Mr. Greene, I presume?"

"That's right. How can I help you, young man?"

"I'm here to talk to you about James Cunningham."

The man's eyes narrowed. "I have no desire to speak to anyone but my lawyer on that matter. Who are you anyway?"

"Cunningham is soon to be my father-in-law."

"Then that insufferable redhead is to be your wife."

Wade narrowed his eyes. "I heard about the names you called Abrianna, and if you repeat them now, you'll have more than a black eye to answer for it."

"Are . . . are you threatening me?" the man sputtered. "I'll have you arrested, as well."

"As one gentleman to another, I only offer that as encouragement to conduct yourself in a more civilized manner. I'm here to ask why you've had Jay charged with attempted murder. You know full well the man made no such threat."

"You weren't here," Greene replied. His manner suggested nervousness as he stacked and restacked the papers on his desk. "Nor do I see any reason to discuss the matter with you. My lawyer has the details of it, and I'm certain he will be more than happy to discuss it with Mr. Cunningham's lawyer—if anyone will even represent such a vicious criminal. The man has murder in his past, and no doubt I barely escaped alive."

Wade narrowed his eyes. "Who told you he had murder in his past?"

"That's unimportant. Now, I demand you leave this office. I won't have anything more to do with you."

Wade stood in silence for a moment, fixing the man with a

hard stare. He could see perspiration forming on the man's brow. "Maybe you're right. Maybe Mr. Cunningham's lawyer will be more than happy to meet with your lawyer. Maybe he'll even see fit to file some charges of his own for bearing false witness."

The door opened to admit a tall, thin man. Mr. Greene got to his feet in an awkward manner. "Glad you're back, Simpson. Usher this man out. He's not to be readmitted, and take him out the back way. I have clients who will be here any moment."

The older man looked at Greene and then to Wade. "Sir, if you will come this way."

Wade decided it wouldn't serve any good purpose to argue. He followed the man through the small house. "Mr. Greene lives here as well as works here?"

"I don't see that it's any of your business, but yes. I am his manservant." The man took Wade into the kitchen and then to a side room where he opened the back door. "Good day."

Wade stepped outside, noting that it had started to sprinkle. He stood for a moment on the back step of the house and wondered what he should do. Maybe it would be best if he left things in Kolbein's hands. After all, Greene seemed to take offense at any mention of Abrianna or her father. There was no sense getting in the middle.

The rain grew heavier, and Wade decided to get over to the hospital and find Kolbein. He pulled up the collar of his coat, then snugged his cap down before heading across the tiny yard to where he'd left the horse and wagon out front. As he reached the edge of the lawn, a searing pain filled his head. Someone had struck him! Spots danced in front of his eyes as he fell to the ground, small pebbles digging into his palms. If he could just see his attacker. But the world spun around him, and his vision blurred. On his hands and knees, Wade thought of Abrianna and fought to keep consciousness. What was going on? He tried to blink and focus once again, but all he could see was a river of red mixing with the rain as it streamed through the rocks and dirt. The pain forced his body to convulse, and everything went black.

"But he should have come home by now," Abrianna argued. "Even if he went straight to work after seeing my father, he would have come home for supper."

"Perhaps there was an emergency in the city," Aunt Poisie suggested. "Very often things happen that we cannot anticipate. Look at what happened with my dear Captain."

"God rest his soul," Aunt Selma murmured, looking up momentarily from her embroidery.

"Amen," Poisie replied, hardly pausing for breath. "I certainly never thought when I waved good-bye to him on that fateful day that I would never see him again. There was no accounting for the storm that capsized his ship and took his life."

"Poisie, I do not think your words are of a calming nature. Abrianna looks as though she is ready to set out in search of a shipwreck."

"I can't help but think something is terribly wrong." Abrianna began to pace the room and tried to rationalize the situation. "He said he would go straightaway to the armory, where they are keeping the prisoners. He promised to talk to Kolbein, as well." She snapped her fingers. "That's it. Maybe he was kept overlong at Kolbein and Lenore's, and they offered him supper."

"That's a possibility." Aunt Selma gave a slight smile. "I wouldn't fret, Abrianna. Wade is a well-respected man who is known for his caution. I'm sure it will just be a matter of time before he comes to tell us all the news."

Hours passed and Abrianna couldn't bear the thought that something might have happened to Wade. She begged Aunt Miriam to let her go in search of him, but all three of her aunts refused. Aunt Miriam even threatened to set up vigil outside Abrianna's bedroom to keep her from sneaking off alone.

"Flora, he would have sent word." Abrianna shook her head. "And it's not so far that he wouldn't have come home for the night."

"Hold still. I can't braid your hair with you bobbing your head about."

Aunt Miriam had ordered them to bed, but Abrianna was not able to put her mind at peace. At the moment she was even calculating how difficult it might be to climb down the waterspout, given that everyone in the house had been ordered to keep watch on her.

With the ribbon finally secured to hold Abrianna's braid in place, Flora stepped away. "There. Now you may shake your head and move it about."

Abrianna got to her feet and went once more to the window. The carriage house remained dark. She bit her lower lip to keep from crying. It would serve her no good purpose to lose control now. "I fear this is my most arduous moment in life." She toyed with the drapery and continued to stare into the darkness, as if wishing Wade there could make it happen. "I have never felt so completely helpless. I don't like it at all."

"My mama used to say that when things look like they could never get better, God always steps in with a plan. I think He probably has a plan, even for this," Flora offered.

Abrianna let go the drape and turned to nod. "I know you

are right and correct to remind me of God's faithfulness. It's just that this is increasingly hard to bear. Wade wouldn't even be out there if not attending to business on my behalf. If something has happened to him, I will never be able to forgive myself."

"You mustn't fret so." Flora took hold of Abrianna's hand. "I know I'm not your dear friend like Mrs. Booth, but I try to imagine what she might say at a time like this. I believe she would encourage you to take your rest and put your fears in God's hands."

Abrianna appreciated the younger woman's attempt to ease her mind. "You are a very dear friend, Flora Ledbetter. Much better than I deserve. Certainly such that I shouldn't pose the request I'm about to pose."

Flora looked at her oddly. "Which is what?"

"I'm wondering if you would help me climb out on the roof and down the waterspout."

"I thought you'd never ask. Of course I will. Should we wait until everyone is asleep or go now?"

Abrianna smiled. "You are perfectly wonderful." Abrianna went to the wardrobe and pulled out her old wool skirt. "This should suffice. I used to have a pair of boys' britches, but Aunt Miriam threw them out when I wasn't here to protest."

Flora went to her trunk and took out an old skirt similar to Abrianna's. Just then the door to the bedroom opened, and Aunt Miriam entered. She assessed the situation and shook her head.

"It's just as I suspected. Abrianna, I believe you would rest easier tonight if you were to share my bed." She crossed the room and took hold of Abrianna's arm. "Leave the skirt. You'll have no need of it. Flora, I will have this room checked on the hour, and if you aren't in bed asleep, you will be expelled from the school." She paused at the door with Abrianna at her side. "Do I make myself clear?"

Flora nodded and looked to Abrianna for suggestions. Abrianna shook her head. "Just go to bed. We have no choice in the matter."

15

Abrianna paced the room and went once again to the front room window. "I cannot bear all this waiting." She looked for any sign of Wade. At breakfast she had gone to Lenore's in hopes that Kolbein would still be home. He had already left, but Lenore sent the Booths' gardener to find and instruct him to go at once to the school. Kolbein came promptly and commanded Abrianna to wait until his return, but that had been two hours ago, and now her patience had run out.

"I'm going to go to the jail myself," she declared to her aunts. "And no one is going to stop me. I'm sorry, Aunt Miriam, but sometimes a lady has to take matters into her hands."

"But you put Mr. Booth to work on the matter," Aunt Poisie reminded. "It would hardly seem beneficial for you to leave and be at some unknown place when he returns."

"But he should have already returned to let me know what was going on." Abrianna shook her head and took up a shawl. "I will just walk down to the armory myself and demand answers."

"You cannot do that, Abrianna," Aunt Miriam said in her patient but stern manner. "The men down there are more of the sort you dealt with at the real estate office. Men in general are not going to do business with a lady. You must wait."

A sigh escaped Abrianna. "It isn't fair. What is the use of coming of age and having money if you can't get anyone to do what you want them to do?"

"But you did," Aunt Selma countered. "You hired Mr. Booth, and he is seeing to the matter. He has proven himself quite capable, despite having come from Chicago." She looked at Poisie, who nodded in approval. Turning her glance back to Abrianna, she continued. "Now you must wait, and though that is most taxing to your patience, it is for the best."

"But I can't just stay here and do nothing."

Liang appeared in the small parlor. "Mr. Booth, he come back."

"Where?" Abrianna hurried to where the young girl stood. She pointed behind her in the hall. Abrianna could see the grim look on Kolbein's face. "What is it? What's happened to them?"

Kolbein pushed past Liang and took hold of Abrianna. "Come and sit down."

"No. I don't want to sit down." Abrianna gripped his arm. "I'm about to lose all reason. Tell me."

He pressed his lips tight and nodded. Nevertheless, he led Abrianna into the parlor. Nodding to the older women, Kolbein appeared most uncomfortable. Finally he spoke. "The news is quite grave, I'm afraid."

"Is he . . . is Wade . . ." Abrianna couldn't even say the words. The thought of him being dead was unthinkable.

"He's alive but injured. Someone hit him over the head."

"Take me to him," Abrianna demanded. "I know you've been long away from Lenore, but I must insist. Take me to Wade, so I can assure myself he's getting proper care."

Kolbein frowned and cast his glance to the floor. "I can't."

His refusal wasn't at all what Abrianna expected. "Then tell me where he is. Where my father is. I will attend to the matter myself."

"Abrianna, perhaps if you give Mr. Booth a chance, he can give you the entire story," Aunt Miriam said.

She squared her shoulders. "He can tell me on the way to the stable. My father showed me how to hitch the smaller carriage, and I will take that to get me wherever I need to go."

Kolbein took hold of her and gave Abrianna a slight shake. "Stop it. You aren't going anywhere. Your father is in jail, and Wade is, too."

"Whyever would they put our Wade in jail?" Aunt Poisie asked. "He is the most virtuous of men and quite well received among people of high regard. Goodness, he even owns two pairs of shoes."

Aunt Selma spoke up. "It must be some kind of a mistake. Perhaps it was another man with the same name. Although I can hardly imagine there being two Wade Ackermans in the same town."

"Perhaps not even the same state," Aunt Poisie added.

Abrianna shook her head and kept shaking it. "Jail? But why? I mean, I understand my father being there, but why is Wade there? What reason did they give?"

"He's been arrested," Kolbein said, then gave a long pause before finishing. "He's been arrested for murder."

Abrianna felt her knees give way. Kolbein's hold on her tightened, and he lifted her into his arms and carried her to the settee. Abrianna fought back blackness. It wouldn't serve anyone if she were to faint. She searched Kolbein's face for some sign of hope. There was none.

"Mr. Booth, do tell us everything." Aunt Miriam came to sit beside Abrianna on the settee. She took Abrianna's hand and rubbed it in a tender fashion. "Everything, Mr. Booth. Do not leave any detail out."

Kolbein remained standing. "Apparently Wade found your father in jail and couldn't get him released because they said he'd been uncooperative and had fought with them. Not only that, but Mr. Greene . . . was pressing charges of attempted murder."

He paused and Abrianna let the words sink in. She nodded, staring at the floor. "Go on."

"Wade went to see Mr. Greene. He wanted to see if he could talk the man out of pressing charges against your father. Greene was livid that Wade would approach him and demanded he leave. Wade did, and once outside, someone . . . someone hit him over the head and knocked him unconscious."

"If Wade was unconscious, how could he have harmed Mr. Greene?" Aunt Miriam asked the very question on Abrianna's lips.

"Mr. Greene's house servant said that Wade came there threatening and ranting. He said it so frightened him that he hid in the pantry while Wade took advantage of his master. He said that in the end, Wade fought with Mr. Greene, and Greene in turn fought back as best he could."

"And he said that Wade killed him?" Abrianna questioned, finally raising her eyes to Kolbein's face.

"Yes. He said that he didn't actually see the murder, but that when everything fell silent, he made his way out to the office room and found Mr. Greene bludgeoned to death and Wade unconscious in the backyard. He believed Wade was attempting to flee the scene."

"Then if he didn't see it, isn't it possible someone else might have done them both in?" Aunt Selma asked.

"It is," Kolbein assured. He squeezed Abrianna's hand. "I know it looks bad, but I think just as you do. I believe someone else was involved. You and I both know that Wade isn't capable of murder."

Her stomach churned, and bile rose in the back of her throat. Abrianna fought it down and tried to steady herself. All of her life Abrianna had prided herself in being strong, in trusting God, but never had a situation been this horrific.

"Is there anything at all I can do?"

"No," Kolbein replied. "It's best you stay out of it and leave this to me. I already have some men looking into the matter. They will help me collect information and hopefully find other witnesses. I need you to just stay calm and out of the way."

Another time she might have protested, but given the severity of the matter, Abrianna knew it was best she listen and obey. "All right. But you will be thorough, won't you? I can pay you to hire as many people as you need."

He shook his head. "I don't want or need your money. Wade is my friend, too. I'll handle it. I just need to know that you'll be here . . . safe."

"We will see to it that she stays here," Aunt Miriam said. "Abrianna can be quite determined, but I've never known her to refuse counsel when placed in such a grave situation."

"Oh, but this is such a tragedy." Aunt Poisie blew her nose into a lace handkerchief. "I am quite overcome. Do you suppose we might send him some cookies? He has always liked cookies."

"I can't take him anything," Kolbein replied. "They won't allow it."

Aunt Selma spoke up. "If there is anything that any of us can do to help, Mr. Booth, you will let us know, won't you?"

"I promise you that I will." He looked Abrianna in the eye. "I will come here every day and let you know what I've learned."

A kind of void engulfed Abrianna's mind. Rational thought was impossible. Nothing in her life had ever prepared her for this moment. Nothing had ever been as seemingly hopeless.

Oh, God, where are you? Why have you let this happen?

Those two questions echoed over and over, but the answers didn't come.

Despite the tragedy Aunt Miriam said that they had to go on with a pretense of normalcy for the sake of the others in the school. With that in mind, the monthly reception for the bridal candidates was held the following Saturday. The day turned rainy and windy, which kept them from hosting the reception outdoors as they had originally planned.

"I know this is difficult, Abrianna," Aunt Miriam began, "but I want you to help at the refreshment table."

Abrianna knew better than to argue. Besides, she didn't have the strength. "All right."

Aunt Miriam took hold of her and hugged her close. "Dear child, I know you think me cruel for forcing you to do this, but I assure you I am not. I, too, have dealt with tragedy in my life, and keeping busy was much better than sitting and imagining all the things that have gone wrong."

Already Abrianna had imagined such hideous things happening to Wade and her father that she couldn't share such worries with Kolbein, much less Aunt Miriam. She held tight to her aunt for a moment and then straightened. "I'm sure you're right. Thank you for directing me."

She took her place behind the refreshment table. *God, please give me strength to endure this.* She bit her lip to keep from dissolving in tears. *I have always been strong and capable. Now, more than ever, I need to draw on those abilities. It will do Wade no good for me to be otherwise focused.*

The reception dragged on for nearly an hour, with all of the students preforming their various musical talents. Abrianna filled cups with punch and offered her best chitchat when someone came for refreshments, but all the while she wanted to run from the room in tears.

"Um, Abrianna, I need to talk to you." Flora's whispered words came as a surprise. "That man, Mr. Welby . . . you know, the one with the big ears?"

Abrianna nodded. "What about him?"

"He wants to see you. He's standing at the back of the room and said to tell you he will meet you downstairs in the first-floor parlor."

Looking out across the ballroom, Abrianna spied Welby in the corner near the door. He nodded her way then left the room. Abrianna had no idea why he'd come, and she was in no mood to deal with any of his nonsense. Even so, she pulled off her apron and decided to go see him, knowing that if she didn't, he was just rude enough to make a scene.

"Do you want me to come, too?" Flora asked.

"No. That won't be necessary. If any of the aunts ask after me, tell them I had to attend to something and I'll be right back."

Abrianna made her way from the room, taking the back stairs in case Welby had paused on the way down to wait for her.

She wanted a moment to compose her thoughts. An idea came to mind. Welby was a powerful man with many connections in the city. Perhaps he could help her. The murder and accusations toward Wade had been splashed across the newspaper, so no doubt he knew all the details of the matter. It gave her a flicker of hope that quickened her steps. She was very nearly breathless when she came to the large parlor and found Priam Welby standing by the hearth, a bouquet of flowers in hand.

"You wished to speak to me?"

"I heard what happened to your . . . to Mr. Ackerman."

She nodded. "No doubt everyone has." She didn't know whether to remain standing at the entry or to take a seat. Perhaps he was only here to offer his condolences, but then again, he hardly seemed the type to waste time on such matters. "Is that all?"

"No." He motioned her to the settee. "These are for you." He handed her the flowers. "I thought it might cheer you." She looked down at the flowers as he continued. "Please sit. I want to discuss something with you."

Abrianna thought to protest but didn't wish to get on his bad side in case he might assist her. She took her place on the settee and continued to hold the flowers. Welby pulled a chair up and sat so close that their knees almost touched. Abrianna felt the heat of his suit, warmed by the fire, and she straightened. The intimacy of the moment made her most uncomfortable. "What is it you've come to say?"

"The situation for Mr. Ackerman is quite serious, as I'm sure you already know. Murder is an offense that upon conviction will demand his life be forfeit either by death or life in prison."

She swallowed hard and nodded, still refusing to look up. If he came here to gloat, Abrianna was afraid she might very well take the fireplace poker to him. She bit her lip to keep from saying anything and tasted blood.

"I am not a man of words, and it seems to me that getting right to the point is probably your preference, as well."

Again she nodded, but this time Welby reached out and put his fingers beneath her chin. With the slightest of pressure he raised her face to meet his. His dark eyes seemed to bore holes through her walls of defense. Abrianna steeled herself. She would not show emotion and give him the satisfaction of seeing her cry.

"Abrianna, you know how I feel about you. I have made it quite clear. I am, as you know, a man of power in this city. I am not without my influences, and I believe it within my power to see your father and Mr. Ackerman set free."

She couldn't help the sharp intake of air. The gasp seemed to echo throughout the room, and only the crackle and pop of wood in the fireplace made any other sound.

Welby grinned in his leering fashion and dropped his hold. "I thought that might get me your full attention. Would you like me to go on?"

Abrianna drew a deep breath. "How could you possibly ask me that? They are innocent. Of course I want you to continue. What can you do to help them? How can you see them set free?"

"As I said, I'm not without my friends. There are also those who are indebted to me." He sat back and despite their nearness crossed his legs. "Guilty or innocent, I believe I can arrange for all of the charges to be dropped."

"How? How would you be able to do this? Our lawyer has found no witnesses to support Wade's innocence. And while my father did in fact hit Mr. Greene, he would never have threatened to kill him. So how can you arrange their freedom?"

He chuckled, which only served to irritate her. "My dear, you are such an innocent. Men and their testimonies are easily bought and sold. I can have a dozen witnesses declare Mr. Ackerman to be nowhere near the murder site."

"And why would you do this?" There was something in his tone that made her want to run from the room.

"I think you already know the answer to that. I would do it for you, because of my feelings for you."

"You would lie and cheat for me? How very noble." She shook her head. "I don't think either Wade or my father would approve."

"Perhaps not, but they certainly can't agree or disagree to the matter if they are dead." He stood and pulled her up with him. The flowers were crushed between them. "I'm through playing games, Abrianna. Either you want them to live, or you're willing to let them die."

She began to shake from head to toe. "I want them to live, of course. I would do anything for them."

"Anything?"

The thought of all that word might encompass stormed through her mind. His sneering smile left her little doubt that he was thoroughly enjoying her discomfort.

"What is it that you want, Mr. Welby?"

"You, of course."

His matter-of-fact answer left her cold, while his grip on her arms seemed to burn. She couldn't find the words to order him out of the house. The thought that there might be no other way to save her father and Wade left her unable to speak.

Without warning, Welby dropped his hold and stepped away. "You have until Monday to decide."

"And what is it that I'm to decide?" she managed to say as he reached the door. She turned toward him, determined to prove that she was stronger than he thought.

He paused and slowly faced her. "You have until Monday to decide if you will marry me. If your answer is yes, then I'll see your loved ones set free. Otherwise . . . well, I'll do what I can to hurry their demise. It's entirely up to you. You hold their lives in your hands."

"But how can you do that?" She fought to keep from sounding frantic, but it was no use. "You appear to know they are innocent, yet you are willing to have them . . . killed?"

He laughed. "I eliminate obstacles, dear Abrianna. I've done so all of my life, and it has gotten me great wealth and position. Now I am willing to use that wealth and position once again in order to have what I want."

"But to have innocent men killed just to get what you want is . . . it's . . . evil."

His eyes narrowed, and his expression went completely blank. "Call it what you will. It really doesn't matter to me. Your father and lover will be dead in a very short time unless you agree to marry me . . . and quickly. I won't brook any nonsense of long engagements. We will marry immediately, and you will be my wife . . . in every way."

He started to leave and added, "Oh, and if you say one word about it either way, the outcome will go against them. This is a matter strictly between you and me."

16

Abrianna was still standing in the front room when Flora found her.

"Is he gone?" she asked, looking around the room.

"Yes."

Flora came to stand in front of her. "Are you all right?"

Abrianna found the shock and horror she'd felt after Mr. Welby's visit was now replaced by anger. Red-hot murderous anger.

Seeming to sense there would be trouble, Flora took hold of her arm. "Let's go to our room, and you can tell me everything."

Abrianna allowed Flora to lead her, but all the while her thoughts churned in rage. How dare he threaten them all in such a ruthless way? Life and death meant nothing to him unless it got him what he wanted.

By the time they reached the bedroom, Abrianna began to understand how a person could plot the death of another. She very much wished Priam Welby would fall off the face of the earth and with little prompting she could be the one to give him a push.

"Abrianna, you haven't said a word since Mr. Welby left."

Flora closed the door to their room. Her gaze traveled Abrianna's frame from head to toe. "And now you're still as a statue. Goodness, what on earth is going on?"

Abrianna inhaled a deep breath and glanced at the bouquet in her hands. Without a word she began to rip the flowers apart. Petals and stems littered the floor. But it wasn't enough. She stomped them into the floor, crushing every last piece with the heels of her boots.

"You're scaring me." Flora took a step back, shaking her head. "Abrianna, please. You can trust me. Please tell me what Mr. Welby did to make you so angry."

The urgency in Flora's voice and tears in her eyes broke the spell of fury over Abrianna. She sank to the floor. "I cannot."

Flora wasn't one to take no for an answer. She came and knelt beside Abrianna. "You must. Otherwise, it will destroy you as you have destroyed that bouquet. I promise you, I shan't say a word to anyone else—no matter how much I might want to."

For several long minutes, Abrianna considered what to do. Flora was right. She had to confide in someone. "Very well. But it is both shocking and ugly. You must make certain you can bear up under the promise that you will tell no one."

"I can bear anything, if it will help you," Flora said, wiping her eyes.

Abrianna nodded, and the story of her time with Mr. Welby gushed out. She left nothing out, even sharing in details the expression on his face. "And then he left. Just like that."

Flora bore a look of disbelief. "What a cad. What a reprobate. He should be horsewhipped." She shook her head and got to her feet. "No, that would be too good for him."

"I quite agree, but that isn't why I told you." Abrianna got up and began to pace the room. "Again, you must promise me that you won't tell a soul!"

"You can count on me." Flora sat on the edge of her bed. "I promise."

"Thank you. I knew you were a kindred spirit. As you know, I'm not generally given over to anger and wrath, but Mr. Welby just seems to bring that out in me. I must say, I am ashamed of my display and hope you will forgive me."

"Of course. But how can I help? There must be a way."

Abrianna considered this for a moment. "I have to figure out how to put him in his place without risking the lives of those I love. He would just as soon see my father and Wade hanged. And I must say that until hearing what Mr. Welby had to say or threaten, as is the case, I didn't think that was even possible."

Flora tucked her legs up under her in contemplation. Abrianna could see no easy answer in the matter. She knew that she only had tomorrow to figure out how to combat Mr. Welby and his intimidating threats.

"Perhaps we could go to the authorities. He can't own everyone in town. There has to be a man of power somewhere who could stand up to him."

"I don't know who that would be," Abrianna replied. Welby had long boasted of having all of Seattle's elite and powerful obligated to him. Telling their story to the wrong person would just get back to Welby and prove Abrianna had talked. She couldn't let that happen.

"I won't be bullied by him," she decided. "It's terrible that he would take advantage of a tragic situation like this. No doubt he has just been waiting for Wade to make some sort of compromising move."

"But God is bigger than this," Flora murmured.

Abrianna stopped her pacing and looked at the younger woman. "God truly is bigger than this, Flora. I get myself so worked up that I tend to forget that. I suppose my faith is much weaker than I knew, and this is just one of those trials to help me grow stronger. But never have I encountered such evil. It was like talking to the Devil himself."

She began to walk again, tapping her finger against her cheek. "This I know, I won't sit by and do nothing."

Flora fixed her with a stern look. "But you can hardly return evil for evil. That would never be right, and unfortunately, a man like that can only understand evil. I've heard others say that about people who live and act without morals."

Abrianna plopped down on her bed. "I believe that evil is all that Mr. Welby understands." A thought came to mind. "Perhaps that could be to our advantage."

Flora perked up. "Go on."

"Well, I'm just thinking that innocence and good are completely foreign to Mr. Welby. He believes he can master any situation by using evil, but remember, the Bible states quite clearly that God can use evil for His good. I can't remember where that's found just now, and it wouldn't change the situation even if I did. Goodness, but my mind is in a whirl." She pressed her hands to her temples. "Sometimes it's best not to worry with the details. It's enough that I know God can turn this around. However, I am quite confident He will need our help."

Flora nodded with great enthusiasm. "He often calls those who are the weakest and smallest to prove His glory."

"Indeed He does." Abrianna jumped up from the bed. "Get some paper and a pencil. We have some plans to make."

"How's she holding up?" Wade asked Kolbein late Sunday afternoon.

"You know Abrianna. At first I thought we'd have to put her in a cell. She was ready to come down here and break the two of you out. Now, oddly enough, she's not saying a whole lot."

Wade knew that this was how Abrianna normally responded when she was gravely worried. That's how she'd been since childhood. It also signaled that she was up to something. "That can spell disaster, Kolbein. She's most likely plotting something. Keep an eye on her."

"Lenore said the same thing, so we're doing our best to watch out for any unreasonable action on her part."

"I keep thinking about Joseph being wrongly accused and thrown into prison." Wade looked down at the Bible Kolbein brought him. "Speaking of which, I don't know how you talked them into this, but thank you."

"I reminded them that practicing your religious beliefs was a constitutionally protected right. I threatened some legal complications, and the chief of police himself gave approval."

"I'm sure glad you thought of it. I kept going over all the Scriptures I've ever memorized and realized with great frustration that it wasn't nearly enough. I'm going to use this time to commit more to memory."

"How are you feeling? Did the doctor say anything further about your head wound?"

"No. He stitched it shut and told me to rest. That was about it. They don't trust me enough around here to take me out on any of the work details, so rest is about all I get done anyway." He put the Bible on the cot beside him. "What about Jay? How's his recovery?"

"Slow. They all but killed him. The doctor said he'll recover, but it'll take time. I took Jay a Bible and promised we'd figure a way out of this."

Wade smiled. "I hope that's a promise you can keep."

"I intend to. The entire thing just seems to lack substance." Kolbein shook his head and took out paper and a pencil. "Let's go over all the details one more time. Maybe there's something you've left out that can help us."

"All right. I don't know what it could be, but I'm willing to do whatever necessary. What doesn't make any sense to me is that nobody knew I was going to stop at the real estate office. I mean, I didn't say I was going to talk to Greene when I left the jail. At least I don't think I did." He put his hand to his head. "It's hard to remember everything. Maybe I did mention that. I wanted to talk to Greene, but it was a last-minute decision to go there. No one could have planned for that."

"I suppose you're right, but even so, there are always crimes of opportunity. It's possible they saw you go in and then decided to use it to their advantage. The butler couldn't say for certain if anything was taken. Apparently Mr. Greene's business affairs were kept private, and the butler was generally not even allowed to clean in the office until everything was locked away. Could be Greene had something going on that no one knew about. All of this is something to explore in greater detail."

"I can't imagine it helping." Wade felt exhaustion creep over him. Ever since being hit in the head, he'd felt done in. His biggest concern, however, was Abrianna. He knew there was nothing he could do to help Jay while in jail, but he knew Abrianna would be doing her best to figure out something she could manage, and that was quite worrisome.

"Tell Abrianna that I'm prayerfully asking God to help her leave this all to you," Wade said after several long minutes.

"Make her promise that she won't get involved. I know her only too well. She'll think she needs to help, and she'll only end up putting herself in danger."

"I agree. I plan to impose upon her to come and help with Lenore. She's home now, and Abrianna could be great company for her. I can't imagine Abrianna would refuse. She loves Lenore dearly, and if I can persuade her that Lenore needs her, I know Abrianna will lend her assistance."

Wade smiled and gave a nod. "That's a perfect plan. Ought to keep her busy."

The door to the small room opened. "Time's up."

Kolbein got to his feet, and Wade did likewise. "I'll do everything I can, Wade. I'll see you again tomorrow. Keep trying to remember anything you can. Even the smallest detail might be important." He looked to the jailer. "Take me to Mr. Cunningham's cell."

Wade watched him go. The door closed with a thud. The sound of the key in the lock made Wade's skin crawl. He was at the mercy of people who thought him a murderer. If the place caught fire, no one would worry about him.

He sat back down on the cot and put his head in his hands. It was all like a very bad dream that he couldn't awaken from. He tried to ignore the headache that seemed to grow stronger by the minute. He picked up the Bible and eased back onto the cot, hoping the reclined position would help ease the throbbing in his head. He stared upward at the ceiling.

"Lord, I sure don't know what this time of testing is all about. I can't even figure how you can be glorified in this, but I want you to know that I'm putting my trust in you, as always." He held the Bible to his chest and closed his eyes. "Sure hope you got a plan, Lord, 'cause I'm all out of them."

Priam Welby waited with great impatience for Liang to retrieve Abrianna. He had thought to let the redhead stew about their meeting all day, but by noon on Monday Welby found he couldn't wait. He knew she would have to yield to him. And if she didn't at first do so, Welby had some ideas of what could change her mind. The entire matter was quite exhilarating.

After waiting for at least twenty minutes, Priam was finally rewarded with Abrianna's presence. She walked to just inside the parlor and stopped. Her blue eyes seemed to darken at the sight of him. She held herself regally, like a queen about to deal with her subjects. He thought it rather amusing, but he wasn't foolish enough to trust that she wasn't up to something.

"Mr. Welby."

"Abrianna." He stepped forward. "Let us go for a walk in the garden. I don't wish to be overheard or interrupted."

She gave him a curt nod and headed across the room to the side door. He watched her as she opened the French doors and felt a strong desire to touch her, to hold her and feel her body crushed to his own. It was hard not to act on that need. He craved her, and his mind and soul demanded to possess her. He'd never wanted anything more, unless it was revenge on his father.

Abrianna stepped outside into the fall afternoon and turned to wait for him to join her. He smiled. Soon. Very soon he would have her. There would be no part of her that he didn't own, and he would make certain she understood that early on in their marriage.

They walked away from the house. Abrianna kept her distance from him. She held on to her dark blue wool skirt and

208

paid him little mind as she maneuvered the cobblestone walkway. Priam found it all rather amusing.

"You needn't act so reserved with me." He glanced overhead at the rainy gray sky. "I know you better than you probably think. I know you have a great deal you wish you could say to me, but you fear I might take offense. I assure you I won't, so you might as well have your say before you agree to our marriage."

She turned and shook her head. "But I have no intention of agreeing to marry you, Mr. Welby."

He smiled. He had expected as much and was ready to make clear to her just how far he'd go to secure their union. "By all means, continue."

"There's nothing more to say." Abrianna took a seat on one of the garden benches. She sat in the middle, making a clear statement that she would not welcome him joining her.

"I think there is." He fixed her with a look that he'd known capable of crumbling the strongest man's resolve. "You see, I don't think you understand. I told you that I would wait until today for your reply, but not because I doubted your answer. I just wanted to give you time to come to terms with the matter. You will say yes, and you will marry me. That is, unless you want to see your beloved Wade and father go to their deaths."

He could see her jaw clench and unclench as she listened to him speak. There was a fire in her eyes that intrigued him. Life with her would no doubt be quite a challenge, but he found himself looking forward to breaking her down.

"I've prayed about this, Mr. Welby. Say what you will, but I know that God will deliver them both. The truth will come out, and everything will be fine."

He laughed out loud. Her eyes widened in shock, but she sat as prim and proper as any fine lady might. "Oh, my dear

Abrianna. You are such a little girl in so many ways. Let me explain this to you so that you have no doubts about the outcome."

Moving to the bench he imposed himself beside her. She didn't want to yield the space but did when she realized he intended to sit there whether she liked it or not. She started to get up, but Welby pulled her back down. "You will sit here and listen to me."

She fought against his hold. "It isn't proper for us to sit so close, especially since I'm engaged to another."

"Like you've ever cared about what was proper, and your fiancé is soon to be dead unless you do what I tell you."

She stopped and turned to better see him. "Tell me what you must, but it won't change anything."

He smiled and patted her hand. "I think it will. Now to make myself quite clear, we will marry. In fact, I've already secured the church and the date. We will marry October nineteenth. It will be a lovely morning wedding with one of the largest wedding breakfasts to be given afterwards. All of Seattle's finest will be there."

She crossed her arms but remained silent. Welby stretched his legs out before him, as if he were there for nothing more than a moment of respite.

"You see, Abrianna, what you don't understand is that your Mr. Ackerman and your father are in jail because I made it happen. I wasn't going to share all of this with you, but I can see it will take exactly that in order to convince you of my determination."

"What do you mean?" Her tone betrayed her irritation.

"I mean I've had you and the others watched very carefully. I needed an opportunity, and one presented itself. Your father's temper got the best of him, and he attacked Mr. Greene. I arranged for the police—actually some very good men of mine who just happen to be on the force—to arrive at your house and take him into custody."

"You?" She shook her head. "Why? Why would you care?"

"Because I saw it as the means to an end. The end being our marriage and the elimination of my competition."

"That makes no sense."

He smiled in a tolerant manner. "But of course it does. You see, by putting your father and Mr. Ackerman in danger of their lives, I can better impose my will upon you."

"But you couldn't possibly know that Wade was going to see Mr. Greene."

"Ah, that one came by sheer luck. I had him under observation with an order to use whatever means to compromise him and see him arrested. When Mr. Ackerman went to see Mr. Greene, my men got word to me that he was there, and . . . well, the rest is history."

"I don't understand." Her eyes narrowed as she appeared to try to reason it all out.

"I wasn't that far away from Mr. Greene's location. My house is just a short walk away. My man came and told me that Wade was at Greene's house. I told him to return and see to it that Wade never left. The man barely got back in time to see Wade coming out the back door. He snuck up and hit him over the head. By the time I got there, he was quite unconscious.

"Of course Greene knew nothing about it. He was too busy with his books. I came into the office with my man Carl— you do remember Carl, don't you?" He smiled at her surprise. "Yes, Carl, the same one who you supposed was responsible for those lovely Chinese girls in my basement."

Her face turned ashen, causing her freckles to seem all the

more prominent. "You? You were the one who put them there? You are the one who left them there to die?" Her voice rose causing him to put his hand on her arm.

"Not so loud, my dear. You wouldn't want one of your aunts to interrupt us."

"I would love for the entire world to interrupt us. You are a hideous man." She glared at him. "And I would thank you to release me."

"I don't believe I will," he said, daring her to challenge him. She tried to pull away, and he tightened his grip. "Sit still."

"You're hurting me."

"I plan to do much more than this to cause you pain if you refuse to cooperate."

She stilled, but her cheeks reddened, and her eyes narrowed. Welby knew he'd just about pushed her to the limit, and he didn't care.

"What you need to understand is this. I have the power to see Mr. Ackerman and your father meet with an untimely death. I will do so if you try to refuse my proposal."

"The court would never just kill them. There are processes you know."

He shrugged. "The court isn't the only one who can determine the end of their lives. Fatal accidents take place in prison all the time. Furthermore, I will systematically go down the line of your loved ones and arrange accidents for each of them until you have no one left to you in this world."

"You would kill innocent people just to force me to marry you?"

He nodded without the slightest feeling of guilt. "I would."

The truth of the matter seemed to hit her all at once. He could see it in her expression. There was a sort of hopelessness in her eyes that she quickly tried to hide.

"I see you finally understand." He let go of her arm and waited for her to speak.

"You can't possibly be that cruel. No one is so completely without conscience about life and death. You surely couldn't kill an old lady."

"I arranged the death of old men, homeless men. Like the men who ended up in the alleyway behind the Madison Building. Friends of yours, if I'm not mistaken—"

She turned on him like a wild cat. She pounded his chest with her fists and would have gone for his face, but he took hold of her wrists. Her face reddened, and tears formed in her eyes as she struggled against his hold. "You killed Charlie and Bill? You were the monster who did that?"

He gave a sneer. "Guilty as charged. I don't say it because I'm necessarily proud of it, but rather to make it quite clear to you that I will stop at nothing to have what I want."

Abrianna's defeat was complete as she slumped against him. He almost felt sorry for her. The shock had to be quite great. Still, it was all a matter of business, and he wouldn't back down now.

"So, you see, I am a man of my word. But you should also know that I plan to lavish you with everything you could ever want. I am, after all, a man of means, and my position in this city requires that I keep my wife in jewels and luxury. You will be the envy of all Seattle. You will have the finest gowns and the most beautiful estate. I will even build you a new mansion if that would please you. See, I'm not so very cruel.

"Of course there are things you will give me in return." He let go of her left wrist and reached up to run his fingers along her cheek and down her jawline. His smile broadened, and he trailed his touch down her neck.

"If you go farther, I will scream and bring all of Seattle down on you," she said, her voice barely audible.

He chuckled and released her. "See, I can be a very understanding and patient man. I also know ways to afford you a great deal of pleasure."

She sat up, and he didn't try to stop her as she moved away. "I seriously doubt that, not that it matters. I only want to keep you from killing the people I love."

"And I promise you, nothing will happen to them if you agree to marry me on the nineteenth."

Abrianna looked at him, as if trying to decide if he was telling the truth. He softened his expression and tried his best to look contrite. "I never wanted to do things this way, but I'm quite besot with you. You must know that."

"All I know is that I am expected to marry a killer. How do I know you'll keep your word? How do I know that once we are married, you won't have everyone I love killed, anyway? Will you kill me, as well?"

"I suppose it's asking too much that you take me at my word. Truly, I am a man of my word. When I promise a thing—it is something upon which you may depend."

She sniffed back tears. "Then prove it. Set my father and Wade free, and I will marry you."

"I can't take that chance. If I set them free you might refuse me."

She stood and looked down at him with narrowed eyes that held more hatred for him that he'd ever seen from another soul. "And if I did, you would simply have them murdered. So my requirement is that they be set free now, or I will never agree to this wedding."

He smiled and gave a slight nod. Getting to his feet he felt a great sense of satisfaction. "On one provision."

"And what would that be?"

"You will say nothing to anyone about this arrangement and the things we spoke of here today. And you will make everyone believe that you are happily doing this of your own accord. I want you to convince them all—those old ladies and even your dear father and beloved Wade—that you are madly in love with me."

She fixed him with a calculated stare. "No one is that great of an actress, Mr. Welby." She shook her head and squared her shoulders. "However, if you will do as I ask and get Wade and my father out of jail and all charges dropped, I will do my best."

"Very well. It will take a few days, but I assure you, they will be cleared of any wrongdoing." He once again tasted victory. Soon he would have everything he desired.

17

Do lies count against you when they're made to the Devil?

The question haunted Abrianna as she did her level best to forget the horrible things Priam Welby had said and done. She could still feel his hands touching her face and neck. She had been afraid that he would take additional liberties, but even that fear was nothing compared to worrying about how she would get herself out of this mess.

She watched her aunts at dinner that night and wondered how in the world she would ever convince them that she loved Priam Welby and desired to be his wife. They would know the truth. They had always been able to read her face and know her thoughts. At least most of the time it seemed they could.

Toying with her roast lamb, Abrianna felt overwhelmed with guilt. Welby was much too strong an adversary. Never in her life had she ever had to deal with such a man.

"You aren't eating much, Abrianna. I know you're worried about Wade and your father, but you must remain strong," Aunt Miriam said in her authoritative way.

Abrianna straightened but refused to look her aunt in the eye. "I will endeavor to do what I can."

"I heard you had a visitor this afternoon," Aunt Selma said.

Bristling at the thought that someone knew about Welby's appearance beside Liang, Abrianna nodded but waited. Kolbein had also stopped by earlier, barely missing Mr. Welby.

"Did Mr. Booth bring you news of Lenore?"

Abrianna forced a smile. "Yes. She's home early. The doctor said her recovery was well ahead of schedule, and he knew she would be happier at home. Kolbein thought perhaps I could come and sit with her throughout the day and keep her company."

"That's a splendid idea." Aunt Miriam passed a basket of dinner rolls in Abrianna's direction. "It will help you to keep your mind busy."

Nothing will ever keep it so busy that I won't be thinking of Wade and Father in jail. Nor will it keep me from wishing Priam Welby would drop off the pier and drown.

She lowered her head. Such ugly thoughts were no better than the ones Mr. Welby conjured. "I will endeavor to help in her recovery." Abrianna put down her fork.

"Perhaps the two of you can work on your wedding gown. There's a great deal to be done now that the pieces are cut," Aunt Selma added.

Aunt Poisie smiled. "Goodness, but it's so hard to imagine our little Abrianna getting married. It seems just yesterday she was but a young girl being baptized."

If only I would have drowned.

Such a thought made Abrianna wonder if a person drowned during baptism would they go immediately to glory, or would there be some sort of divine investigation. Surely not. Since

God knew everything, He would have to have known that such a drowning would take place.

"Abrianna, did you hear me?"

She looked up and met Aunt Miriam's stern gaze. "No, ma'am."

Her aunt's eyes narrowed momentarily then relaxed. "I asked if you would like us to baste part of the gown tonight so you might try it for a fitting in the morning?"

"No, that's all right. I'm sure we have plenty of time." She rose abruptly. "If you don't mind, I'm rather tired. I have a great deal on my mind to sort through, and I would just as soon make an early evening of it." She didn't wait for permission but hurried from the room, knowing that if she stayed there for even another minute, she would tell them everything.

The bedroom she'd known for the last year or so offered little comfort. There were so few memories here, and while it was quite a lovely home, it had also come to them by way of Priam Welby.

"Goodness, but that man is a millstone around my neck." She sat down on her vanity chair and tried to force her mind into neatly organized thoughts.

"If you don't want me to stay, I'll go," Flora said.

Abrianna hadn't even heard the door open. She shook her head. "No, please do stay. You're the only one I can talk to just now. I am afraid that things have taken a turn for the worse."

Flora quickly closed the door. "Is this about Mr. Welby?"

"Yes."

Flora came and knelt beside her. "Tell me everything, and then we will figure out what to do."

"There isn't much to figure," Abrianna replied. "I have to marry him."

Wade stared in dumb silence at the announcement in the paper. He looked at Kolbein and then reread the piece again. "Abrianna and Welby? They're going to get married?"

"I don't know what to say. Lenore and I were just as stunned by this, and Abrianna won't talk to anyone. I spoke with Mrs. Madison, and she said Abrianna has all but dismissed the subject. She has stated plainly that she was mistaken in her agreement to marry you and that it was only her confusing feelings for Welby that made her hesitate to set a date with you in the first place."

Wade threw the paper across the room. "Get her down here. I want to talk to her. I've no doubt this is all some sort of game she's playing. Maybe he's promised her help to get me out of jail. Maybe he's threatening her with something."

"I thought of that, too, but she won't see me. She won't see Lenore. Lenore has sent four different requests that Abrianna come to the house, but each was returned unopened."

He felt his anger deepen. "That story about her confusing feelings can't be true. She couldn't stand Priam Welby. She knew he was trouble even when he was pestering her to court him. There is no chance she would just up and marry him."

"But I checked. The church is reserved, and the minister assured me that October nineteenth is to be the day of their wedding."

Wade got up so fast it sent his chair flying backwards. It made a clatter when it hit the ground, causing the guard to unlock the door and peer into the room.

"What's going on in here?"

"Mr. Ackerman simply got up too fast. Do leave us. I have important matters to discuss with my client."

The officer frowned but did as Kolbein instructed. Meanwhile, Wade began to pace. "That's less than a month," he said, as if there had been no interruption.

"I know, Wade. I know. I'm trying to get to the bottom of this, but right now worrying over you and Jay has taken precedence. I don't even know if I can get you out of here in a month."

"They aren't going to hang me tomorrow, Kolbein. You need to find a way to get to her. You have to ask her what this is all about. Either she hates me and has been playing me for a fool all along, which I don't believe, or something has happened to make her think that she has to do this. I know Abrianna. She would never marry Welby unless she were being forced to do so."

Kolbein nodded. "I agree. I'll speak to her aunts and see what we can arrange."

Abrianna hadn't had a chance to tell her aunts about the upcoming wedding to Priam Welby before they read the announcement in the paper. She had refused to leave her room or allow them entry for two days—something she had never done in all of her life. During that time she didn't eat, not that she had much of an appetite. She told Flora to let everyone know she was fasting and praying. This was the only way she was certain to be left alone, but it was also true. If she turned this over to God in fasting and prayers, He would surely see her sincerity and give her guidance. But after the time was up, Abrianna felt no more certain of what she should do than when she began.

Now she sat facing the trio of old ladies, much as she imagined the man responsible for the Great Seattle Fire had felt when facing his interrogators. The old women knew her—better than anyone, save Wade. They would badger an answer out of her if need be, so Abrianna did her best to take an authoritative upper hand. Something she'd never have dreamed to do prior to this moment.

"What is the meaning of this?" Aunt Miriam demanded to know.

Aunt Poisie bobbed her head, worry plastered across her face. Aunt Selma added her thoughts on the matter.

"Have you gone completely daffy?" The raised tone of her voice sent the cats scrambling from the room.

Abrianna might have laughed at her aunt's use of slang, but the situation was far too serious. She had practiced what she would say to them, but now that the moment came, her mind went blank. She tried to steel herself to be firm but loving.

"You are engaged to Wade. You cannot simply up and engage yourself to another man. Imagine what Wade must be thinking," Aunt Miriam declared. "Furthermore, you clearly rejected Mr. Welby's courtship. You cannot simply pick it back up like a dropped handkerchief."

"It's true," Aunt Poisie said. "You cannot."

Abrianna waited to say anything until they concluded with their initial comments, which went on for nearly twenty minutes. Finally they fell silent and looked at her for answers. Abrianna drew a very deep breath and folded her hands.

"I realize that I have caused you grave concern, and that was not my intention. As you all know, I wrestled with the idea of marrying Wade from the beginning. I have certain trepidations about marrying a friend so dear. I would not wish to see our relationship ruined."

"Bah! This is the only thing that is going to ruin that relationship. You must see that," Aunt Miriam replied. "I honestly fear you may have a fever or some other injury to your head. This isn't rational thought at all."

Abrianna knew that nothing she said would ease their minds. She didn't want to lie to them, either. So instead, she got to her feet. "I'm a grown woman," she declared, sounding harsher than she'd ever been with them. "I do not need to explain myself to any of you."

She saw the hurt expression on Aunt Poisie's face. She always had been the most sensitive of the trio. It was nearly her undoing, but then Abrianna imagined the woman laid out in a casket. Priam Welby wouldn't care at all how much her aunts were hurt in this matter. He would only remind her that he would have them killed if she was less than convincing.

"I am sorry that you cannot trust me to know what I'm doing. But even so, I will not be treated like a child." She softened her tone and expression. "You are all so very dear to me, and it is my utmost desire that you will trust me in this matter. I love you all very much, but this is important to me."

"Do you love him?"

Aunt Miriam's matter-of-fact question left Abrianna uncertain how to answer. She couldn't very well tell them that she was going along with this farce in the hopes that she could figure a way out, but neither could she convincingly lie about something so important.

"Do you think I would marry someone if I didn't?" Abrianna shook her head. "I don't wish to discuss this any longer. I have a lot to accomplish in a very short amount of time."

As if to prove her point, Liang appeared. "Mr. Welby here with some ladies. You want me to tell him to go?"

Abrianna shook her head. "No. I will see what he wants."

For once she was almost grateful that Welby had imposed himself on them. Abrianna made her way to the front foyer where Priam Welby stood with a half dozen women. Unfortunately, her aunts followed close on her heels.

"I wasn't expecting you," she said as pleasantly as she could.

He smiled. "My darling, you are radiant. I believe our betrothal agrees with you." He nodded to the older women. "I have come so that we could start immediate preparations for your wedding gown. These are the best seamstresses in all of Seattle. They will measure you and fit you for a dress to outmatch any other."

Abrianna smiled. "That was quite considerate of you. However, I've already begun work on my gown."

"Oh, do show us what you have in mind," Welby insisted.

It wasn't a suggestion but rather a command, and Abrianna knew better than to choose this as one of her battles. "But of course. Although it is very unusual for the bridegroom to see the wedding gown before the day of the wedding. Bad luck, don't you know?"

He smiled and took hold of her arm. "We will never have bad luck." He looked over his shoulder. "Join us, ladies."

Seeing he wasn't to be dissuaded, Abrianna sighed. "Very well. I will lead you to the sewing room."

She headed for the stairs, and Welby kept pace with her, holding tight to her arm, as though she might somehow escape. There was only one student working in the room when Abrianna entered. Elizabeth looked up and smiled. "I'm afraid I've made a mess of things."

"No matter, Elizabeth," Aunt Miriam replied. "Would you mind leaving us?"

Elizabeth got quickly to her feet. "Not at all." She gave a nod and left the room.

Abrianna pulled away from Welby and went to a long table where basted pieces of her gown lay. She took up a picture of the pattern and presented it to her would-be husband.

"Oh no." He shook his head. "This is much too simple. We must have a gown of great extravagance. I absolutely insist. I am, after all, paying for this wedding, and I want to show you off. All of Seattle must see you as the queen I intend you to be."

Abrianna was glad her back was to her aunts. She couldn't hide her expression of anger. Welby would know how she felt but no one else would. Of this, she was quite determined.

"What exactly did you have in mind?" she asked sweetly.

Welby chuckled. "That's why we have these dear ladies with us. I will leave the choices of material and color and laces and such to you. However, they know what I expect." Abrianna joined him in looking at the women. The team of seamstresses nodded.

"There you have it," Welby said. "Now I must be off to arrange the shipment of flowers for the church. I think you'll be pleasantly surprised at what I have in mind."

"I'm sure I will be surprised," Abrianna replied, purposefully leaving off any reference to it being pleasant.

"Do you mean to take over the entire wedding?" Aunt Miriam asked.

He turned to her and smiled. "I have so longed for this event that I told Abrianna I wanted to help in the arrangements. She graciously is allowing me to put it all into play." He looked to Abrianna, as if daring her to discount what he'd said.

"I prefer it this way," Abrianna replied. At least that much was true. She wanted nothing to do with this farce.

Welby seemed satisfied with her answer. Abrianna thought with that he might leave, but instead he fixed her with a determined glance. "One more thing. I will be picking you up for supper at six."

"She will need a chaperone," Aunt Miriam declared.

Welby shook his head. "I think not. After all, we will wed in less than a month. No one will think anything of it."

"I will," Aunt Miriam replied.

"Well, that is a pity. But I must insist," Welby said firmly.

"We will be just fine, Aunt Miriam," Abrianna said with a smile. "You mustn't worry. I'm certain that Priam will look after me with the greatest of convictions regarding my chastity and well-being." She looked at the man and batted her eyelashes as she'd seen some of the coquettish women of the school do with their beaus. "Won't you?"

He was momentarily taken aback, and Abrianna wanted to gloat. Let that fix him for the moment. She would show him that there was fight left in her yet, but she would have to be very careful if she was to beat him at his own game.

"I will see to it that Abrianna is kept quite safe," he replied, looking to the three women. "If you'll excuse me, I must attend to business." He lifted Abrianna's hand to his lips and placed a kiss there. It took all of her strength, but Abrianna refrained from shuddering and instead smiled at him. "Until tonight," he whispered.

In the end, God bestowed a beautiful blessing on Abrianna. Welby was tied up with work and couldn't take her to supper, after all. She received the message from him shortly before five, along with a dozen long-stemmed roses. She left both on the front table for all to see. Then she secluded herself in her bedroom and prayed that everyone would leave her alone.

"Maybe they'll think you're heartbroken," Flora suggested. "I can let them all know at supper that you were taken with a headache if you'd rather not come down."

"That would be best," Abrianna admitted. "I'd just as soon stay here."

"I'll bring you something to eat," Flora promised. "But before I go, have you thought of anything that will help you get out of this? I've been fretting since this latest development. I don't know how a man like that might be bested except to use his own words against him."

"I know, but there's little possibility of getting him to recount what he told me regarding all his evil deeds." Abrianna began undressing. She dropped the wool skirt to the floor. "He certainly wouldn't admit it to anyone else."

Flora hurried to help her by unbuttoning the back of her blouse. "Maybe you could make him put it in writing. You know—that way you'd have something to use against him. You could demand it, telling him that it's only right that you have some control, as well."

"I'm sure he would never be that foolish." Abrianna felt the last button give way and pulled the blouse forward. Flora meanwhile began unlacing her corset. "Whatever you do, Flora, you must be careful to say nothing that will give us away. Welby would surely see to someone's death if he knew I'd shared everything with you.

"I suppose I should have better considered his temper before allowing you to know the details of his threats, but I couldn't help myself, and for that, I do apologize. I would never risk your life even to ease the woes heaped upon me. That would not be the actions of a good friend, and that is exactly what I hope to be to you."

"Oh, but you are," Flora assured. "You are most dear to me." She finished with the laces and came to face Abrianna. "You must know that I cherish our friendship. I would have run away from here long ago if not for you."

Abrianna gave her somber nod. "I do understand. I wish I could run away now. However, this situation is most grievous and will call for bravery and fortitude. We have no one but ourselves to count on."

"And God," Flora reminded.

"Of course. I know we have Him. I just hope He hasn't held my deception against me." Abrianna shook her head. "I know He didn't hold Rahab's lies against her when she sought to protect the two Hebrew spies. Goodness, she was even of questionable repute, yet God blessed her by putting her in the lineage of Jesus. I would hope if He could forgive her all of that, He will forgive me, as well. After all, I am doing this for the betterment of many souls."

"I can't help thinking He would," Flora said thoughtfully. "As you say, it's not for yourself that you have done this. Yours is a most unselfish and sacrificial act. I believe God looks at your heart in these matters."

Abrianna nodded. "I hope you're right. I suppose by the nineteenth we shall know."

Flora looked confused. "How do you suppose that?"

"If this works out, and Welby is exposed, then I'll know all is forgiven. If not and I find myself wed to that monster, then I'll know that even God couldn't abide my choices."

18

Abrianna stood gowned in one of Lenore's finest hand-me-downs. The extravagant evening dress was layered silk in a burnt pumpkin color that was overlaid with a buttery cream-colored lace. The neckline was cut quite low in a V-shape, but for modesty, the same cream lace was inset to the neck where a band of the pumpkin silk held it in place. It gave the appearance of a choker type necklace, especially after Abrianna pinned a cameo in the center. To finish off the outfit, there was a stylish hat and gloves that came to the elbow. She looked, as Flora had said earlier, finer than a twenty-dollar gold piece.

Welby demanded she accompany him to dinner that evening, and finding no excuse to do otherwise, Abrianna had readied herself for the event. When a knock sounded at the door, she was certain Welby had arrived early. Instead, it proved to be Brother Mitchell and the other elders of the church.

Liang admitted the three men and directed them to the main parlor before going in search of Abrianna's aunts. Abrianna acted momentarily as hostess, seeing to their comfort.

"Miss Abrianna, you look quite lovely," Brother Mitchell declared. "I understand that you have changed your mind about marrying Mr. Ackerman."

"Yes," she replied but offered nothing further. "Would you care for refreshments? I can have tea brought, as well as cakes." She moved toward the door in anticipation.

"No, we won't be here long. We came to speak to your aunts about Mr. Ackerman's situation."

Abrianna immediately felt a pang of regret. She should offer Wade a defense and show her support. Even if they thought she had abandoned him. "I hope," she began, "that you aren't being persuaded to think less of him. This entire matter with the arrest is nothing more than a misunderstanding. His lawyer, Kolbein Booth, believes it to be someone's underhanded plot to see Wade discredited. We anticipate that the charges will be dropped anytime now."

"We have had our concerns. There are questions from the congregation, as you must realize." Brother Mitchell looked most uncomfortable.

"There will always be someone questioning something," Abrianna said with a smile. She tried to make light of the situation. "Goodness, but most of the congregation have issues they would rather not come to light. I would think in a situation like this, where the accusations are so evidently false, they would stand behind Wade in support."

"I believe most will," Brother Mitchell said.

"Indeed," Brother Williams said, nodding. Brother Adams did likewise.

"I'm glad," Abrianna said, feeling that she'd done all she could to support Wade's innocence. "I firmly believe that Wade and my father will soon be released. I am certain of it."

"So you didn't change your mind about marrying him because you thought him guilty?" Brother Adams asked.

She frowned. "Is that what people are saying?"

"I haven't heard such," the man admitted, "but it was something that did come to mind. Everyone knows that your aunts have nothing but the highest standards. I thought perhaps they had asked you to refuse him."

"Not at all. They do not believe Wade guilty any more than I do. As I said, I'm certain the truth will come out very soon."

"We are praying for just that," Brother Mitchell replied. "We wanted to speak to your aunts on the matter."

"Of course." Abrianna noted the time as the mantel clock began to chime the hour. "I'm afraid I must excuse myself, gentlemen. I have a previous engagement." She left them in the parlor just as her aunts came down the hall.

"Abrianna, I do not condone this arrangement of you going out to supper without a chaperone." Aunt Miriam reached out to take hold of Abrianna's gloved arm. Aunt Selma and Aunt Poisie nodded but said nothing.

Hating the worry in their expression, Abrianna longed only to ease their mind. "You all have raised me to be a good woman of high morals. I promise you that I will not do anything to shame you. Please trust me in this matter."

"It's not you I worry about." Aunt Miriam's mouth was set in a grim line as she drew a deep breath and released Abrianna. "I wish I understood what was going on."

Abrianna nodded. "I know. I am sorry." She hurried on toward the front door, worried that if she remained even a minute more, she would break down and tell her aunt every detail of Welby's threat. She was glad Aunt Miriam didn't press further but instead murmured something to the other two before the trio made their way to the parlor. Abrianna breathed a sigh of relief.

She reached the front door just as the knocker sounded.

Opening the door, Abrianna found Priam Welby. He seemed surprised to see her.

"My dear Abrianna. May I say that you are clearly the most beautiful woman in all of Seattle?"

"Say what you will. You seem quite good at that." She picked up her small reticule and moved past him. "Let's get this over with."

He chuckled and followed her to the closed carriage. A liveried driver sat at attention in the driver's seat, while a groomsman stood by the open carriage door. Abrianna allowed the man to hand her up into the conveyance. She took a seat, only then remembering that she'd left her shawl behind. It was already chilly and no doubt would be even more so by the evening's conclusion. However, rather than deal with a delay, she decided to say nothing.

Welby joined her in the carriage, wedging himself into the seat beside her. She had hoped that her position in the middle would dissuade this, but the man was most demanding. Abrianna moved as far away as the seat would allow, which wasn't anywhere near far enough.

"If I didn't know better, I would think you were trying to escape me."

"You know full well that's exactly what I'm trying to do." Abrianna rearranged her silk and lace skirts, and the carriage began to move. "I may put on a show for the world around me, but here, inside of this far-too-private quarters, I want to make my feelings clear to you."

"Yes, well, be that as it may"—he sounded most amused—"in time you will find yourself yielding to me in every way."

"And what of my father and Wade? Why haven't they yet been released?" She looked at him hard. "Are you backing out of the arrangement?"

"Not at all. I have it on the best authority that they will be released tomorrow."

She felt her heart skip a beat. *Please, God, let it be so.*

"Are you certain?"

He looked at her with a leering grin. "Do you suppose I would risk losing you?"

Abrianna let go a sigh of relief. If he was telling the truth, half the battle was won. "How did you arrange it?"

"Like I said before, I wield a great deal of power in this town."

"Threatening others like you did me?"

He laughed. "With whatever means I need to get the job done. Now let us change the subject to something more pleasant—our wedding."

She looked away to gaze out the small window. Her fingers toyed with the edge of the burgundy velvet curtain, uncertain what to say. She waited for him to continue, and when he didn't, Abrianna looked back to find him watching her.

"What about our wedding?"

"I have decided we will allow your aunts to host the wedding breakfast at the school. They seemed so disappointed in not being able to make your gown, and when I mentioned having the wedding breakfast handled elsewhere, they were positively downcast. I want them to know that I am not a heartless man."

"More lies." She shifted her reticule to her left wrist. "I don't know how you sleep at night."

He leaned closer. "Sleep has never been my favorite thing to do at night." His breath was warm and smelled of liquor. He ran his hand down her arm. "You truly are more beautiful than I ever gave you credit for. I suppose it was that dowdy and childish way you dressed yourself. From now on how you dress . . . or undress . . . is going to be up to me."

233

Abrianna pulled away as best she could, but Welby would have none of it. He grabbed her to face him, almost pulling her off the carriage seat. Her arms were all but crushed together in his hold. He tried to kiss her, but Abrianna turned her face away, causing him to take hold of her face instead. It was the opportunity she'd hoped for.

"You will learn to endure, if not enjoy, my affections," he said, his lips only inches away from hers.

"And you will learn to conduct yourself as a gentleman." Abrianna pressed her point home with the tip of a boning knife atop his thigh.

Welby very carefully let her go and glanced down at his leg. She held the knife in position. He slowly held out his hands and grinned. "I suppose I should have expected such nonsense."

Abrianna shook her head. "You will respect my virtue and my values until we are married. After that, I will do my wifely duty but nothing else. I will not shower you with affection nor even give pretense to liking you, Mr. Welby. God knows that in dealing with you, I've told enough falsehoods to last me a lifetime."

"If I were Ackerman, you'd no doubt feel differently."

She withdrew the knife and replaced it in her bag. "Wade would never take advantage of me in such a way. He has done nothing but respect me. We've shared a few kisses, but even those were innocent. You have in mind to dishonor me and take liberties with me that I will not allow."

"I could force you. You realize that, don't you? It wouldn't be at all difficult to knock that little knife from your hands. Oh, I might suffer more than a nick in my trouser leg, but I would endure. You, on the other hand, would most certainly be less successful."

"I'm not afraid of you, Mr. Welby." She narrowed her eyes. "Keep that in mind. I hold great concern for my loved ones, as you well know, but for myself . . . well, let's just say that I'm no man's fool. Not yours or anyone else's. In spite of what you might think, I can take care of myself."

The carriage drew to a halt, and Welby's man quickly opened the door. Abrianna drew a deep breath and forced a smile. "Just remember, Mr. Welby, you aren't the only one who has a friend in a powerful position. My hope is in the Lord."

"Well, He doesn't seem overly concerned about your plight."

She relaxed her tense muscles, and this time her smile was born out of confidence. "You'd be surprised, Mr. Welby. I have come to learn that God will not be mocked. He will deal with deceit in His own way and in His own time."

Wade looked at the uniformed officer who unlocked his door and told him he was free to go. It was almost like a cruel joke. He'd had dreams like this, but they always ended up with the guards leading him to the gallows.

"Come on, Ackerman. I haven't got all day."

Wade stepped from the room that had been his cell and saw Kolbein waiting for him down the hall.

"I'm really free to go?" he asked, approaching his friend.

"You are. All charges against you have been dropped." Kolbein handed him a coat. "It's turned rather cold."

Wade pulled the jacket on. "What about Jay?"

"He's waiting for us in the carriage. The judge was amazingly lenient. He gave him time served and a small fine for assault." Kolbein shook his head. "The attempted murder charges were all but apologized for. None of it makes much sense to me, but since it resulted in the charges being dismissed, I'm taking it as a gift from God."

Wade climbed into the carriage while Kolbein had words with the driver. Jay sat against the far corner, looking considerably better than the last time Wade had seen him. "You still look like you went a few rounds with the local boxing champ."

"Feel like it, too." He moved with great difficulty. "Ribs still hurt like the dickens."

Wade sat back and shook his head. "I don't know why this has happened to us, but I do intend to get to the bottom of one thing."

"Abrianna?"

"Yes. I have no idea what she's up to."

"I don't believe she loves Welby," her father said.

"No. I don't either. Kolbein says, however, that she isn't talking much to anyone. She hasn't even gone to see Lenore. Kolbein also said that Mrs. Madison tells him that Abrianna is so often in the company of Welby or his lackeys that they never have much of a chance to speak to her alone. Not that she allows for it, anyway. Apparently Abrianna has been quite reclusive when at the house and refuses to answer anyone's questions."

"That's not like her."

"Not a bit," Wade replied. "Since when has Abrianna ever hesitated to share her mind on any matter? I have an idea that she's done this to somehow benefit getting us out of jail."

Jay frowned. "Do you really?"

"I do."

Kolbein climbed into the carriage and looked at Wade. "You do what?"

"I think that Abrianna had something to do with getting us out, and I think it has to do with her agreeing to marry Welby."

Kolbein nodded. "Lenore and I think the same, but she isn't speaking to us. She's not speaking to anyone, with exception to Welby and maybe Flora."

"Flora? Eloise's niece?" Jay asked.

"One and the same. According to Mrs. Madison, Flora is very often in Abrianna's company. The two share Abrianna's bedroom."

"Then if Abrianna won't talk, perhaps Flora will," Wade said, giving the matter consideration. "I'll see if I can't corner her when we get home. Unless, of course, I can get Abrianna alone."

"Welcome home, Wade . . . Mr. Cunningham," Mrs. Madison declared. The old woman had tears in her eyes.

"Yes, welcome home." Eloise surprised them by embracing Jay, but at the sound of his moan she quickly released him. "Oh, I'm so sorry. That was quite thoughtless of me."

"No matter," Jay said. His grin assured them all that he wasn't displeased. "I'm honored to see that you've come all the way from Tacoma to celebrate our return."

The old ladies embraced Wade one by one while the others congratulated him and Jay on being cleared of the charges. The only person who was obviously missing was Abrianna.

"Mr. Welby appeared here at noon to pick Abrianna up for a dress fitting. He told us they were to be present at an afternoon tea with the governor, who is here regarding some sort of community business. After that they were going directly to a party being hosted by one of the city officials," Mrs. Madison explained.

"But first they were going to have a quiet supper," Miss Poisie added. "Whatever that means."

Wade felt his anger getting the better of him. He knew men like Welby and didn't figure it meant anything good. "How can you just let her go like that?" He knew the question was unfair, but he was at a loss as to what else to say.

Mrs. Madison shook her head. "It is not our choice or desire. We have prayed long and hard for Abrianna to come to her senses. She doesn't love him—of that I'm certain."

"I am, too." Wade looked around the room. "I think we all are." His gaze fell to Flora who instantly looked away.

"It's left us quite filled with sorrow," Miss Poisie said. "She even snapped at me the other morning when I asked her if she was happy that Mr. Welby had moved the wedding breakfast here."

"Here?" Wade asked.

"Oh yes." Miss Poisie's head bobbed. "He was to have it elsewhere, but as a favor to us, I suppose, he's allowed it to be here. He did require it be of the utmost elegance and beauty. He plans for over two hundred people to be present and has hired a caterer to furnish all of the food. He said it wouldn't be right for us to have to work on Abrianna's wedding day."

Wade gritted his teeth. It wasn't going to be Abrianna's wedding day. Not to Welby. Never. He looked again at Flora. She slipped away from the group and disappeared. He was more certain than ever that she knew something. Now it was just a matter of getting her to explain.

"There's something else." Mrs. Madison looked most uncomfortable. "I would prefer to speak to you alone, Wade. Will you join me in my office? The rest of you go on about the celebration. There are refreshments and cake. Let us make merry as best we can."

But her tone was anything but merry. Wade was certain he'd

never heard or seen the woman be so downcast. He followed her into the small office and waited for her to speak.

"I don't know quite how to say this, but Abrianna . . . well, Mr. Welby to be exact, is uncomfortable with you living here so near to Abrianna. He said it wasn't proper and that people would talk."

"Rather like the pot calling the kettle black, isn't it?" He barely held his anger in check.

She nodded. "Be that as it may, I don't know what else to do." She sat down, and it was only then that Wade noticed tears in the old woman's eyes.

He went to her side and knelt. "I'm sorry. We both know that something isn't right. We know that she doesn't love him, and that for whatever reason, she thinks she has to do this."

"She won't even talk to me. She's never done this before. I think of all the times she's given me cause to worry, none of them frightened me as much as this."

Wade took hold of her hand. "Try not to fret. We have eighteen days to get it all figured out. For now, I'll get my things and stay elsewhere. I don't want there to be any additional pressure on Abrianna to do something stupid. Welby is the sort who will make everyone miserable if he doesn't get his own way."

"The Booths have said they will take you in."

Wade nodded. "I will take advantage of that, then. Please don't worry. I promise you, I will take care of everything."

19

Lenore reclined on a chaise lounge while Kolbein paced the beautifully polished oak floor. Wade watched their faces as they recounted all they knew in regard to Abrianna's sudden decision to marry Welby.

"It's been impossible to get her to come see me." Lenore twisted her hands. "I have tried many times, but there's been no reply."

"There has to be a way." Kolbein rubbed his chin. "What is it that Welby wants most?"

"Abrianna." Wade was losing his patience in the matter.

"Besides that," Kolbein replied. He stopped midstep. "He wants power."

"And approval of the socially elite," Lenore added. "Or at least the pretense of it."

"She's right." Kolbein's expression was one of intense thought. "I wonder . . . yes, I know a way we can get Abrianna to come here, but it will require Welby come, as well."

"How?" Wade asked.

"We'll host an engagement party. We'll do it right away." He looked to Lenore. "I'll have it completely arranged with the housekeeper. I don't want you lifting a finger."

"I don't have to lift a finger to plan a party." Lenore smiled. "I will arrange it, husband."

"But how are you going to make it such that it will assure Welby's attendance? He might not know that I'm here, but he knows how you two feel about Abrianna marrying him."

"It won't matter. I'll put the governor and mayor and anyone else with power and social position on the guest list. He wouldn't dare refuse to attend."

"But there's so little time." Wade shook his head. "How is that going to help us?"

"Well, the way I see it, if we can get Abrianna here, then Lenore can talk to her alone, and if not Lenore, then you."

"He'll never attend a party where I'm also in attendance," Wade replied. "He'll be far too worried that Abrianna might speak to me."

"He won't know you're here," Kolbein said. "I'll make a personal invitation to him and in the process mention that no one knows exactly where you are. That should make him feel more at ease. Meanwhile, you hide out wherever you like. Don't tell me, so I don't have to lie." He grinned. "This is a very big house."

Wade shook his head. "I don't know how this will make a difference, but I'm game to try."

"That is sure one fancy dress." Flora walked to the dressmaker's dummy and Abrianna's newly finished wedding ensemble. She fingered the lace overlay and shook her head. "Never seen a bustle that big or a train that long. Got to be about a thousand little pearls sewn in all that material."

Abrianna nodded. "So I've been told." She came to where Flora was and gave a sigh. "It's such an ostentatious gown. I cannot imagine any bride wanting to wear such a thing. Grief, but it's ugly."

Flora nodded. "I was afraid to call it that. I didn't want to hurt your feelings."

"It doesn't hurt my feelings at all. It's not the gown I wanted." She pointed beneath the abominable overlay. "That's the gown I prefer, the one I had planned to wear when I married Wade. If I had any real guts, I'd show up at the church wearing it alone."

Flora turned to her. "Abrianna, we're no closer to figuring out how to get you out of this. I've looked over our notes, and I can't see any way out."

"I know." Her words rang with resignation. "I fear I've dug myself in too deep this time. Welby rarely leaves me a moment to myself, and when he's not around, he's having me watched." Tears came to her eyes. "I don't know what to do. I can't even think clearly."

Flora hugged her. "We have to figure a way out. Don't you think maybe we should get some help? You have a lot of folks who care deeply about you."

"And all of them are at risk. No, I can't put this off on any of them. It's bad enough that I've included you."

A tear slid down her cheek. Flora, too, looked as if she too might burst into tears. "We have to be strong, Flora. We have to continue to pray and listen for God's direction. We don't have many days left, but I have to hold fast to my belief that God will deliver me. Otherwise . . ."

Flora looked at her and shook her head. "Otherwise what?"

Abrianna drew a deep breath. "There is no otherwise. Flora, be a dear and leave me for a time. I'd like to sit here and pray."

"Of course. I have some chores to do, anyway." She hurried to the door of the sewing room. "I'll be praying all the time." She stopped and shook her head. "Wade doesn't hate you, Abrianna. I'm certain of that."

"Thank you. You are a good friend. Much better than I deserve." Abrianna waited until Flora had gone before going to the door and locking it. She had no desire to answer anyone's questions or to face her aunts.

She returned to the wedding gown and ran her fingers down the sleeve. Then, without concern for Priam Welby's feelings, she picked up a needle and thread. Next she retrieved a small stool and sat down beside the dressmaker's dummy.

She pushed aside the heavy overlay and lifted the hem of her original gown. Wade was the only man she would ever love. Welby would know that, too. If something didn't happen to get her out of this mess, she would end up in a loveless marriage that would no doubt be the most difficult situation she'd ever faced. Welby was cruel and didn't care how anyone else felt. He would inflict pain just to put her in her place and make certain Abrianna knew he was her master.

With tender care, Abrianna began to stitch her initials into the hem of the satin gown. The embroidery was barely noticeable. She'd never been all that good at fancy work, but the needle seemed to glide in and out of the material as if held by divine hands. Once the A had been completed, Abrianna moved the needle over a space and added a W and then another A. Even if the stitches were spotted, she could declare them simply to be A for Abrianna and W for Welby rather than Abrianna and Wade Ackerman.

She tied off the stitch with a knot and surveyed her work. At least this way, if all else failed and she was forced to marry

Welby, she would have this reminder that Wade was truly the one she loved.

Like I would ever need a reminder.

"I told Mrs. Madison to send Flora to the carriage house apartment to find you," Jay told Eloise Snyder. He looked to Wade. "Once she gets here, she'll find out too late that we're determined to get the truth out of her. Mrs. Madison was all for that."

Wade nodded. He'd snuck back onto the property, being very careful that no one had seen him. "Good. I intend to get to the bottom of it. If I know what's going on, I'll have a better chance of getting Abrianna to tell me everything. The party is tomorrow night, and I can't very well wait any longer."

"She'll talk," Eloise replied. "I'll see to that." The determined look in the woman's eyes made Wade glad he wasn't the one about to face interrogation.

"Aunt Eloise? Are you here?" Flora called out from the other side of the door.

Eloise went to open it while Wade ducked out of sight. He heard the exchange and waited for just the right moment to reveal himself.

"Hello, Mr. Cunningham. Aunt Eloise, Mrs. Madison sent me to find you."

"Sit down, Flora." Eloise's tone was quite firm.

"What's wrong?" the younger woman asked.

"We need to have a talk."

"Did I do something wrong?" Flora asked, her voice quivering.

Wade decided that was a good time to reveal himself. "You

haven't done anything wrong, Flora. I'm pretty sure you've been doing what you thought best for your friend, Abrianna."

The younger woman's eyes grew wide, and a look of discomfort crossed her expression. Wade took the chair beside her and reached out to take hold of her hand. "I know Abrianna confides in you. I know, too, that you have probably sworn to keep all of her secrets. But, Flora, whatever secrets she's keeping this time may very well backfire on her. You do realize this, don't you?"

For a moment Wade thought the girl would refuse to speak. She lowered her face and remained silent for the longest time. When she looked back up, there were tears in her eyes, and Wade felt confident she was ready to talk.

"I know you don't want to betray her, Flora. But keeping someone from making a mistake that might even cost them their life isn't a betrayal—it's a rescue and a loving act. I know you don't want to see Abrianna married to Welby. None of us do."

She sniffed and nodded. Wade patted her hand. "So in order to keep that from happening, you have to tell me everything. Start at the beginning."

Flora looked to her aunt and Jay, as if for reassurance. Jay knelt down beside her. "Flora, we know Abrianna doesn't love Welby. We're pretty sure, too, that she wouldn't be doing any of this if it weren't for her thinking it was going to benefit somebody else—like me or Wade."

She nodded again and bit her lip. After another few minutes she spoke. "It's truly horrible. I promised I would say nothing. She'll never trust me again. She might even end our friendship, and I cannot bear that."

"She doesn't need to know you said anything," Wade replied. "If we work it right, Abrianna herself will be the one who ends up telling me everything. But it will be better if I know ahead of time what's going on. That way, maybe I can get an idea of the needed solution."

Flora looked uncertain but eventually nodded. "All right. I'll tell you."

"Of all the underhanded meanness," Kolbein declared after Wade finished telling everything that Flora shared. "Welby ought to be strung up, not only for the killings he's been responsible for, but for the torment he's put poor Abrianna through."

"I know. By the time Flora had finished, I think all of us were so stunned, we hardly said two words."

"And to think she's been carrying this around with her since your arrest." Kolbein shook his head. "No doubt she thought it was something she could manipulate. That's the trouble with Abrianna. She always thinks she's bigger than any problem that can come her way."

"Not this time. Flora said Abrianna cries herself to sleep almost every night. I'm pretty sure she knows this won't have an easy solution."

"Tomorrow night we'll find a way for you to be alone with her." Kolbein glanced toward the door. "I don't want Lenore to know all of this. She'll just fret, and she's still recovering."

"I agree. Lenore doesn't need to know the details. However, I think she may be needed in order to get Abrianna separated from Welby." Wade considered the matter a moment. "Maybe Lenore could be present at the party and then feign needing rest. She could ask Abrianna to help her upstairs."

"No. Everyone would know I wouldn't leave Lenore to be helped by someone else."

"Perhaps you could be busy elsewhere. Maybe not even in the room at the time. In fact, your leaving could be Lenore's signal."

Kolbein nodded. "That's possible. But what's to keep Welby from offering to help, as well?"

"I suppose you're right. What else could we do to get Abrianna to a more isolated part of the house without Welby at her side?"

Kolbein sat down and smiled. "You know, we're looking at this all wrong. Lenore is about to go into her confinement from society. Perhaps the baby is the angle we need to look at. Maybe Lenore could ask Abrianna to come see the nursery. Welby might ask to go along, but then I could approach with someone of value to him and interrupt the moment. You know, there is someone in town I think Welby would be itching to know. He's an investor from Chicago and a friend. I could make certain Welby gets introduced and amply intrigued."

Wade nodded. "That just might work. Welby might be concerned about letting the two women be alone, but if the value of staying with you is greater, then there's a good chance he'll let Abrianna go."

Kolbein grinned. "I think we have a plan."

20

"I expect you to stay at my side throughout the evening."
Priam Welby helped Abrianna from the carriage and studied their surroundings. Lights shown from nearly every window in the Booth house, giving it a cheery appeal. Carriages lined the drive, and groomsmen and liverymen were being entertained under a large tent on the lawn. The entire estate spoke of wealth and good taste. He looked back to Abrianna. "Shall we go?"

Abrianna took his arm, but with her free hand tightened her hold on the mantle she wore. "Don't you think folks will find it strange that you are unwilling for me to visit with the ladies? After all, the men are certain to separate off to discuss politics, and you said there was to be some important investor here from Chicago. I can't imagine he'll wish to speak with you about your business ideas if I'm hanging on your arm."

Welby considered her words. She made a good point, but he feared leaving her alone. "And what's to keep you from saying something about our situation to your friend Lenore?"

"What's stopped me all along?" she snapped. "It's not that I haven't had opportunity to speak to her or my aunts or anyone else." She raised a hostile gaze and awaited his response. "You know me very well—at least you say you do. Had I wanted to, I could have managed to find where Wade went and talk to him, as well."

He let a slow smile spread across his face. "I suppose you're right. The repercussions of your talking to the wrong person are quite sufficient. I tend to forget how much you care about the people you deem as loved ones. I've never felt that way about family or friends."

"That doesn't surprise me," Abrianna said as they began up the steps to the front door. "It's a wonder your family would even have anything to do with you."

His grip on her arm tightened. "You would do well to keep your thoughts to yourself, Abrianna. My family is not a topic of discussion that I wish to share."

"If you keep tightening your hold, I'm bound to be black and blue. Given that this gown is sleeveless, the entire party will see your abuse and question it."

He loosened his hold. "Just remember what I'm capable of."

"Grief, but it would be impossible to forget."

The butler admitted them and announced their arrival. Kolbein Booth and his wife Lenore came forward in greeting.

"Abrianna . . . Welby," Booth said with a nod, "we are so glad you could come this evening. Lenore and I wouldn't have felt right if we hadn't given you a party."

"We are quite honored," Welby replied. He looked to Abrianna. "Aren't we, my dear?"

"Yes." Abrianna pasted on a smile. "Most honored."

Lenore stepped forward and embraced Abrianna. "You look wonderful, and that mantle is beautiful. Is it new?"

Abrianna nodded. "It was a gift from Mr. Welby. He has

arranged an entire wardrobe for me, but most of it is still being made."

"There were only so many seamstresses available," he said with a chuckle. "But as I told those I could get my hands on, Mrs. Welby needs to be gowned according to her station."

He took the high-collared mantle from Abrianna's shoulders, and Lenore gasped. Welby knew it was no doubt because of the lavish diamond and emerald necklace clasped around Abrianna's neck. Of course it could also have been the rather low cut of Abrianna's bodice. She hadn't been pleased with the immodest arrangement and had insisted on covering herself with some sort of netting, which Welby had quickly cast aside earlier that evening in order to present her with the necklace. Her aunts had been horrified, and he found it all rather amusing.

"Another gift?" she asked.

Abrianna nodded. "Mr. Welby is quite generous."

"You'll put the rest of us to shame, Welby." Kolbein Booth's tone was teasing, and Welby couldn't help but enjoy the attention.

"She is too beautiful to leave unadorned. I thought with that beautiful hair of hers, emeralds would be perfect, and I must say they are quite pleasing. Of course, sapphires would set off her eyes." He gave Abrianna a hungry gaze. Her milky white skin seemed to glow against the glittering jewels and the stunning gown of ivory brocade and glistening gold tulle. To his surprise she produced a feathered fan and opened it to shield his eyes from the low neckline.

"Abrianna, you look stunning," Booth replied. "Come and meet our guests." He took hold of his wife. "I think there are some people here you will be very happy to see." He led the way into a side room that stretched the full length of the house.

It was a grand room of beautiful paintings, plush furnishings, and numerous flower arrangements. Welby found it impressive, but even more so the people in attendance. The governor and several other well-known political figures stood near one of two fireplaces. Welby glanced around the room, wondering if anyone would have been foolish enough to invite Wade Ackerman. There was no sign of him anywhere in the city, but that didn't make Welby relax his guard. He'd continued having Abrianna and the school watched twenty-four hours a day.

"You have a beautiful home, Booth," Welby offered.

"Thank you, Mr. Welby. As I mentioned earlier, I have a friend here from Chicago who would love to meet you and hear your ideas for Seattle."

Welby nodded, quite pleased that someone was finally acknowledging his vision. Abrianna remained at his side in silence unless directly spoken to. She was all beauty and graciousness, and Welby felt a sense of pride in the way things were working out. It wouldn't be long at all until he could laugh in the face of his father, proving what a fool the man had been.

Abrianna knew the evening would be most difficult to endure. She was uncomfortable in the inappropriate gown and even more embarrassed at the gaudy necklace Welby forced her to wear. She'd tried to protest that the jewelry didn't go well with the color of her gown, but he'd hear nothing of it. The man was without a doubt the most depraved and irritating man she'd ever encountered.

Throughout the evening Abrianna kept her guard in place, fearful that at any given moment Lenore or Kolbein might see a chink in her armor. Lenore was no fool, and Abrianna knew that keeping her from the truth would be difficult. For that reason, Abrianna was almost glad that Welby refused to let her from his sight.

They had been at the party for nearly an hour when Kolbein approached with a tall, distinguished-looking man at his side. He introduced the man as Samuel Albright, his friend and associate from Chicago.

"I must say I've looked forward to meeting you," the man greeted Welby. "I believe we have much in common, and since I have come to Seattle looking for ways to invest my money, I would very much enjoy a moment or two of your time."

"I'm happy to comply." Welby looked like the cat who'd caught the mouse. He smiled and turned to Abrianna. "May I present my fiancée, Miss Cunningham."

"I am pleased to meet you, Miss Cunningham. I understand that you and Mrs. Booth are good friends."

She smiled at the blond-haired man. "Yes. Lenore and I have known each other since our girlhood."

As if speaking her name drew her to their side, Lenore appeared. "Mr. Welby, I wonder if I might impose. I would very much like to show Abrianna the new nursery. Might I steal her away for a few minutes?"

Abrianna stiffened. She felt certain that Lenore was doing this to have a chance to speak privately. Welby looked momentarily uncomfortable, but it passed in a flash.

"Of course. I'm sure she would love to see it and perhaps even get ideas for our home."

Heat flushed Abrianna's face, causing her to look away. She could only pray that the onlookers thought it from embarrassment and not disgust.

"Come, then." Lenore took hold of Abrianna. "It's the room

just across the hall from our bedroom. I think you'll be pleased with the progress we've made. Of course, I've had to arrange the final stages with the help of our staff. Kolbein refuses to let me do anything, although the doctor says I am quite mended."

"I'm glad to hear that." Abrianna kept her thoughts closely guarded. "I've been most concerned and apologize for my absence. Welby keeps me quite busy with . . . well . . . with everything." She gave a little laugh. "And I thought Aunt Miriam was good at busywork."

"That gown is rather . . . well . . . it isn't what I expected you to wear," Lenore said without warning.

"It's definitely not what I wanted to wear." Abrianna spoke without meaning to. "However, it pleases Welby. So that's what matters." Hoping to get Lenore's mind off her attire, Abrianna changed the subject. "So how are you feeling? I've been quite worried."

They reached the second floor, and Lenore hurried them down the hall. "I'm doing very well, thank you. The doctor said I am the picture of health and vitality."

She opened the door to the nursery and motioned Abrianna to enter ahead of her. Abrianna gazed around at the beautiful room. Lenore had impeccable taste, and the nursery benefited greatly from her tender care.

"It's lovely," Abrianna admitted. The pale green of the walls was accented perfectly by the white sheers and darker green draperies. A beautiful hand-carved baby bed drew her attention, and Abrianna crossed the room to touch the light oak wood. "This is quite the piece. Is it an antique?"

"Stop it this minute."

Abrianna turned. "What?"

Lenore looked at her with an expression of exasperation.

"Stop playing this game with me. I want to know what's going on, and I want to know right now."

"I'm sorry." Abrianna steeled herself as Lenore crossed the room and took hold of her shoulders. She hadn't expected Lenore to be quite this forceful.

"We both know you don't love Priam Welby. And I want to know why you're marrying him."

Abrianna knew she couldn't fool Lenore. It was the biggest reason she'd avoided her friend. "I know that my choice seems strange, but I'm asking you to trust me." She drew a deep breath. "Believe me when I say that I am deeply sorry that I've been so distant. I have missed you—greatly."

Lenore's eyes filled with tears. "Oh, Abrianna. I do wish you'd talk to me and tell me what's going on."

Abrianna nodded. "I know, but for now please try not to worry. I read the other day that worry is thought to cause great strain on the heart."

"Then yours should be about to break." Lenore shook her head. "Wait here. I'll be right back."

Abrianna nodded and turned back to gaze at the baby bed. She couldn't help but wonder what it might have been like to bear Wade a child. Now, in light of everything that had happened to her, all the previous worries about ruining their friendship, their different ministries, and having children of their own no longer mattered. She had already ruined what they had.

She swallowed back the lump in her throat. If only God would show her the way out of this mess. *I never meant to make so many mistakes. I only wanted to see my loved ones out of danger, so why won't you show me how to get myself out of danger, Lord?*

She heard the door open again and squared her shoulders.

She would have to be strong. God would surely give her wisdom and show her what she needed to do.

"Abrianna."

At the sound of Wade's voice, Abrianna whirled around and all but found herself wrapped up in the train of her gown. She could see the determination in his eyes and knew that even if she could lie to the rest of the world, she could never keep Wade from realizing the truth.

Folding his arms, he leaned back against the door and fixed her with a look that suggested he was ready to do battle. "I want answers. And I want them now."

21

"Where's Lenore?" She tried to make her words sound cold and indifferent but knew she failed miserably. Her voice sounded shaky, even in her own ears.

"She's outside standing guard," Wade replied. He stood completely still, just watching her. "We arranged this entire party around the hopes that I could finally get you alone. Do you have any idea how much you've hurt me? And not because of this farce of an engagement, but because you didn't trust me enough to talk to me about whatever it is that's going on."

Abrianna felt a wash of fear go over her. If Welby found them together, he would make her pay—make them both pay dearly. "I have to go. I have to go now."

"You aren't going anywhere until I get some answers." He narrowed his eyes as he watched her. "You at least owe me an explanation."

She fought back her emotions. A longing rose in her so strong that it was all Abrianna could do to keep from crossing the room to throw herself into his arms. She wanted nothing more than to feel him embrace her and hear him promise her that everything would be all right.

"I'm afraid that I have no explanation for you. I am . . . strong-willed, as you have often said." She looked at the floor, trying desperately to remember if there was another way out of this room.

"There's no other exit, if that's what you're thinking."

She determined that she wouldn't look him in the eye. He was all that she wanted—the only one she loved. Being this close to Wade left her feeling so conflicted in her determination that Abrianna couldn't think clearly. Her strength melted into a puddle at her feet. "I am a woman of independent means now. And . . . I've reached my majority. I . . . uh . . . can make up my own mind about what I want."

"And what is it you want, Abrianna?"

You. But she didn't speak the word aloud. It had been dangerous to even allow the thought.

The memory of stitching his initials in her wedding gown hem came back to haunt her. She bit her tongue to keep from blurting out how much she loved him, how terrified she was that Welby would see him dead. Tears flooded her eyes.

"Abrianna, I know you don't love him. I know you don't want to marry him."

She kept her gaze on the floor. If she raised her face and he saw her tears, he would know that everything he said was true. She heard his boots on the floor and knew that if he touched her, she would fall apart, but for the life of her she couldn't move.

He took hold of her shoulder with one hand and raised her chin with the other. Abrianna closed her eyes tight, which only served to send the tears down her cheeks.

"I love you, Abrianna, and I know you love me." His voice no longer sounded demanding. Instead, it was like a whispered promise of hope. "I know that you would only agree to marry Welby if he threatened you with something."

A sob broke from her, and Abrianna collapsed against him. There was no use in fighting it. She couldn't bear to go on hurting him. "I'm sorry, Wade. I'm so very sorry. Please forgive me."

He wrapped her in his arms and held her while she cried. Without saying a word, he gave her more tenderness and hope than she'd had in weeks. "Tell me what's happened," he whispered.

She knew their time together wouldn't be long. There was no sense in lying to him or putting him off. Abrianna raised her face but didn't even try to break his embrace. "I'm afraid that I've rather made a mess of things—again."

He smiled in his lazy way. "I know. That's why I'm here."

It was easy after that. Abrianna raced against the clock to give Wade a complete understanding. Wade didn't condemn her or get angry. He simply listened and took it all into account before even speaking.

"And now, any moment Welby will be up here looking for me, and you cannot be here, Wade. He'll kill you, and I cannot bear the thought of your death." She glanced to the closed door and back to Wade. "You have to go."

"I was afraid it was something like this," he finally said. "It was the only sense I could make of it all. Your father and Kolbein both agreed that it would have to be something of monumental concern for you to act this way."

"I'm completely perplexed as to what I can do," she admitted. "If I refuse him . . . refuse to marry him, he says he'll arrange an accident for one of my aunts. Worse still, he has promised to end the lives of everyone I love if I do anything to stop this wedding."

"Nevermind what he says. You aren't going to marry him. You're going to marry me." He drew out a handkerchief and wiped her cheeks. "Get a hold of yourself. We haven't much more time. If Welby sees you like this, he'll know that something's amiss."

"But what am I to do? The man all but forces himself on me, as it is."

Wade's expression darkened. "He hasn't—"

She shook her head. "Nothing's happened. The only time he tried something, I took my knife to him."

Wade's eyes widened. "You what?" A grin replaced the grim expression. "That's priceless. I wish I could have seen his face."

"I told you I could defend myself," she replied with a shrug.

"Oh, Abrianna, I do love you." He gave her a quick kiss on the forehead just as Lenore opened the door.

"He's coming up here. You have to go, Wade." She hurried into the room. "I'll be with her."

Wade gave Abrianna one last look. "Trust me, Abrianna. I'll work out the details. If you find anything that can lend proof to his part in the murders, secure it and have one of your aunts get it to Kolbein."

She nodded and Lenore put her arm around Abrianna's shoulders as Wade slipped from the room.

"You've been crying, Abrianna. He'll be here any moment so just say nothing. I'll do the talking."

Abrianna nodded and let Lenore turn her toward the baby bed. She heard footsteps behind her but didn't attempt to turn back around to see who it was.

"Oh, Abrianna, I'm so glad that everything is all right. I was worried that you didn't truly love Mr. Welby, but now I see by your tears of joy that you do. Now we can be ever so happy and raise our children together. I know you will be a wonderful mother."

"I think she will be, too."

Welby's words caused Abrianna to stiffen, but Lenore gave her shoulder a squeeze. "There, see? And you were worried that he wouldn't want children right away." Lenore turned them to face him. "I told her I was certain every man would want children to carry on his legacy."

Abrianna sniffed and smiled, hoping Welby would accept her friend's words as an explanation for her tears. Much to her displeasure Welby crossed the room and put his arm around her. Drawing her near, he held her most possessively.

"I do want children, and I intend to see that we have them . . . as soon as possible." He gave a crude little laugh that left Abrianna sickened at the thought. "Now come along, my dear. We should rejoin the party. After all, it is in our honor."

Abrianna nodded. "Thank you for your encouraging words, Lenore."

"That must have been quite the performance. I must say, I was very impressed with you tonight. Not only did you manage to act the doting bride-to-be, you completely convinced your dearest friends that I am the man of your choosing." Welby's smug expression was almost more than Abrianna could bear.

"I told you I would do what I could." She leaned back against the carriage seat in absolute exhaustion. "I find it's easier to fool people when they trust you."

He chuckled. "Having never had anyone who trusted me, I've found force and threats to be far more promising."

Abrianna shifted uncomfortably. She'd gotten into the carriage and plopped onto the seat without making much provision for her bustle and train. Now she found herself trapped against his imposing frame without any give in her skirts.

"You smell like flowers." He buried his face against her hair. "When we are married, I shall buy you every imaginable scent for your bath." He drew in another deep breath. "You truly do something to me, Abrianna."

"Oh, stuff and nonsense. Don't even try to sound like this is anything but an arrangement of you imposing your will on me. There's no love between us, as you well know, and I would appreciate it if we could at least be honest about that fact when we are alone."

He straightened and looked at her oddly. For a moment Abrianna thought he almost looked hurt. Then he shook his head. "Your girlish notion of love and romance will quickly be forgotten when you come to realize what real passion and desire are all about. I'm going to enjoy educating you to that reality."

The carriage stopped, but this time there was no groomsman to quickly open the door. Abrianna hoped that Welby would remember the last time he tried to get too familiar in the carriage. The problem was, this time she didn't have her knife.

Much to her relief, however, Welby simply pulled back and opened the door.

"I would have taken you to my house for some more intimate conversation, but I promised to meet with someone at my club."

Without another word he climbed down and held out this hand to assist her like any proper gentleman might. Abrianna pulled her mantle close with one hand and reached out to take his hand with the other. To her surprise, however, he put both hands on her waist and lifted her from the carriage. He lowered her very slowly, keeping her pressed against him. Then, just as her feet touched the ground, Welby buried his hand in her hair and forced her head back. Her mantle fell to the ground, and the cold rush of air caused Abrianna to gasp. His lips crushed hers in a demanding kiss, leaving Abrianna certain she was going to be sick. But instead of fight, she stood completely still, refusing to show any reaction whatsoever.

When Welby pulled away, he looked confused and stepped back, assessing her without a word. Abrianna waited for him to say something. Instead he bent down and retrieved the mantle. Taking hold of her elbow he led her up the porch steps and deposited her at the door.

He handed her the cloak and turned to walk away. "Good night, Abrianna," he called over his shoulder. "Driver, take me to my club."

She hurried to get inside and put the closed door between her and Welby. She was thoroughly disgusted by his kiss and touch. She shuddered and hurried up the stairs, hoping that if her aunts were still awake, they wouldn't attempt to stop her and ask questions.

Flora awaited her like a faithful sentry. She looked at Abrianna and shook her head. "I saw what he did. I heard the carriage pull up and looked outside. It was all I could do to keep from throwing a rock at him."

Abrianna closed the door and leaned against it with a sigh. "I wish you would have." She pushed off the door and crossed to her vanity. Taking up a bottle of perfume, she pulled out the stopper.

"What are you doing?" Flora looked as confused as she sounded.

"I'm removing Mr. Welby from my lips." With that she took a healthy swig of the perfume, swished it around her mouth, and then spit into the washbasin. Abrianna gave a shudder again. One tasted just about as bad as the other.

"I've never seen anyone do that." Flora's tone was one of awe.

She shrugged and replaced the stopper on the perfume. "I was desperate." She pulled the pins from her already messy hair. "Now, then, there has been a most advantageous turn of events." Abrianna kicked off her shoes.

Flora sat down on her bed. "Tell me everything. Will it alter the future for you?"

"I think it will. Wade surprised me with a visit tonight."

"At the party?" Her eyes grew wide. "What did Mr. Welby do?"

"He didn't know Wade was there. Lenore took me upstairs to see her nursery, even though I knew it was for the purpose of pestering me for the truth." Abrianna let her hair tumble down her back. "Please come release me from this awful gown."

Flora was immediately at her back working the fasteners. "Do go on. I'm dying of curiosity. I have sat here all night—well, except for when I was at the window or pacing. Anyway, I was worrying all night about you."

"As only the dearest of friends would," Abrianna replied. "It was a great trial to be sure, but I played my part quite well. I believe even Mr. Welby thought I might be having a change of heart toward him."

"No!"

Abrianna laughed. "Perhaps I should speak to Kolbein's sister about going into the theatre. She's an actress, you know. Or maybe you didn't. When Kolbein first came to Seattle, it was in search of her. I'll tell you all about it one day." Abrianna dropped the gown to the floor and stepped out of it. "I wonder if you are up for an adventure."

Flora looked at her with great interest in her expression. "Such as?"

Abrianna's lips curved upward. "Such as breaking into Mr. Welby's house."

22

Abrianna was relieved to find that one of Mr. Welby's windows was unlocked. Without making a sound, she and Flora gained quick entrance and then stood in the silence of the darkened house to let their eyes adjust to the dark.

"Do you know what room this is?" Flora whispered.

"I have no idea. I'm not at all familiar with this house, but I know that Welby's office faces the front, so I presume it might be just down the hall."

Abrianna felt her way around the room until she reached what she hoped was the hall door. She opened it just a crack, and light slanted across the dark room. "This is the way." She waited, listening for any sound of someone nearby. "Come on."

She slipped around the door. "Close it behind you." Flora nodded and did as instructed.

With the stealth of a cat, Abrianna tiptoed down the hallway. Fortunately, there was only one door on the side of the house that faced the city. She tried it and smiled when it yielded. "This is it." She looked back over her shoulder. "This is his office."

They hurried to get inside and closed the door. Abrianna let out a long breath. On the far side of the room a fire had been lit in the hearth. It kept the room warm and at least marginally lit. "We'll have to work by firelight. We absolutely cannot risk any other light."

"What exactly are we looking for?" Flora asked in a barely audible voice.

Abrianna moved to the desk. The hair on the back of her neck bristled, and she froze. In the hallway came the sounds of footsteps. "Quick, hide behind that chair." She motioned to Flora and then dove under the desk.

Someone with black trousers and shoes that reflected the fire's glow moved across the room and to the hearth. Abrianna held her breath as that same person poked up the fire and added another log. Then just as quickly as he'd arrived, the man left and closed the door behind him.

Sweat trickled down the side of her face, and only then did Abrianna realize how frightened she was. She knew that Wade would never have approved this venture, but he did say that she should look for proof. Carefully, so as not to make a sound, Abrianna crept out from under the desk.

She immediately spied Flora sneaking a look from behind the chair. "I think it's clear."

Flora stood. "This is quite a stimulating adventure."

Abrianna nodded and began to pick up papers that were strewn on Welby's desk. Would he be so foolish as to leave anything in plain sight? Probably not. She sorted through old correspondence and invoices but saw nothing that could aide them in their efforts. She tried the drawers of the desk and found them locked.

"I know nothing of breaking into a locked desk. How about you?" She looked to Flora.

"No. I'm afraid that is not one of my skills."

Abrianna considered the matter for a moment. If she tried to force entry, there would be no doubt that someone had been there. "I hate to just go without further search." She glanced around the room. Tall bookcases lined one entire wall, but otherwise there was little furniture besides the chairs.

She knew that whatever damaging material Welby might have must be in the locked desk. Just then the unmistakable clip-clop of a horse could be heard coming up the cobblestone drive. Abrianna felt her heart skip a beat.

"He must be arriving. Come. We have to get back to that room and get out of here. If he finds me here, I'm certain to be worse for it."

She moved to the door with Flora right behind her. Cracking open the door, Abrianna checked the hall. There was no one yet. She pushed Flora through the opening and then followed, drawing the door closed as she went.

They scurried down the hall and had just gained entrance to the dark room when voices sounded. Abrianna closed the door as quietly as possible. She could hear a man's voice, but it wasn't Priam Welby's. She strained at the door for just a moment to hear the words, but it was impossible to make out anything being said.

"Come on," Flora encouraged. "We don't want them to find us here."

Abrianna knew she was right. It had been a complete waste of time to come, and now they were still in jeopardy of being found out. She hurried to the still-open window. She helped Flora through and then allowed Flora to help her from the outside. Now all they had to do was get home without being seen.

Wade paced the floor of the Booths' music room and considered all that he'd shared with Jay Cunningham and Kolbein. The trio had gathered with the sole purpose of figuring out how to put an end to Welby's hold on Abrianna.

Kolbein spoke first. "I think there has to be a way to get Welby to reiterate his threats. And if we can get him to do it in the company of witnesses, then we will have him."

Wade stopped and looked at his friend. Kolbein didn't look as though he'd had any more sleep than Wade. None of them looked too good. "Welby's too smart for that. I doubt he'd even be honest in front of the old ladies, much less anyone else."

"Then maybe we arrange it so he doesn't admit it in front of anyone," Kolbein replied. Both Wade and Jay looked at him and waited for him to say more. "I think the trick will be to set up the situation so that Welby has to threaten Abrianna again. He needs to say exactly what he said before and admit to ordering the murders. Wherever we do this, we could have someone in authority within hearing distance."

"That's going to be hard to do. Welby is very careful. He isn't one to leave anything to chance."

"It will be hard," Kolbein agreed, "but not impossible."

"Well, the way I see it," Jay began, "it'll need to be somewhere he won't expect it. That way we'll catch him off guard. Folks like Welby usually make their mistakes when they're forced to think out a matter quickly."

"He's right." Wade took a chair for the first time since they'd started talking. "Welby is used to having everything prearranged. He doesn't often leave much to chance."

Kolbein rubbed his chin. "That leaves us just one place for the ambush."

"Where?" Wade looked at his friend and could see he clearly had a plan.

"The wedding."

Wade shook his head. "No. I want this thing resolved before then."

"But don't you see, Wade, that's the only place where we can be assured of catching Welby off guard. He'll be consumed with making certain the wedding goes off without a hitch."

Wade let go a heavy breath. "All right. So how do we do this?"

Kolbein laid out a brief idea. They bandied the details for over an hour, until all finally agreed as to how they might make it work.

"Jay, you explain it to Abrianna." Kolbein stretched. "She'll have to make Welby repeat the things he's done, not just the threats he's made. If he confesses to murder, he will go to prison. If he confesses only to threatening murder, he will no doubt be able to get out of it."

"All right. I'll tell her tonight." Jay's expression was one of grave concern.

Wade couldn't shake his apprehension. "Is there any way for us to have an alternative plan?"

"What other plan do you suggest?" Kolbein shook his head. "It's taken all our imagination to come up with this one. I don't see any other way to rid ourselves of his threat than to have Welby confess to murder."

"I suppose you're right. I guess I need to turn this over to God." Wade shook his head. "It's just got to work."

Abrianna wasn't surprised when her father said he needed to speak with her that evening. She had just returned from yet another party with Welby and wanted nothing more than to rid herself of the clothes he had imposed upon her.

"I know you're tired," her father said, "but this won't wait."

She nodded and followed him into the kitchen. She wrestled with the train of her silk evening gown and positioned the bustle as she sat sidewise on one of the wooden ladder-back chairs at the kitchen table. Leaning to the side, Abrianna breathed a sigh.

"These gowns were not designed with the comfort of women in mind." She glanced down at the low neckline and in a very unladylike manner pulled it up with both hands. It didn't budge.

Her father surprised her by going to the counter and retrieving a flour sack dish towel. "Maybe this will help."

Abrianna smiled. "Thank you." She draped the towel around her neck like a bib. It covered her exposed body perfectly. "That's much better. Now what do we need to discuss?"

Her father took a seat at the table. "We had a meeting today—Kolbein, Wade, and me. We have a plan in mind for you."

"Oh, I'm so glad. I've been so anxious in waiting to hear something these last few days. What have you come up with? I do hope it is foolproof."

"It's going to take some work on your part," her father explained. "You've got to get Welby to say all those things again about how he arranged murders and such. He can threaten you and even talk about killing someone you love, but if he doesn't admit to the murders from the past, he won't be held for long."

"I don't understand how having him repeat anything is going to help."

Her father put his elbows on the table and folded his hands together as if for prayer. "We need to have him repeat his deeds and threats in a place where he can be overheard by folks in authority. We tried to figure out something that would work

prior to the wedding day, but nothing came to mind. We figure
this trap will have to be sprung right before the ceremony—at
the church."

Her heart sank. "You mean I have to go forward with this
pretense?"

"I'm truly sorry, Daughter. It seems the only way. Knowing
the kind of man he is, he won't be easily distracted, and we
need him distracted enough that he gets careless."

Abrianna sighed. "Go on."

"The wedding day will be most hectic, and Welby will be
feeling pretty assured of his situation. Especially if you make
him believe that you've given up hope of doing anything else."

"He knows that already. He also makes sure that I remember
it."

"That will work to our advantage. Kolbein plans to arrange
a place for you to wait for the ceremony to start that will also
have a place where we can hide folks."

"Hide folks? From what?"

"From Welby. See, we have it in mind that you will send for
Welby just before the ceremony starts. You will have to make him
believe that you're nervous and can't go on with the ceremony."

"That won't be hard." She shook her head in disgust. "I can
easily manage that."

"But here's the hard part." Jay lowered his arms. "You have
to get him to repeat the things he told you about ordering folks
killed. Kolbein is going to have the authorities there waiting.
Once Welby admits to you what he did and that he'll do it again,
then we'll have him."

"It's as simple as that?" Abrianna began to clearly see a way
out of this mess, and it excited her to no end. "That sounds
easy enough. Why didn't I think of that? Flora and I talked

about how it would be ideal to use his words against himself, but we had no thought of how to do it. This will be perfect."

Her father frowned. "There's a possibility that he won't repeat what he told you for fear that someone will overhear. He's no fool. If he won't repeat it and insists on the wedding, then just comply and—"

"I will not marry that man."

"I wasn't going to suggest you marry him," Jay said. "I won't allow you to marry him. That's for certain. Wade added something to the plan just before I returned home. He suggested that if Welby won't listen, then you should tell him that you will yield and marry him. Make him believe you, just as you've done. Make sure he is willing to leave you alone for a few moments, and Wade will slip in and steal you away, if need be."

"How adventurous. However, that would leave Mr. Welby able to hurt my aunts. I cannot do that." Abrianna knew that Welby would have little trouble finding ways to torment and harm the old ladies. He would know that word would get to her, and he would make certain he caused just enough trouble to bring about her return.

"Father, I believe that this is a one-chance situation. If Mr. Welby won't repeat his words, I'll have no other choice than to see to it he can never do this to anyone again."

Her father smiled. "As brave as you are, I really don't think you're capable of murder."

Abrianna knew that, as well. "No. I'm not. But he is, and if it costs me my life, it will be worth it to keep the rest of you safe. I'll simply create a situation so he has no choice but to kill me. That way you and the witnesses can arrest him for my murder."

"Wade would never let you do that," her father replied.

"I know. And that's exactly why you will say nothing about it to him. I need your word on this, Father."

"She's an awfully brave young woman to suggest such a thing," Eloise Snyder said as she and Jay sat together on the porch swing later that night. "Do you suppose she would really go through with something so dramatic?"

"I do, unfortunately. I haven't known Abrianna long, but what little time I've spent here has proven to me that the girl is rather fearless when it comes to ensuring the safety of those she loves. Just look at all the nonsense she's gotten herself into already."

Eloise nodded and took hold of Jay's hand. "Try not to worry. We'll pray and pray hard that Welby will have no fear in repeating his threats."

Jay relaxed at the sound of her soft-spoken words and encouraging ways. He put his hand atop hers. "You know, there's something I'd like to discuss with you. Something other than my daughter's wedding."

"All right." She looked at him with a smile. "What is it?"

"Our wedding." He grinned and held tighter to her hand. "I want you to marry me, Eloise. I've known it for a time now, but I felt it was the gentlemanly thing to wait. I wanted to give you time to be sure of your feelings. I've waited long enough, however. Seeing the mess these young folks have gotten themselves into, I want nothing to come between us."

"Oh, Jay." She drew his hand to her cheek and pressed it close. "You know I feel the same. I will happily marry you."

"I'll never be a rich man."

"I don't care. I'll happily live over the stalls with you. As long as we're together, none of the rest matters."

"I'll work hard and see us fed and housed. I'm not a lazy man, to be sure."

"I've never imagined you could be. Honestly, Jay, I've given the matter a great deal of consideration. I've been prepared to pose the question myself should you fail to do so. I've sold my house in Tacoma. It will give us a nice start. Unless, of course, you find it appalling to use your wife's money."

He chuckled and drew her close. "As long as you come with the package, I'll take whatever comes with you. Riches or none. Health or sickness. I am prepared to love you no matter."

"And I am prepared to love you . . . no matter." She lifted her face and met his gaze. "And I do love you, James Cunningham. More than I ever thought possible."

He pressed a light kiss on her lips. "I love you, my dear Eloise."

23

"Dare I hope that you're actually enjoying yourself?" Welby asked Abrianna on Thursday evening.

She shrugged. "The music is lovely and the food delicious, although I have no appetite. I suppose it's just my constitution, what with all that is happening." They sat tucked in the corner of a beautiful restaurant where a small orchestra played classical music and the waiters were dressed as fashionably as the patrons.

Abrianna wore a gown of navy blue brocade trimmed out in black jet. It was one of the gowns Lenore had recently given her. The neckline was modest, and the long sleeves added warmth. The style was of the latest designs from Paris, although Welby thought it much too chaste. His perversions only served to rile her sense of dignity.

"I suppose you have considered that you'll need to have your things delivered to my house prior to the wedding, as we are to reside there immediately. Of course, I have much of your new wardrobe already scheduled to be brought there."

The very thought filled Abrianna with horror. She did her best to keep from frowning. They were less than two days from the Saturday wedding, and all she could think about was the one chance they would have to catch Welby in his lies.

"You look perplexed."

"I suppose I am. You haven't given me very much time to accomplish everything needed. I'm afraid I haven't even begun to pack."

He chuckled. "Well, you'll have tomorrow. I can send over some servants to help you with it."

"That's not necessary." Abrianna forced herself to sound nonchalant about the matter. "We have a houseful of people who can help me. I just didn't think about it."

"It's all I've been able to think about." Welby leaned closer. "I have to admit that when all of this started, I merely wanted a means of getting back at a lot of people. My father in particular. Now, however, well . . . I don't suppose you'll believe me, but I find you impossible to put from my mind."

Abrianna shook her head. "I hardly see how marriage to me will help you in that situation. I don't know your father, and he definitely doesn't know me."

"True enough, but that will soon be rectified, as I will explain. You are of a sterling reputation, and while your ministries to the poor have caused some to think you rather reckless, most of the people who know you hold you in high esteem. Added to that, your family in Seattle has also been highly esteemed."

"But what of my father? You have taken great pleasure in reminding me of his twenty years in prison. That can hardly impress your father. Won't it harm your standing?"

He laughed. "Not at all. You see, once we are married, I intend to make a great show of the grave injustice done to James Cunningham. I will have newspaper stories covering what happened to him and how he found himself falsely accused. It will lay a good foundation for me as I press for better laws requiring additional evidence in all murder cases. This, I've decided, will be the perfect lead into my political career."

"Political career?" She looked at him in disbelief. "With all you've got going on—illegally, that is—how can you even think of politics?"

"Oh, my dear Abrianna. You are sweetly naïve. All politicians are masters of the illegal. How else do you suppose they accomplish all that they do?"

"I presumed that men who put themselves into positions of elected office accomplished the will of the people."

"Granted, there are some who do. However, for every honest politician there are at least twenty others who are in their offices purely for personal gain. I intend to be among their number and see to it that the office serves me instead of the other way around.

"As for my father, there is a long-standing debt he owes me. I have worked very hard all these years to finally see that old man put in his place."

Abrianna frowned. "You must hate him a great deal."

"I do. He threw me out of my home without a penny to my name, and all for what he perceived as an unforgivable lapse in judgment." Welby sat back in his chair, and his expression grew hard. Abrianna did her best not to shiver at the look of pure hatred in his eyes.

"I have carefully invested my money and bought my support where it could be had. Once we are married, we will go to him and I will deliver to him the truth of his failures face-to-face."

"I still don't see how that has anything to do with me."

"Well, perhaps it doesn't have as much to do with you as it used to. I once felt certain that showing my father that a respectable woman of society would have me as a husband would prove something to him. It came purely as a welcome surprise that you turned out to be an heiress, as well." He gave her a smug look of satisfaction. "A very welcome surprise. I believe it will show those friends of his a thing or two after they all boasted of their connections when I was young. Ultimately, I will show my father that I have gained far greater wealth than he will ever know. And finally, I will reveal to him that I have had his business associates and friends in my control for some time." He smiled, but it didn't reach his eyes. "Then he will regret not only what he did, but he will despair of his very life before I'm through with him."

Abrianna thought to tell him that he would never have any benefit from her money, but she knew it was best to let him think whatever he wanted. Instead, she questioned him about his father.

"Do you really suppose it was easy for your father to take a stand? It sounds to me that he had his values and wanted to teach you something about them. Perhaps he always intended for you to come back and seek forgiveness."

"I will never ask any man for that. Nor any woman."

She shivered at the implication. "And what of God's forgiveness, Mr. Welby?"

He shook his head. "I won't ask for His, either."

"But why not?"

Welby picked up his wine goblet and swirled the contents for a moment. He tossed back the remaining contents, then shrugged. "I won't give Him the satisfaction of rejecting me like my father did."

Abrianna tried to focus on the meal but found that what little appetite she had mustered up was now gone.

She suppressed a yawn that drew Welby's attention. He offered a sympathetic smile. "I suppose I haven't given you a great deal of time to rest during all of this. You must understand, of course, that I couldn't risk leaving you too much time to yourself. You might have plotted against our marriage and me."

"I'm not really as horrible a person as you believe me to be. Not that you care to know my heart."

He considered her a moment. "You're wrong. I hope you might believe me when I say that I am sorry that things had to take this course. I would much rather have had you fall in love with me and desire this union."

She could almost believe him. His words and expression seemed genuinely contrite, but Abrianna wasn't going to allow herself to feel anything for him but regret. "I'm sorry, but I'm so very tired. I wonder if you might consider taking me home."

He nodded. "Of course. I want you well rested for Saturday." He signaled the waiter. After arranging for the bill, Welby got to his feet and helped Abrianna to hers.

She let him help her with her cloak and didn't move away from him when he took hold of her elbow. Abrianna figured once they were in the carriage, he might try to kiss her or worse and so decided to approach the subject of her purity once they were alone.

The carriage had barely begun to move when Abrianna spoke. "I want to thank you for understanding my desire to remain pure until we . . . until our marriage. I could not face myself, much less a church filled with people, and wear white, if I were not . . . not unspoiled."

He chuckled. "You have some strange notions, my dear."

"Nonsense. I think you would find most women think as I do," Abrianna said. "Besides, you must consider my belief in the Bible. The Bible makes it clear that fornication is a sin." She tried not to be embarrassed about the topic of their conversation but to stand on the truth. "I desire to come to my husband without blemish on my reputation or my convictions."

"Yes, but were we to . . . fornicate, as you put it," he said, sounding amused, "it would be less than two days before we were legally wed."

"I understand that, but what if one of us were to die? Any number of things might happen, although I certainly do not anticipate it." She tried to sound casual about the entire idea. "If I were to allow your desires, we would be forever changed. At least I would be. And if I were the one remaining and you were the one who died, I might even find myself with child. I could never find acceptance in the public eye as an unmarried woman having a baby."

"I suppose you make a good point. However, I think you overestimate your unmarried sisters around the world. Believe me when I say that many a young woman finds herself happily engaged in amorous games prior to her wedding."

"Well, I'm not one of them. And I only brought it up to thank you. I know it was not your desire to put off such things. But I do appreciate that you have acted in an honorable way . . . for the most part." She cringed. She hadn't meant to add the latter and could only hope it hadn't offended him.

"If being a virgin on your wedding night is that important, then I will give that to you as my gift. It hasn't been easy knowing that I could have forced the matter, given all that I have available to me."

"I realize that you could have threatened someone I love with an accident or death. Perhaps it shows some decency in you that you have considered my feelings on the matter."

He laughed most heartily. "Your naivety knows no bounds, Abrianna. There is nothing decent about me."

The carriage came to a stop, and Abrianna breathed a sigh of relief as the groomsman opened the door and Welby climbed out. She had no idea how she might have answered Welby's last statement. It quite amazed her that the man took such pride in being evil. She drew a deep breath and rose. She only had to get through tomorrow and then her ability to play a part would determine her entire future.

"No," a still, soft voice seemed to whisper to her heart. *"I hold your future."*

She smiled and nodded as Welby helped her down. God held her future. Her actions were of little consequence if God was not in control.

Abrianna entered the house to find her aunts awaiting her return. Her father had told her that he would inform her aunts of the wedding-day plans so they would not despair of the situation. She knew they had been very hurt by her unwillingness to confide in them.

"We would like to speak to you for a moment, Abrianna," Aunt Miriam declared.

"Of course." Abrianna draped her cloak on the banister before following the trio into the small private sitting room. A fire was burning out in the hearth, but the room was still toasty and warm.

"We were going upstairs to prepare for bed, but your father came to us and explained what has been going on." Aunt Miriam sat down beside Poisie on the settee. Aunt Selma took the chair opposite them and nodded.

"I am sorry," Abrianna said in a hushed voice, "that I could not say more. In fact, I doubt it is wise for us to say much even now. I find that Mr. Welby has spies in the most unlikely places."

"Surely not here!" Aunt Poisie put her hand to her throat. "Goodness, but I couldn't sleep at all if I thought that. Perhaps we should all take up weapons?" She posed the thought as a question and looked to her sister for confirmation.

"I don't believe he has anyone here, but I would practice caution," Abrianna replied. "I never meant to hurt any of you, and I have been most grieved by the fact that I have. Please know that I am sorry, and I hope you will forgive me."

"Of course," Aunt Miriam said. "We could never hold anything against you. We love you." Aunt Poisie bobbed her head in approval.

"Indeed we do," Aunt Selma added. "You were placed in a most difficult position, and it is to our utter despair that we realize we play a small role in it. Had you not felt our safety compromised, you might never have made the choices you did."

Abrianna held up her hand. "Let's say nothing more. If all goes well, we can discuss it at length after Saturday."

"Agreed." Aunt Miriam got to her feet. "Is there anything we might do to help?"

"Just pray." Abrianna looked into each of their faces. "I know God has control of this matter. I know there was a reason that things happened as they did. I can even see where He has tempered my pride and self-confidence. I know that I was often of the belief that there was nothing I could not handle by myself. I realize the mistake in that. Now I can see that there is nothing God cannot handle, and I am only an instrument in His hands."

Aunt Miriam came to her. She placed a light kiss on Abrianna's forehead. She stepped away and gave one of her rare smiles. "That gives me great peace."

"It gives me peace, as well," Aunt Selma said. She hugged Abrianna close. "We will all endeavor to bear this as best we can." She joined Aunt Miriam by the door.

Aunt Poisie came forward and took hold of Abrianna's hands. "Just as David slew Goliath with God's help and direction, you will see your giant slain." She frowned. "Well, perhaps not slain but at least conquered. Yes. Conquered is a much better way of saying it. After all, there has been more than enough killing." She gave Abrianna a quick peck on the cheek, then joined the others.

Once they had gone, Abrianna gave a sigh. Flora would be waiting for her upstairs, eager to hear all about the evening's events. The young woman had been a great source of comfort prior to the others knowing what had taken place between her and Welby, but tonight Abrianna had no desire to talk about the evening. Her mind churned with thoughts of Saturday and all that might take place at the morning wedding. She knew there was a risk that everything would fall apart. There was even a risk she would die.

She looked around the small sitting room. "If my life is the price, Lord," she prayed in a whisper, "then I willingly lay it down for those I love." The thought gave her little satisfaction, however. She didn't want to die. She wanted a life with Wade. She wanted to minister with him, bear his children, and grow old together.

One of Aunt Selma's crocheted doilies caught her eye. Abrianna lifted it from the back of the chair and studied the pattern. She'd never been any good at crocheting, no matter how much time Aunt Selma had taken to teach her.

Abrianna smiled sadly and replaced the doily. She had wasted a lot of those lessons because of stubbornness and a lack of desire to know what her aunts longed to teach her. If things went the way she prayed, Abrianna vowed to spend the rest of her unmarried days learning whatever they desired to teach her. It was the least she could do for three old women who loved her more than life.

She blew out the lamp and moved down the darkened hall to the stairs. She was about to pick up the lamp her aunts had left lit on the foyer table when she saw a shadow move in the hall. Abrianna went to see who or what it might be and found herself suddenly wrapped in a tight hold. She suppressed a scream at the familiar scent of cologne.

"I thought you'd never come," Wade whispered against her ear.

"You scared a dozen years off my life. Oh, Wade, how I've missed you and our talks." She couldn't see his face well, but she knew it by heart. Reaching up she put her hand to his cheek and felt the stubble. "You need a shave."

He laughed. "I've been much too worried about you to tend to shaving."

"Nevertheless, you need one." She frowned. "How did you get in here without someone seeing you? You know that Welby has this place watched."

"I do. But they are looking for a dashingly handsome young man who will walk up the drive and knock at the front door. They hardly expected me to be hiding in the school's omnibus for your father to drive me in unseen."

"So you are a dashingly handsome sneak. How wonderful." She laughed in spite of her worry about him. "Next thing I know you'll be climbing up the lattice and appearing in my bedroom. Which reminds me, had I only agreed to elope with you, we might not find ourselves in this predicament. I must say, God has taught me a great lesson in giving up my desire to master and control my life. I will happily let you take charge in the future."

"Ah, Abrianna, how I love you." Releasing his hold, he stepped back. "I've missed you so much, and I can't bear to see you in the company of another."

"Well, hopefully it will be concluded soon. Have there been any changes to our plan?"

"No. Kolbein has figured the perfect place for you to be when you send for Welby. It's a large room, but a good portion of it has been utilized for storage. There are old altar pieces and large furnishings that have been kept there. They will allow us to remain hidden until we can spring the trap on Welby."

"But how will you get in there unseen?"

"Kolbein has that all figured. We will go well ahead of time and hide in one of the locked rooms well away from the main part of the church. There are a series of rooms that connect to each other, and this is one. We will wait until the ceremony is just about to start. You will send your father to fetch Welby, and we will sneak in and take our places. When Welby comes, you will give the performance of your life, and we will capture Welby in his confession."

"Oh, Wade, I do hope and pray this all works out the way you plan. I'm so afraid."

"I know, sweetheart. But believe me, I won't let anything happen to you or anyone else, if I have any say in the matter."

She sighed and stepped closer to wrap her arms around him. With her cheek resting against him, Abrianna felt his strength give her courage. "I love you so dearly. Facing all of these trials makes me realize how silly it was to fear marriage ruining our friendship. It makes me also see how foolish it was to worry about money or anything else."

"It's made me see that, as well. I was a fool to be so wrapped up in my pride. Do you forgive me?"

"Of course. Do you forgive me?"

"Do you really have to ask?"

He put his hand in her pinned-up hair, much as Welby had done the night he'd forced his kiss on her. Wade bent her gently backwards and pressed his mouth to hers. Abrianna felt her heart pound so hard that she felt certain Wade could hear it. She tightened her hold on him and let the warmth of his kiss spread a fire throughout her body. For a moment she found herself not caring at all what might happen. Thankfully, Wade still had the presence of mind to realize the danger at hand. He straightened and, once certain that she was steady on her feet, let go his hold.

"When this is over with, we're getting married," he said in a matter-of-fact manner. "Wedding or no wedding. I don't want to wait any more than is absolutely necessary."

"Me either," she whispered. "But I think we'd best not meet like this again. Your kisses do something to me, and I don't trust myself."

He chuckled. "I was thinking the same thing."

Abrianna drew in a deep breath. "Good night, then." She stepped away but found each step harder than the next. She couldn't understand what was happening to her, but it was hard to remember her standards and beliefs in light of the passion that single kiss had awakened. She felt completely helpless in her longing. Turning back, she whispered his name, but there was no response. Disappointment and relief washed over her, and for a moment she stood wondering what to do. Her senses gradually returned, and without further delay she headed for the stairs.

24

Abrianna waited for Flora and Eloise to put the finishing touches on her hair. She had chosen a Grecian arrangement, where her dark red curls could be drawn up and pinned at the front and side, while allowing the rest of her hair to spill down her back.

"You look beautiful." Eloise took a step back. "Pity it has to be wasted on this occasion."

"It is indeed a pity." Abrianna tried not to sound overly nervous. "Let's finish this. Flora, will you attach the train and then help me into the overlay?"

The younger woman nodded and quickly went to work with the beautiful cathedral train. "This is fit for a queen's coronation," Flora declared.

"Perhaps when this is all over, I could send the gown to one of the crowned heads of Europe," Abrianna mused. "Imagine it arriving and the royal stewards trying to decide why a woman in America would send them such a concoction of fabric and lace. There are a great many princes and princesses, I've heard. Seems most every country over there has several to spare. Even so, I doubt they'd want this mess."

Flora giggled. "They already believe all Americans to be fools. I read that much in one of the newspapers last year. I had wanted to visit Europe prior to hearing such things. That just seemed rude and uncalled for."

"Well, let them have their notions." Eloise set the crowned veil atop Abrianna's head. The circlet of pearls fit perfectly over the crest of the pinned curls. Eloise held the bulk of the veil aside while Flora helped Abrianna into the lace overlay. When everything was in place, they stood back to admire their work.

"You may not have chosen this style," Eloise declared, "but you look truly beautiful. Should I pull the veil over your face?"

Abrianna gazed into the cheval mirror that someone had thoughtfully placed in the room. She had to admit the image reflected there was of a royal princess rather than a mischievous hoyden who frequented the docks to feed old sailors.

"No. There's no need. I must speak face-to-face with Welby."

"The man certainly spared no expense," Eloise said, handing Abrianna her gloves. "Even these gloves are edged with pearls."

"Pity he didn't use the money to benefit the poor or help those in need. When I think of the money this gown costs and how it could have been put to much better use, it sickens me. Maybe not as much as actually marrying Welby, but it's close."

A knock sounded on the door, and all three women started at the noise. Eloise went quickly and admitted Kolbein. "It's time, Abrianna. The men are ready. I'm going to let them in back there." He pointed to where she'd been told there was another door. "It will only take a moment, and we will all be in place, so send for Welby now."

She nodded. "I'll have Flora go get him. Do you know where he is?"

Kolbein nodded. "He's speaking at the back of the church with Jay. Jay thought to keep him busy there for easier access."

"Good." Abrianna turned to Flora. "Please go tell Mr. Welby that I must see him. Go slowly and give the men time to hide." She looked at Eloise. "You go and get out of harm's way."

Eloise leaned over to kiss Abrianna's cheek. "I am going to be praying for you. You won't be alone, just remember that."

Abrianna nodded and turned to say something to Kolbein, but he had already disappeared. She glanced toward the back of the room but saw nothing amiss. There wasn't even so much as a stirring coming from that area.

Eloise and Flora left the room, and Abrianna drew a deep breath and began to pace. She hadn't thought of how cumbersome it would be with the long train attached, but she did her best to look a nervous wreck by the time a second knock sounded on the door.

"Who is it?"

"It's me." Welby's voice was barely audible.

Abrianna swung open the door and watched the man's expression change from disturbed to awe. He stood completely silent, spellbound for several moments. "You look more beautiful than I could have ever imagined. I must say without any doubt whatsoever, you are the most beautiful woman in Seattle."

Abrianna shook her head and walked away from the door in what she hoped looked like a fit of fear. "I can't do this. I can't do this," she muttered.

Welby followed her into the room and closed the door. "I'm sorry. What did you say? Why did you send for me? Aren't you afraid of causing bad luck for our marriage?" He laughed, causing Abrianna to whirl around.

"Surely you jest. This entire ordeal has been nothing but

bad luck." Abrianna wrung her gloved hands. "I can't do this, Welby. I cannot go out there and lie to all those people—to my loved ones and to God. I can't."

Her words took a moment to sink in, but when they did Welby shook his head. "You will. I'll have you dragged down the aisle if necessary."

"You wouldn't dare," Abrianna countered. She fought to think fast. "Think of the public humiliation you'd face. Why, you'd never have a political career if you were known to force a woman into marriage."

He crossed the distance between them in two long strides. Taking hold of her at the shoulders, Welby shook her hard. "You aren't going to ruin this for me now." He raised his right hand back, as if preparing to slap her.

"I'm sorry. You can beat me if you choose, but I cannot go out there and marry you."

He calmed in an unnatural silence, and for a moment Abrianna thought he might hit her, but then he slowly lowered his hand. "We have an agreement about this. I got your beloved Wade and father out of jail, all charges dropped, or have you forgotten?"

"I haven't forgotten anything." Abrianna let her fear show. She felt a trembling start at her knees and work its way up through her body. "I especially haven't forgotten that you are heartless and evil."

Welby let go his hold on her. "You know what I'll do."

Abrianna knew she would have to choose her words carefully to get Welby to remind her of his terrible deeds. "You can hardly have them falsely accused of murder—again." She looked at him for a moment, daring him, praying to God that he would take the bait.

"No, but I can have them killed."

She was partway home. Kolbein said it was absolutely necessary, however, for him to admit to the other deaths he'd arranged. It wouldn't be enough to just threaten murder. "Like you did poor old Charlie and Billy Boy and the others. Poor Mr. Greene. He didn't deserve to be beaten to death."

"Perhaps none of them did." Welby shrugged. "But they're just as dead."

"And all because you found it necessary. Who are you to determine a man's life? You aren't God."

"I am in this situation." Welby narrowed his eyes and pointed his finger at her. "You are going to walk down that aisle and marry me, and you will do so with a smile on your face, or I will systematically start eliminating your family members."

"Will you do the deed yourself?" She asked sarcastically. "Or will you get that brute of yours to do it?"

Welby gave a sinister smile that chilled Abrianna to the bone. "I will do whatever I need to. Carl proved most useful to me in seeing the others dead. It's amazing how much a man can get done when people simply follow his orders." He took hold of her jaw and squeezed tightly. "But Carl isn't the only one capable of killing, and you should know that by now. I will tell you something I didn't before, but now I think it's important you know. Perhaps it will convince you to stop this nonsense."

He let her go but didn't move away. "Carl wasn't the one who killed Greene. I did, and if you don't do exactly as I demand you to do, I will personally kill those old ladies you love, and furthermore, I will make you watch."

Abrianna willed herself not to move, but with this last statement she couldn't help but back up a step. She waited, hoping that the authorities would spring into action, but before anyone came to her rescue the door opened and Aunt Miriam came in with Selma and Poisie right behind her.

"Goodness, Mr. Welby, what are you doing here? Don't you know that it's bad luck to see the bride before the wedding?"

"You shouldn't be here." Abrianna was terrified that Welby would kill one of them here and now just to prove himself to her.

"They're here at my insistence," Kolbein said, coming into the room behind the trio. His entry surprised Abrianna. She had thought him to be hiding with the other men. "We were listening at the door and heard everything."

"You'll have a hard time proving it," Welby said.

"No, he won't" came another male voice. This one from behind them. Abrianna turned, as did Welby, to see who it was that spoke. "Priam Welby, you're under arrest for the murder of Guyland Greene."

In one fluid movement Welby took Abrianna in front of him like a shield. One arm held her tight while he pressed something into the middle of her back. "Move and you're dead," he whispered in her ear.

"Let her go," Kolbein demanded.

"I have a gun." Welby moved a few steps back toward the door, where Abrianna's aunts had been. Abrianna tried not to move with him, to make it difficult for him to keep his hold and pull her along, but he was far stronger than she'd given him credit for.

"Let her go now, Welby. We have police surrounding the church." This came from the same well-dressed older man who'd announced Welby's arrest. Wade stood right beside him.

Welby took another step back. "I'm honored that the chief of police—a man who would not be bought—would arrest me personally. I'm afraid I must decline your request. You have been a thorn in my side since the beginning. If you think I'm going to give in and allow you to take me to jail, you're a fool."

"And you're a fool if you think we're going to stand by and let you kill this young woman. You've already confessed to murder, and there is really no reason that my men won't put a bullet in your brain if you so much as attempt to leave this church." The police chief smiled. "You are had, Mr. Welby. Something I've looked forward to for a very, very long time."

Welby leaned closer to Abrianna's ear. "They think I won't kill you. They think they can save you."

A loud clunk sounded from somewhere behind Abrianna, and to her surprise Welby's hold loosened. Then before she knew it, he collapsed to the floor, tearing the veil and crown from her head as he went. Abrianna jumped away from him as best she could in the weighty gown and moved toward Wade. She saw the stunned look in Wade's eyes and then noted it was on the faces of all the men. Turning, she realized what had taken them all by surprise. Aunt Poisie stood over Welby's still body, hammer in hand.

"Well done, Miss Holmes," Kolbein said in absolute awe.

As the shock wore off, some of the men began to chuckle while Aunt Miriam and Aunt Selma went to stand beside the younger woman.

Aunt Miriam fixed her sister with a sober gaze. "I thought we agreed you'd leave the hammer at home, Poisie." Her tone was that of a chastising mother to her child.

"Sometimes, Sister, I simply have to listen to my own good sense," Poisie replied. She put the hammer back into her large reticule and raised her gaze to the others. "This time it served me quite well."

"It's true." Aunt Selma allowed her gaze to dart from person to person. "I often felt that same way when Mr. Gibson made unreasonable suggestions."

"God rest his soul," Aunt Poisie murmured without looking up.

"Amen," Aunt Miriam and Selma replied.

Abrianna stared in wonder at the entire scene. Welby lay moaning on the floor as he regained consciousness, while her aunts stood over him like faithful watchdogs.

Somewhere in the midst of all the commotion Abrianna's father had come into the room, Eloise and Flora close behind him. "Are you quite all right?" Flora came quickly to Abrianna's side. "I was ever so fearful for you. Did you get him to confess?"

"She did," Wade replied for her. "She managed it quite professionally. You should be proud of her."

"Oh, I am." Flora looked at Abrianna with wide eyes. "She is the bravest woman I know."

Wade nodded. "Me too." He smiled at Abrianna and winked.

The authorities managed to get Welby to his feet. Welby put his hand to his head. "Who hit me?"

"Unimportant," the police chief replied. "What is important is that you understand we are placing you under arrest for the murder of Guyland Greene. We also have your man Carl Neely. Your days of blackmail, vice, and murder are at an end."

Welby's brows furrowed, but whether in pain or confusion Abrianna couldn't be sure. "You arranged all of this, didn't you?"

"Not me." Abrianna point to her beloved. "Wade was responsible. He's my knight in shining armor."

"It was a combined effort." Wade put his arm around Abrianna. "One that I hope we never have reason to repeat."

"Well, given all that Mr. Welby's admitted to," the police

chief said as his men led Welby away, "you won't have any more trouble from him. Now, if you'll excuse me, I need to see to a proper reception at the armory for Mr. Welby."

Aunt Miriam came to Abriannna and took hold of her hand. "Are you all right, my dear?"

She managed to nod. "I'm just relieved it's all over."

"What should we do with all those folks in the church?" Jay asked.

Aunt Miriam considered this a moment. "It seems a pity to have them all assembled for a wedding and not have one. Then, too, there's the wedding breakfast. Mr. Welby has paid a great deal of money, and it would be most sinful to waste all that food." She looked at Wade and Abrianna. "Perhaps you two should marry. I know the judge will be happy to supply the proper papers."

"No." Wade shook his head. "I wouldn't expect Abrianna to do that."

"Sister makes a good point," Aunt Poisie interjected. "You could forego the church and marry at the house. The skies are clear, and the gardens are still quite lovely. You could marry there or in the ballroom where the wedding breakfast is awaiting."

"I think it would be great irony," Aunt Selma added. "Just think of it. Mr. Welby's money will pay for your wedding."

Aunt Miriam fixed them with a hint of amusement. "Don't let pride stand in your way. You've already seen where that gets a soul. I think it would be the perfect way to put the ugliness of this ordeal behind us."

Wade looked at Abrianna. "What do you want?"

She smiled. Suddenly nothing else mattered as much as becoming his wife. "You, of course." She looked to Flora and her aunts. "I won't go another day without him. Take me home, where we can rid me of these ghastly attachments."

"You heard the lady." Wade lifted Abrianna in his arms. He frowned and shifted her with a groan. "You must be wearing ninety pounds of material."

"At least." She felt sorry for him. "So why don't you let me go?"

He shook his head, his gaze never leaving hers. "Never."

25

Most of those in attendance at the church had eagerly followed the family to the Madison Bridal School for the wedding of Wade Ackerman and Abrianna Cunningham. Since the wedding was to take place here, it was qute a simple matter to arrange for the chairs to be moved to the garden for all of the guests. People seemed at ease and much happier than they had at he church.

With Priam Welby in custody, the people felt compelled to speak their minds. Abrianna had this on Flora's assurance. It seemed no one actually liked Priam Welby, and most were ready to testify against him if the opportunity arose.

"Ready?" her father asked.

Abrianna put her hand to her hair one final time. Only moments ago she had worked with Flora to rearrange flowers in her hair instead of the tiara and veil. "Do I look all right?"

He grinned in pride. "You look perfect."

They began the short walk along the garden's cobblestoned path. Abrianna had rid herself of what she came to call "The Welby Appurtenances." Instead, she wore the gown she'd helped to design and make for her wedding to Wade, the one Welby deemed far too plain, the one she now deemed her something new. She traded the beautiful pearl-encrusted heels Welby had insisted on for a pair of simple white satin slippers that Lenore loaned her. It was her something borrowed.

For something old and blue, Abrianna pinned Aunt Miriam's sapphire broach to the bodice of the gown. The broach had been a gift to Abrianna on her eighteenth birthday. She seldom wore it, but today seemed the perfect opportunity. She wore no additional jewelry, nor would she, until Wade slipped on the emerald and diamond ring that once belonged to his grandmother. Abrianna had taken the ring off when Welby forced his hand, but now she would receive it back for good.

Abrianna tightened her grip on her father's arm. He smiled down at her in a reassuring manner. After all she'd been through that morning, Abrianna hadn't thought she'd be nervous to walk the aisle to Wade. But she was. Her old concerns came back to haunt her.

Am I really ready for this?

Lenore, despite her well-rounded figure, walked just before them and turned with a smile when she reached the front where Wade and Kolbein waited with the judge.

Abrianna's father stopped short of giving her over to Wade. He kissed her cheek. "I love you, Daughter."

"I love you, Papa." Tears welled in her eyes. He looked at her in surprise. Abrianna smiled. "I've wanted to call you that for a while now. Do you mind?"

His eyes moistened. "Not at all. I'm honored."

As she was handed over to Wade, Abrianna couldn't help but shift her attention. Wade's brown eyes seemed to stare right through to her soul. Goodness, but this man could evoke such a whirlwind of emotion and thought. She trembled at the realization that soon they would be man and wife. She would belong to Wade Ackerman, body and soul. The thought caused her momentary panic. Her earlier misgivings came back to haunt her. *What if I fail at this? I've not gained the skills my aunts tried to teach me. I know so very little about running a household or being a wife.* She bit her lip. Wade gave her a smile and turned to face the judge as he began the ceremony.

The judge cleared his voice. "Dearly beloved . . ."

Still Abrianna's doubts continued. *I suppose this is my moment of no turning back. Not that I want to. I love Wade, and he loves me. I know I'm meant to be his wife, but I feel so inadequate. I've made so many mistakes, and I'm so headstrong. It won't be at all easy to put aside my will and be obedient. I've never been good with obedience, yet now I'm making a vow to obey. Oh, Lord, help me.*

Abrianna felt her knees weaken. She couldn't help but notice the look of love in Wade's expression. He didn't seem at all nervous. How was that fair? How was it that he could stand there and be as calm as could be? She drew a deep breath. There was no need to get up in arms about it. Thankfully one of them had their wits about them.

"Will you, Abrianna, have Wade . . ."

Her mind whirled in a dozen directions at once. What if this turned out to be a bad idea? What if Welby's money somehow tainted the ceremony?

Oh, I'm being so ridiculous, Abrianna berated herself. *I'm marrying my best friend, and God's blessing is greater than any curse given by Priam Welby.*

The judge cleared his voice and leaned forward. "You need to say, 'I do.'"

Abrianna startled. Realizing she hadn't been paying attention, she nodded. "I do."

She looked to Wade and then back to the judge. "Sorry."

The judge continued. Wade squeezed her hand, and Abrianna felt her tension fade just a bit. He had so much patience when it came to dealing with her. How like him to put aside all of her mistakes and poor judgments and devote the rest of his life to her. God knew she had pushed him to the limit more than once, yet Wade continued to accept her—to love her, flaws and all. A rush of tears came unbidden, and Abrianna fought to keep her emotions in check. She didn't deserve the love Wade offered her, but she intended to take it and be as worthy of it as possible.

The ceremony concluded with Wade securing the ring on her finger and pledging her his all. "You may kiss your bride," the judge said with a fatherly smile of approval.

Wade took her face in his hands. "I've wanted to do this all day." He kissed her with great tenderness, and Abrianna felt a surge of wonder rush over her. They were really and truly married and would spend the rest of their lives together. The marvel of it all made her head spin. Or maybe it was the kiss.

The wedding attendees surprised Abrianna by applauding. For a moment she and Wade pulled apart and gazed out at the people. Wade chuckled and put his arm around Abrianna's waist. "It would seem they approve," he whispered in her ear.

"I feel as though we're on the stage and have just completed Act I. Who ever heard of applauding at a wedding? Goodness, is this to become the new tradition?" She felt her cheeks grow hot.

Aunt Miriam was the first to come to their side. She kissed Abrianna on the cheek and then did the same for Wade. "I couldn't be more pleased."

"Nor could I," Aunt Selma declared and embraced Abrianna and then Wade. "You two make the most beautiful couple. I don't think I've ever seen two people better suited to each other."

Aunt Poisie wasn't to be left out. "I am happier than I have been in years. You two are meant for each other." Her eyes seemed to sparkle with the joy she clearly felt. "I could only be happier had my beloved Jonathan been in attendance. God rest his soul."

"Amen," Aunt Miriam and Selma murmured.

Poisie shrugged. "But we shan't contemplate our sorrows. This is your day, and though it started on a most disparaging note, it has been redeemed. What man meant for evil, God meant for good."

"Indeed," Abrianna's father declared. He stepped forward to join them with Eloise on his arm. "I never thought I'd live to see this day." His eyes met Abrianna's. "Your mama would have been real proud."

Abrianna felt a momentary ache in her heart at the mention of her mother. She had reflected on her the night before, wondering if she would have had any sage advice to offer Abrianna. Again, doubts began to creep in. Lenore had told Abrianna that her mother had gone on and on about the proper duties of a wife to her husband and household the night before her marriage to Kolbein. Having grown up in a bridal school, Abrianna felt certain she should already know these things, but for the life of her she couldn't remember much at all. Perhaps it was the gravity of her ordeal with Welby, or maybe it had something to do with her never paying serious attention to her aunts' instruction. Whatever the reason, Abrianna could only pray that God's mercy would extend to bridal etiquette and wifely instruction.

She gave a heavy sigh. "I don't even remember how he takes his coffee."

"What did you say, dear?" Aunt Selma asked.

It was only then that Abrianna realized she'd spoken aloud.

She looked at Wade, fearful he had heard, but he seemed completely oblivious in his conversation with Poisie. She turned her attention back to her aunt. "It wasn't important."

Abrianna and Wade very quickly found themselves unable to move as the rest of the congregation surrounded them to offer their best wishes. Abrianna wanted nothing more than to sit down and contemplate all that she had faced that day, perhaps even talk it out with Wade, but there was no time. As soon as the guests moved away, Aunt Miriam directed Abrianna and Wade to take the back stairs up to the ballroom. "We will direct the guests up the main stairs momentarily. I've arranged for the chairs to be moved back upstairs, and once everyone is assembled we can begin the breakfast." She left them without waiting for a reply.

Abrianna sighed. The day was nowhere near to being over.

"I'd like to think that was a sigh of happiness, but I'm pretty sure it's more along the lines of exhaustion," Wade said, his expression one of sympathy.

"It has been an extremely fatiguing day. I must say I never figured to be wed to you like this." Her brow furrowed. "Not that I'm unhappy, mind you. I just think it most unusual. I barely slept last night. I was terrified that I'd never get Welby to admit to his wrongdoings. Then at the church I was almost certain that I would lose my nerve and make a mess of everything. Then there was Aunt Poisie and the hammer. Goodness, did you ever imagine she could do something like that? I might have expected it from Aunt Selma or Aunt Miriam. Both of them have been active in the discipline of students and dealt with strong-willed husbands, but Poisie's demeanor has always been more timid and—" She couldn't finish her thought because Wade pulled her into his arms and kissed her again. This time the kiss was more passionate and held the promise of more to come.

"There. I thought that might quiet you." Wade let go his hold. "You think too much."

Abrianna looked at him for a moment and nodded. "You are right on that account. I am sorry. I'm afraid it's just one more of my flaws you will have to bear up under. You know full well that I am given over to contemplating matters in great detail."

"So much so that you very nearly missed completing your vows."

"I am sorry for that, too. I'm afraid I can hardly think clearly, and when my mind is like this, I do tend to ramble on and on. You know that, as well."

"I do know that. And that is why I'm prepared to kiss you into silence as much as possible." He chuckled and took hold of her hand. "Of course, I also enjoy listening to you and hearing your thoughts on the world at large. Right now, however, I believe our wedding guests are waiting to toast us."

"I wish we could just be done with all of these formalities. I'd much rather skip the nonsense and just get on with . . . well . . ." She fell silent, realizing that Wade might take her comment to mean that she was overly desirous to get him alone. She bit her lower lip and dared to raise her eyes to his.

"Well? You were saying?" His arched brow and grin were enough to leave Abrianna feeling mortified and more nervous than before. She felt her face grow hot.

Shaking her head, she drew in a deep breath and wished the ground might open and swallow her up. "I think I've sufficiently put my foot in my mouth. No need to continue."

He roared with laughter and pulled her along with him through the back door of the house. They made their way up the two flights of stairs and finally reached the crowded ballroom. Aunt Selma quickly came to their side and guided them to the head table.

Abrianna slipped into a seat beside Lenore and sighed. "I am completely exhausted. Goodness, but I've never known a more demanding day. It would surely have been easier to help re-lay the streets of Seattle."

Lenore smiled and reached over to take hold of Abrianna's hand. "But not as rewarding. I'm so happy for you and Wade. The baby is, too. He's not stopped doing somersaults since you said, 'I do.'"

"Do you suppose he really knows what's going on? Goodness, but now you have me referring to the baby as he."

"My guess is that he feels my joy," Lenore replied. "That is enough to please him, I'm sure. I can hardly believe this day has finally come. It seems just yesterday you were attending me at my wedding, and now I've been able to do the same for you. We are no longer schoolgirls, but wives."

"And soon you will be a mother," Abrianna said, smiling.

"And you might well be one soon yourself. Wouldn't that be amazing if you found yourself with child right away?"

Abrianna swallowed hard and nodded. Amazing wasn't the only word that came to mind. The idea of the intimacies to come and the consequences of such times left her feeling rather shaken. Aunt Miriam had sat her down to discuss the details of wedded intimacy only moments before the wedding ceremony. She apologized to Abrianna for the brusque and blatant manner of explanation but assured her things would take their course, and there was really little more she needed to know, since men most often had a natural instinct about such things. Abrianna was aware of some things related to marriage, but hearing them from Aunt Miriam left her with more questions than answers.

Her father interrupted her thoughts by calling for everyone's attention. Abrianna turned from Lenore and focused on what her father had to say.

"I want to offer a blessing on the happy couple." He smiled at Abrianna, and she thought she glimpsed the sheen of tears in his eyes. "I wasn't able to watch my daughter grow up, but seeing the beautiful and accomplished young woman she's become, I have to say that I could not have done a better job. I know her mother would praise the three ladies who took Abrianna as their own and raised her into the perfect young woman she's become."

Abrianna dropped her gaze to her hands. Perfect wasn't a word she often found associated with herself. Her father was kind to suggest such a thing, but she knew better. Misgivings regarding her ability to make Wade happy continued to grow, and Abrianna began to doubt if she'd make it through the meal without being ill.

Her father concluded his comments just then. "Wade and Abrianna, I wish you only happiness. I pray a blessing on your marriage. I pray that your life together will be one of harmony and trust. That you will give each other the benefit of doubt in times of difficulty and that you will be stalwart in your support and defense of each other. Above all, I pray that you will trust God with your every need." He raised his glass. "May your love endure all of life's trials."

There were murmurs of approval from the audience as they shared in the toast. Abrianna felt Wade take hold of her hand.

"You're trembling," he said in a barely audible voice. "And your fingers are like ice."

"This is a most prodigious time for me. My entire life has just changed, and the impact of it is quite overwhelming." He squeezed her hand, but she couldn't bring herself to look at him.

There were so many blessings offered that Abrianna lost track of the words and the time. The food was served, and as Priam Welby had demanded, it proved to be the finest cuisine available. Tray after tray of savory meats were offered, along with beautifully prepared dishes of tantalizing concoctions that Abrianna couldn't even identify. How was a person supposed to know if she wanted to try something if she didn't know what it was?

Biting into a delicate puffed pastry with salmon mousse, Abrianna realized she was quite famished. The tightness in her stomach eased as she continued to eat. A light supper the previous evening had been her last meal, and now it was nearly eleven o'clock. Despite not knowing what had been put on her plate by the white-coated serving staff, Abrianna dug in with such gusto that even Wade noticed.

"Why are you eating so fast? You still in a hurry to get me alone?"

She choked for a moment, coughing and sputtering in a most embarrassing manner. Taking a quick sip from her glass, Abrianna worried that someone might have overheard him. Glancing around, she was relieved to see that no one seemed to have heard. She finally looked at Wade and found him grinning. "I'm hungry," she admitted, trying to hide her embarrassment. "After all I've been through, surely I deserve a decent meal."

He chuckled. "And here I thought it was passion, not starvation that guided your heart."

"You're impossible," she said. "As if this day wasn't stressful enough, your teasing is about to be my undoing."

A small orchestra had been arranged at the far end of the room and began to offer strains of beautiful music to add to the pleasure of the meal. Abrianna remembered that Welby had intended there to be dancing, but she hoped that Wade wouldn't expect her to spend the afternoon in such activity. Her anxiety was fading in the face of exhaustion. All she really wanted was a long nap. She raised her napkin to her lips to hide a yawn. Thankfully, no one seemed to notice.

Abrianna finished her plate of food, and as she did, Aunt Miriam appeared and motioned the couple to follow her. Grateful to do something other than endure the gazes of the wedding attendees as she did her best to hide her fatigue, Abrianna allowed Wade to help her to her feet. They followed Aunt Miriam down the back stairs to the first floor.

"As you know," she began, without any hint of discomfort, "it is tradition for the bridal couple to leave the breakfast for a time . . . alone." She drew her hands together as if she were about to recite a poem or sing a song. "It stems from days of old when it was important to offer proof of a bride's virtue, as well as to solidify the marriage contract with consummation." She gave them a nod. "I will return to attend the party. Wade, I trust you can take over from here."

"Of course," he replied, throwing Abrianna an amused wink.

Without another word, Aunt Miriam took her leave. Abrianna watched her hurry back up the stairs and disappear. She looked up at Wade and shook her head. "Well, I wasn't expecting that."

He touched her cheek and chuckled. "And what were you expecting?"

She shrugged. "I don't suppose I know. I've been to many a wedding breakfast or brunch, but I've never really paid much attention to what became of the bride and groom." She frowned. "Do they really expect that we would . . . that you and I . . . well, do they really expect that? While they all just sit there and eat and wait? I don't think I've ever heard of anything more appalling."

He drew her close. "Let them expect or presume whatever

they will. We're married now, and it doesn't matter." He led her through the kitchen and out the back door.

"Where are we going?"

Abrianna had faced many ordeals and trials in her life with great strength and boldness, but the idea of what was soon to come left her feeling weak and uncertain. At least she wasn't focused on her exhaustion anymore, but this was hardly better.

Wade didn't stop walking until they had reached the carriage house. "I thought you might like to see your new home."

"My new home?"

"It was your father's idea. He talked to me just before the wedding when the elders approached me to let me know they still wanted me in the pulpit. Apparently the congregation was in no way concerned that any of the previous charges were based in truth. Anyway, he thought it might be easier if we took the carriage house for our home until we could decide where we wanted to live. Your father moved his things to a room in the main house while you were preparing yourself for the ceremony. And although I'm not supposed to know it, Eloise took it upon herself to spruce up the place for us."

"She did?" She looked him in amazement. "That was most industrious of her. Very kind, too."

"Indeed. Would you like to see for yourself what they did?"

She looked over her shoulder, remembering what her aunt had said about giving them time alone. "I suppose it's expected."

He laughed and took hold of her hand. "Don't sound so excited." Together they climbed the steps. At the top, Wade pushed open the door and surprised Abrianna by whisking her into his arms. "Time to carry you across the threshold."

"Wait!" Abrianna put her hand on his arm. "I have something to say."

He nodded with a lopsided grin. "You usually do. Go on."

"Well, I know that I treated you very badly in that Welby ordeal. I felt I had to do what I did, but it grieved me to hurt you. I was overcome with sorrow at the very idea of causing you pain and perhaps even losing you."

"You could never lose me, Abrianna. Haven't you figured that out yet?"

She smiled. "I'm beginning to see that, but I want you to know that even when I thought it hopeless and could see no way out but to marry Mr. Welby, I was thinking of you and the great love I held for you." She reached down and pulled up the hem of her wedding gown. "I stitched our initials into the hem. See?"

He looked at the material. "Where?"

"I did the stitching to match the color of the gown so that no one would readily notice. You see, I thought if nothing else, I would have that part of us. I would wear the gown I had planned to wear for our wedding, although it would be covered over with all that other nonsense of lace and beading, and our initials would be forever joined in the gown. You were always there in my heart, Wade. You always will be."

He looked again at the stitching. "I see it now. A and W and another A." He lifted his eyes to her face. "You never cease to amaze me, Abrianna Cunningham . . . Ackerman."

"I just wanted you to know . . . in case . . . well, should I prove to be a disappointment to you or fail to be the wife you had hoped for."

"You are already exactly the wife I hoped for, Abrianna. I was so terrified of Welby hurting you. I hated that you had to go through all that you did on my account, but I also admired you for your strength. I love you, and nothing else matters now but that we're together."

"Well, like I said. I just wanted you to know."

He kissed her on the nose and chuckled. "There's something that I want you to know, as well."

She straightened just a bit in his arms, quite curious. "And what's that?"

He leaned close to whisper against her ear. "I like my coffee black with just a little sugar."

Her eyes widened. "You heard that?" She groaned and shook her head. "I am completely mortified. It seems I am always to be making a scene and embarrassing myself and my loved ones. Perhaps with you by my side, I will somehow manage to do better and elude trouble, but it's doubtful."

Wade gave her a little toss into the air, eliciting a squeal. She grabbed for his neck. He laughed heartily and tightened his hold. "Ah, Abrianna, trouble just naturally seems to find you, but you needn't be self-conscious or mortified. I'm your husband and best friend. I came into this knowing full well what I was in for." He pressed his mouth to hers for a rather quick kiss before adding, "Besides, what fun would it be if you didn't always keep me guessing what you will do next?"

"Well, you did promise me we would have fun." Feeling her tensions ease, she relaxed her hold and her fingers lightly stroked the hair at the nape of his neck.

"I did, didn't I? Well, then I say we get on with it." He crossed the threshold without further delay. "Welcome home, Mrs. Ackerman."

26

"We are here today to open the new facilities for the indigent and homeless," Brother Mitchell declared. "The church is proud to sponsor this endeavor, and with the funding and pledge of ongoing support from so many in the community, we feel confident that this shelter will offer hope and biblical counsel for all who seek its refuge. Pastor and Mrs. Ackerman will now cut the ribbon."

Wade looked at Abrianna and handed her the scissors. She took them, and Wade closed his hand over hers as they cut the ribbon together. Cheers went up from the gathering of church congregants, members of the community, friends, and family. Perhaps the most unexpected attendee came in the form of Priam Welby's father, Vernon Welby, who, upon hearing of his son's grievous deeds, had come to Seattle on several occasions. First to see his son convicted of murder and sentenced to life in prison, and then to oversee the dissolution of the younger Welby's holdings. He had even made a healthy contribution to the shelter, with the promise of regular support. Even more surprising was that he and Aunt Poisie seemed to have taken a liking to each other, and Abrianna couldn't help but wonder if her aunt would soon find herself a married woman, after all.

"This is going to be a great help to our city." The mayor stepped forward to offer Wade and Abrianna his congratulations. "I must say, Mrs. Ackerman, your devotion to the poor has put me to shame."

"We all have our calling, Mayor. However, it is also our duty as Christians to see to the needs of the poor and orphaned."

Just then, several of her beloved orphans appeared at her side. The eldest, Toby, had recently told Abrianna how he and the others had pooled their money to rent a small apartment. "Looks real good, Miss Abrianna," Toby said, nodding toward the two-story building. "I'm thinkin' folks will be real happy to stay here."

"I think so." She gazed at the brick structure with pride. "There's room for everyone. Sleeping quarters for women and children only on the upper floor. Rooms for the men, as well as the dining hall and kitchen, on the first floor. I believe it will adequately serve the intended purpose."

Toby smiled. "I know it will. Now nobody will have to sleep out in the cold and rain." The other boys nodded, and their admiration of Abrianna was more than evident.

A couple of old sailors made their way to Abrianna and Wade. They pulled their caps from their heads and smiled. "This is a right good place, Miss Abrianna," one of them declared.

"I'm so glad you like it. I hope it will be a haven for you and the others when they have nowhere else to go."

"You're wonderful, Miss Abrianna," thirteen-year-old Bobby said, rushing her with a bear hug. "Now none of us will have to be afraid ever again."

Her heart melted at his declaration. "No, you don't have to be afraid. But please remember, I'm not wonderful. I'm just trying to be obedient to the calling God put on my heart. I haven't done this because I'm a good person. It was and will continue to be a lot of work, but it isn't about me, and I don't want you putting me up on a pedestal."

Bobby stepped back and nodded. "It's about serving God and loving our fellowman."

Abrianna was glad he remembered what she had been telling them all along. "It is, and I am very glad that you boys have all chosen to volunteer to help us. We wouldn't be able to keep on top of a place this size without volunteers."

Lenore and Kolbein came to offer their congratulations. Kolbein held their six-month-old son, Daniel Kolbein Booth. The boy looked a great deal like his father, with wavy brown hair that formed tiny ringlets near his neck.

"I can't believe this day has finally come." Abrianna couldn't help but smile. "And I have you to thank as much as anyone. You have always believed in this cause, and I know God will bless you because of it."

"He already has, Abrianna." Kolbein smiled at Lenore.

"I'm so proud of you," Lenore said, leaning to kiss Abrianna on the cheek. "You have remained faithful to what God wanted you to do."

"I couldn't have done it without all of you and, of course, without Wade." Abrianna smiled at her husband. These past months together had proven one very important thing to her. Life was full of conflicts and ordeals, but they were much better borne with someone else.

Wade put his arm around Abrianna. "Don't let her fool you. She didn't need me at all. I've never seen anyone more organized and capable of commanding not only the city officials, but also the contractors and inspectors. Abrianna wouldn't tolerate anyone slacking in their duties. She's pretty amazing."

"I'll say," Kolbein replied. "I wouldn't be where I am today had I not met this beautiful redhead. But for her and the Madison Bridal School I might never have married Lenore."

Wade extended his finger to Daniel, who quickly latched on with a squeal of delight. "He's sure gotten big. Before you know it, he'll be walking."

"And then we'll be in for it," Kolbein said with a smile. "I'm certain he will be just as rambunctious as I was as a child. My mother used to regale me with stories of my adventures."

"Well, before long," Wade said, giving Abrianna a conspiratorial wink, "perhaps we can provide him with a playmate."

Lenore's eyes widened. "Are you . . . expecting?" she asked Abrianna.

Abrianna had looked forward to sharing the news with her dear friend and nodded. "We are. The baby should be born sometime around Daniel's birthday."

Lenore hugged her tightly. "Oh, what joy! Of course you will have a son, and he and Daniel shall be the best of friends."

"It might be a girl," Abrianna offered with a giggle. "And maybe they will grow up to fall in love and marry. Wouldn't that be amazing?"

"Amazing isn't the word that comes to my mind," Wade said with a moan. "I don't want to even think of having to keep control on a miniature Abrianna."

Kolbein laughed and gave Wade a slap on the back. Daniel tried to take that opportunity to lunge from his arms. "Oh no, you don't," Kolbein said, pulling Daniel back securely.

Lenore reached out and took the boy in her arms. "So long

as you both deliver safely and remain in health, we shall be glad for either one. This is such a happy day."

Abrianna caught Wade's prideful gaze and felt her heart nearly burst with love. Her life was almost perfect, and gone were all those nagging doubts about whether their friendship would endure marriage and whether or not she might make an adequate wife.

"Look, your mother and father are motioning for us to join them," Kolbein said to Lenore. "It looks like they have someone for us to meet."

"Don't they always? Father is so determined to see you as the next governor or senator of the state," Lenore declared. She looked to Abrianna. "Please excuse us for now but promise me you'll come to tea on Monday. We have a great deal to discuss and plan."

"I will do my best," Abrianna assured. "It will all depend on how busy we are here."

Once they had gone, Abrianna wasn't surprised to find Aunt Miriam and Aunt Selma had come to join them. "I presume you told them about the little one?" Aunt Miriam asked.

"Wade did, actually. I didn't even have a chance."

Wade shrugged. "I figure the father has just as much a right to be proud and make such announcements."

"Indeed," Aunt Miriam replied. She glanced around the grounds. "It would seem the shelter is a great success. There have been large donations made to the church for the funding of the day-to-day operations."

"God will provide. He always has." Abrianna felt a deep sense of joy in the assurance that God would always guide her so long as she allowed Him to.

Wade lowered his voice. "It would seem Miss Poisie is quite

enthralled with Mr. Welby. I wonder if we will soon be enjoying a different kind of celebration."

"It is possible," Aunt Miriam said in her stoic manner. "However, we must first get through the annual ball this evening before we give ourselves over to too much thought on that account. Thankfully, Eloise has organized the girls to handle the decorating and refreshment preparation. Otherwise, with Poisie so clearly distracted and my rheumatism acting up, I'm afraid poor Selma would be on her own to see to all the details."

"Not that I couldn't manage if needed," Aunt Selma replied, "but I am grateful to leave it in the hands of others. I find that having free time to explore some of my own interests, such as reading for pleasure, has been most beneficial."

Abrianna stepped closer to her aunt. "I heard about an interesting novel called *Kit and Kitty* by R. D. Blackmore. The heroine is the daughter of a scientist."

Aunt Selma shook her head. "That is certain to lead to sorrow."

"But it's a romantic story. Perhaps the hero helps her to overcome the negative influences of science."

"I suppose I could look into it," Aunt Selma replied. "I do enjoy a good love story."

"Nevertheless," Aunt Miriam interjected, "we are most blessed that your father and Eloise have taken on so much of the daily operations of the school. I find it far more enjoyable to teach a class or two and worry about little else. In the past few days—"

Several startled screams disrupted whatever Aunt Miriam was about to say as a soaking-wet Flora flew past them in a cacophony of squawking and barking. In her arms she battled two rather unhappy hens that flapped wildly against captivity. Behind her, causing equal distraction, were four rather worked-up mutts, who seemed to have an undue interest in the chickens.

Throwing an apologetic glance over her shoulders, Flora continued through the crowd with the barking dogs very nearly on her heels. Abrianna couldn't help but giggle. Flora reminded her much too often of herself. She looked at Wade and could see he thought much the same.

"That girl is even more difficult to settle down than you were," Aunt Miriam admitted. "It will be a long while before Miss Flora can be presented for courtship." She shook her head, making a *tsk*ing sound.

"She is our greatest challenge," Aunt Selma added. She looked to Abrianna. "I am so glad you left your wild ways behind you."

"Oh, I wouldn't say she exactly left them behind her," Wade said with a devilish gleam in his eyes. "Abrianna will always be given to her whims and wild ways. I find myself frequently having to keep an eye on her. She is constantly plotting and conniving to do something that she knows none of us would approve. Why, just the other day she—"

Abrianna pulled his face to hers and kissed him in a most public display. Aunt Miriam gasped, causing Abrianna to finally release Wade. She looked at her aunt with a shrug. "I've found this to be one of the best ways to shut him up when he tends to ramble on and on about things that are of no concern or interest to anyone but himself." She smiled sweetly at Wade.

He drew her back into his arms and threw her aunts a wink. "I have found that being talkative has its rewards and intend to improve upon my oratory skills in the future." He looked down on Abrianna. "So you should prepare yourself, Mrs. Ackerman. You may very well spend a great deal of time silencing me."

"An arduous task, to be sure," Abrianna said with a sigh, then happily yielded to her husband's kiss.

Tracie Peterson is the award-winning author of over one hundred novels, both historical and contemporary. Her avid research resonates in her stories, as seen in her bestselling HEIRS OF MONTANA and ALASKAN QUEST series. Tracie and her family make their home in Montana. Visit Tracie's website at www .traciepeterson.com.

More From Bestselling Author Tracie Peterson

To learn more about Tracie and her books, visit traciepeterson.com.

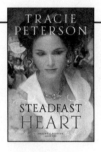

Don't miss Lenore and Militine's stories! Brought together by the Madison Bridal School in 1890, three young women form a close bond. In time, they learn more about each other—and themselves—as they help one another grow in faith and, eventually, find love.

BRIDES OF SEATTLE: *Steadfast Heart, Refining Fire, Love Everlasting*

Three LONE STAR BRIDES seek out marriage for very different reasons. They each face difficult choices and obstacles on the road ahead. But they also find friendship and adventure, as well as romance and a place to call home.

LONE STAR BRIDES: *A Sensible Arrangement, A Moment in Time, A Matter of Heart*

You May Also Enjoy...

Entering her fourth season, Lady Miranda Hawthorne secretly longs to be bold. But she is mortified when her brother's handsome new valet accidentally mails her private thoughts to a duke she's never met—until he responds. As she tries to sort out her growing feelings for two men, it becomes clear that Miranda's heart is not the only thing at risk for the Hawthorne family.

A Noble Masquerade by Kristi Ann Hunter
HAWTHORNE HOUSE
kristiannhunter.com

At Irish Meadows horse farm, two sisters struggle to reconcile their dreams with their father's demanding marriage expectations. Brianna longs to attend college, while Colleen is happy to marry, as long as the man meets *her* standards. Will they find the courage to follow their hearts?

Irish Meadows by Susan Anne Mason
COURAGE TO DREAM #1
susanannemason.com

When Brook Eden's friend Justin, a future duke, discovers she may be an English heiress, she travels to meet her alleged father. Once there, she finds herself confused by her emotions and haunted by her mother's mysterious death. Will she learn the truth—before it's too late?

The Lost Heiress by Roseanna M. White
LADIES OF THE MANOR
roseannamwhite.com

BETHANYHOUSE